DEADLANDS

T0020939

DEADLANDS

A NOVEL

VICTORIA MILUCH

LAKE UNION
PUBLISHING

This is a work of fiction. Names, characters, organizations, places, events, and incidents are either products of the author's imagination or are used fictitiously. Otherwise, any resemblance to actual persons, living or dead, is purely coincidental.

Text copyright © 2023 by Victoria Miluch
All rights reserved.

No part of this book may be reproduced, or stored in a retrieval system, or transmitted in any form or by any means, electronic, mechanical, photocopying, recording, or otherwise, without express written permission of the publisher.

Published by Lake Union Publishing, Seattle

www.apub.com

Amazon, the Amazon logo, and Lake Union Publishing are trademarks of Amazon.com, Inc., or its affiliates.

ISBN-13: 9781662511288 (paperback)
ISBN-13: 9781662511004 (digital)

Cover design by Richard Ljoenes Design LLC
Cover image: © Matilde Rubio / ArcAngel

Printed in the United States of America

DEADLANDS

1

We don't hear the car as quickly as we should because of what I've brought Wulf here to see—a curve of metal jutting out of the sand, just beyond a scattering of creosote. The rest of the object is buried, wedged too deeply in the dirt to know its size or shape. We aren't far from the settlement here, no more than an hour walking if you weave through the cacti and brush in a straight line. Two days ago, when I first found the object, its surface was just a glint I thought was mica. The desert had been rearranged recently by a dust storm, the minerals in the dirt mussed, and I thought maybe I'd found an interesting rock worth taking. It was only after I dug that I started to unearth the edge of a container. That's what I tell Wulf I think the object is—some kind of container, possibly with something inside—but he insists on acting uninterested, on pretending he doesn't care.

"Did you tell Dad?" he asks.

"No," I say. "Why would I tell Dad?"

"If it's not important, what are we here for?" he says, belligerent, but I catch his eyes darting to the ground, flitting across the metal.

"What do you think it is?" I ask.

"Probably just trash."

"Buried like this with nothing else around it?"

He shrugs and crosses his arms. I watch his eyes sweep across the spiny shrubs of our desert, the knobby hills with their hard, round cacti, the dry mountains that always loom in the distance. Wulf is younger than I am, but he'd be taller if he stood up straight. When he stands, his shoulders curl inward like they're meant to fit inside a shell.

"Even if it's trash, Dad would find a use for it," I say. "It looks like good metal."

"He doesn't like you poking around," says Wulf.

"Says who?"

Wulf's eyebrows tip down. "You know he doesn't."

"Dad didn't mind when I found that stash of chicken wire," I say. "He's still using it to fix the fencing. And I bet there's something useful in here, too, or valuable. Why else would someone bury it?"

"Why would someone bury something that's valuable?"

"So they could come back to it. Maybe it's guns. Or an emergency stash of food. There's a woman who found a chest of old paper money years ago, buried on the land she lived on. It wasn't worth anything anymore, but still."

"How do you know that?" Wulf frowns.

"I read it."

"Where?"

I'm about to say, but it occurs to me that he might be trying to trap me, that he thinks I was doing something I wasn't supposed to be doing, like poking around Dad's office, maybe even using the computers. Instead, I shrug like him and keep quiet. There's a tight ball of anger that's formed in my chest, close to where my heart beats. When I inhale, it expands, and when I exhale, it cleaves tighter, slowly making it harder for me to breathe. Wulf doesn't make a move to leave, but he doesn't say anything, either, he just keeps staring at brownish parts of the ground that are anything but the object I've brought him here to see.

That's when we hear the car. When we know it's too late to hide, because we can already see it, a hulking green vehicle creeping toward us. There's nothing to do but wait for it to drive up to us, listen to its wheels crunch across the sand and spit up small rocks. We wait motionless, like two small mammals frozen from dull animal instinct.

The windows of the car are caked with dust, but the windshield is clean enough to see through. There's a large half-moon wiped clear of dirt, and through it we can see two people. One of them is the woman who's driving. The other is a man holding on to his seat as the car wobbles over the uneven ground, because there's no road here, just patches of dirt that are clearer than others. The man stares right at Wulf and me, his gaze moving evenly between us. I'm glad for the ball of anger in my chest because it makes me braver than I am, makes me stare back at him without flinching. The car pulls up next to us, and then the woman brakes. The man rolls his window down, the glass squeaking.

"Hi there!" he says.

For a few long seconds, neither Wulf nor I say anything. I glance over at my brother and see his face empty and stiff. He's scared, I realize, and somehow this, too, makes me less afraid.

"Hi," I venture.

The man smiles. His lips are cracked and large for his face, dried-up pinkish grubs. His pale cheeks and nose are sunburned. "What's your name?" he asks.

"Georgia," I say.

Wulf turns his head sharply to me. "Shut up," he says.

The man gives Wulf a cursory glance. He says: "Do you two live here?"

"None of your business," Wulf says.

The man laughs, and Wulf stiffens. He rocks from his heels to his toes, and for a moment it seems like he's about to take a step forward, to punch the man in the jaw or just wave his pocketknife around to threaten him into going away, but he doesn't.

The door to the driver's side of the car squeaks open, and the woman steps out. She reminds me of a lizard, the way her loose, colorless clothes blend into the landscape, the quick way she moves her head to scan her surroundings.

"We're looking for a trailhead," she says. "Do you know of any around here?"

"A trailhead?" Wulf asks. He steps back, caught off guard. No doubt by the revelation of speaking to a woman who isn't me.

"There aren't any trails around here," I say.

The woman frowns, but the frown is so small, she's not even trying to look upset. "We heard from some people back in Phoenix that we could find some old trailheads up here," she says. "They dropped us the GPS location." She waves the phone she's holding in her hand as if to prove it, though the screen stays blank.

"Phoenix isn't near here," Wulf says.

"It's not that far away." The woman smiles. "Four, five hours driving, I'd say?"

Wulf doesn't say anything.

"You two aren't hiking, are you?" the man says, stepping out of the car. He moves more carefully than the woman, like he's worried about what he's going to step on. He doesn't blend in like she does, with the bright-red T-shirt he's wearing. He sticks out like an emergency flare, I think, and then a rush of fear sweeps through my body as the reality of these two strangers standing here, of them talking to us, registers. The man is suddenly right beside me, staring down at the metal object poking out of the ground.

"What's this?" he asks, and looks up at the woman. "Vanessa, did you see this?"

The woman—Vanessa—glances down. A slight frown passes over her face, and then she returns to scanning the quiet desert. I watch her for a moment, trying to glean if she knows anything, but she's looking the wrong way.

The man squats down and runs his finger along the object's rounded edge. "Did you bury something?" he asks.

"I didn't bury it, I found it," I say.

"Let's stay focused, Nick," says Vanessa.

"Why do you think we aren't hiking?" Wulf speaks up, his voice confrontational.

"Simple," Nick says, standing. "You don't have water bottles with you."

"We weren't thirsty," says Wulf.

"Plus, nobody hikes up here," says Nick. "Nobody even comes here."

"Except you, apparently," Wulf shoots back.

Vanessa makes an impatient sound. "Look, all right, we'll be honest with you if you'll be honest with us," she says. "We're looking for a place that's supposed to be around here. An abandoned commune built in the late twentieth century. It was called Oddinaya at one point, then Mesquite Acres, then something else, I think—but that was a long time ago. You probably wouldn't know it by those names. Or by any name, for that matter. It'd just look like a bunch of concrete and adobe buildings, mostly underground, maybe around ten or fifteen of them. I thought it'd be in a state of disrepair by now, but maybe I'm wrong about that. Maybe it's not as abandoned as I thought it was. I know there's nothing else around here. Does it sound familiar, what I'm describing? Is—am I wrong in guessing that you live there?"

I stare uncomprehendingly at Vanessa for a moment, and then it hits me. She's talking about our home. The concrete and adobe buildings she's talking about are the ones we live in, the abandoned settlement, the one we've settled into the way a hermit crab makes a sea snail's shell its home. Its new names shimmer in my mind, as though Vanessa has brushed away the dust of a century and the past is glinting bright beneath her hand. For a moment, the shrubs and mountains and cacti surrounding me all wobble, the terrain I know so well turns alien and unsettling. Then I blink, and the world rights itself again, but it's altered. It shines with a newness, a dangerous edge of possibility, sharp as a whetted knife.

"I guess you're not hiking either," I say.

Nick barks out laughter that sounds appreciative, and Vanessa's mouth twitches.

"Do you live here by yourselves?" she asks.

I can feel Wulf's eyes on me. He's volleying the question to me, unsure how to answer.

"We live with our dad," I say.

"Well, how do you think your dad would feel about a couple of visitors?" Vanessa says.

"What do you want?" Wulf asks harshly, and I can hear the fear in his voice, a tremor.

"I just told you," Vanessa says. "We've been looking for a place around here."

"Why?" says Wulf.

"We're intrepid explorers," Nick says.

"I'm a writer," says Vanessa. "I'm working on a project, a long essay about these kinds of places—old desert communes and farms, people trying to make the desert habitable before it was a deadland."

Wulf looks at me, and I look back at him. Neither of us wants these strangers to see us deliberating or uncertain. We can't talk to each other, but I try to communicate with my brother anyway. We don't have a choice, I try to tell him with my expression. We know how Dad feels about intruders, but they've only ever been a distant idea, an abstract threat. Now that two are standing before us, we don't know how to deal with the danger. And even if it means revealing more than we ought to, there's no other option than to bring them to Dad. Wulf's face is creased, still angry. I don't know if he understood me, and I can't read what his face is saying. I'm about to take matters into my own hands when he breaks eye contact.

"Fine," he says. "Do you want to walk there?"

Nick grins. This makes his face scrunch up, turning his eyes into slivers with creases around them. The sun catches the gray in his curling light hair. He looks slightly older than Vanessa, whose plain face looks like she could be twenty or forty.

"Wouldn't it be faster if we drove?" says Vanessa.

"There's no road," I tell her.

"That's okay. The car's been handling it just fine up to now."

The four of us pile into the car, Wulf and I in the back, and Vanessa turns on the engine. "Lead the way," she says. Wulf tells her where to drive, and she maneuvers the car expertly across large rocks and vegetation. Nick is humming softly from the front passenger seat, an upbeat tune grossly unsuited to the tension inside the car.

It feels like we're in the car with them for a long time, but Wulf's watch tells me that only ten minutes have passed by the time we start seeing signs of our settlement. The few mesquite trees that grow around our buildings, the outline of the structures visible behind the spindly branches. From the back seat, I watch Vanessa and Nick take in our home as we get closer, watch their heads turn as their eyes sweep across the ramada, the cactus gardens, then the low concrete structures that mark where our buildings descend underground, where it's always tolerably cool and dry even on days when the temperature is over 130.

Wulf gets out of the car first, opening the door before the car is even fully stopped.

"Dad!" he calls at the buildings.

The rest of us pile out of the car and wait. Nick bends down to pick up a thorny twig and fiddles with it, twirling it between his fingers. I stare at it in his hand, wondering if he's going to prick himself. Vanessa puts on a pair of sunglasses and tilts her head toward Nick, murmuring something that makes him smile vaguely.

"Dad, there's some people here!" Wulf calls again.

When Dad finally emerges from his office, I try to see what Vanessa and Nick see: A thin man, the duct-taped shoes on his feet, his sparse hair that's nearly the same tan color as his skin. His wire-rimmed glasses, the careful, stiff way he carries himself. He looks slight against the vastness of our desert, even against the sturdy concrete of the buildings, and I wonder if that's what Nick and Vanessa notice, or if they can already feel his commanding presence.

To my surprise, it's Nick who takes another step forward and extends his hand.

"Nick Wright," he introduces himself. "And this is my wife, Vanessa."

"Isaac Reno," Dad says impassively, shaking Nick's hand.

Vanessa says: "I'm sorry for disturbing you like this, but we're—well, let me start by saying that I'm a writer."

"How interesting," Dad says in the same impassive tone. "We love the written word here. We inherited a whole library when we came to this settlement that we're quite fond of. Many of the books are outdated, of course, but they've aged well. No mold here in our dry air."

Vanessa smiles, nodding uncertainly.

"So what brings you here?" Dad says.

Vanessa looks like she's working hard to keep up with Dad, to figure out what he's already figured out or decided about her. She says: "Like I said—well, I guess I haven't exactly said it—but I've been working on a project, an essay about these kinds of places. Communes or little farms set up in the desert, about the people who built them and why. I didn't realize anyone lived here now. I wouldn't have shown up like this if I had."

"Is that right?" says Dad mildly. "I would have guessed that it would be all the more reason to visit if you had."

"I guess that's true," Vanessa says, laughing lightly.

"Curiosity," says Dad.

"Sorry?" says Vanessa.

"Your object can't be monetary, since I can't imagine your project—you'll forgive me—holds significant worth financially. Therefore, my next best guess is that it's curiosity. A quixotic need to find answers to questions provoked by the ways and reasons why people lived here. I'm not sure if you'll find those answers. There isn't a lot we know about these early inhabitants, these people we consider all-but-ancient dwellers. We don't pay them much thought, to be frank."

Vanessa ventures a smile again.

"Oh, we're certainly grateful to them," continues Dad. "Misguided as they were, whoever originally built this place did an acceptable job of creating structures that make life possible here, given their time period and their technological constraints. Making improvements has certainly been easier because of the foundation they put in place."

"Why do you say 'misguided'?" Vanessa asks after a pause.

"Well, from the mere fact that their home was abandoned, we know that their aims weren't realized. From the size of the library and the area they cleared, it's obvious that there were plans for expansion. Perhaps someone wisely thought better of it. Would you call it sustainable to live in a region that receives less than four inches of rain per year? Granted, it was likely more back when the settlement was built, but a desert is still a desert."

"You're doing it," Nick says.

"Ah, but you're forgetting the other half of the equation," Dad says. "I'm doing it, but how many others are? Four inches of rainfall collected and harvested carefully is plenty for me and my family, along with prudent use of our groundwater well and the moisture I've learned to pull from the air. But for cities? For farms or communes?" He shakes his head. "They're no better than an invasive species in the desert. What would you call Phoenix these days?"

"The last city in the Arizonan deadlands?" Vanessa offers.

"A war zone in our war against nature," Dad pontificates. "Too hot for planes to fly in and out of safely on a regular schedule. Drained of enough water to sustain it. Nearly abandoned, like so many of our coastal cities—cities that were also mistakes, albeit mistakes that are easier to understand, considering we couldn't have predicted how we'd make the oceans rise with our stubborn carelessness. Building coastal cities is more forgivable than trying to recreate lawns and golf courses, as our forebears did, on a piece of land that should have been left to snakes."

"Are there a lot of snakes here?" Nick asks breezily.

Dad smiles. "Why don't we give you a tour of our home? I assume your original curiosity about this place must now necessarily extend to my life here. You must have many questions. Beowulf, Georgia, would you show our visitors around? Then we'll all have supper."

"That's very kind," says Vanessa.

"Really kind," echoes Nick.

Wulf and I take them to the large building we use for storage, the one we call the glass house. It's the only one that's fully aboveground, and, inexplicably, one of the walls is made of glass. In the summer it's too hot to spend more than a few minutes inside, but now it's spring, and the temperature isn't too bad yet. It's mostly empty apart from crates that hold mesquite flour and the large steel drums where we store our surplus water. Vanessa eyes these supplies, then peers at the set of stairs that lead to the dark basement, where we store everything else. Wulf leads Nick and Vanessa through one door and out the opposite one, eager to finish a task I know he thinks should have been left up to only me. He walks us to the buildings we live in, gesturing at them carelessly. Vanessa and Nick peer down at the thick stairs that lead down to the front doors, take in the squarish structures of dirt-colored concrete and reddish adobe with little windows that let just enough light in.

"I've seen photos of buildings like these," says Vanessa.

"I haven't," says Nick. "Can we get a peek inside?"

"No," says Wulf.

"You can see mine," I say.

"No, he can't," Wulf snaps.

"How old are you two?" asks Nick.

"Nineteen, about," I say. "Wulf's three years younger than I am."

"You two bickering made me think of me and my sister," says Nick. "We're about that same difference in age. Couldn't stand each other until we were in our thirties. Now at least we're on civil terms."

"What's that building over there?" asks Vanessa.

She's pointing to the building Dad uses for his office, where he keeps his computers and disappears for the majority of the day. Wulf's a regular visitor now, descending along with Dad, but I've tapered off my visits so much that at this point I couldn't even describe in detail what's down there, the exact number of desks and chairs, the electronics and their arrangement, Dad's graphs and maps and stacks of books and papers.

"It's our dad's," Wulf says, in a voice so final that nobody presses.

Nick and Vanessa are polite about the nopal field and cactus garden we show them. Nick asks if we eat them, and I point out which ones are edible.

"You just pick these off and eat them?" he asks, bending down by a barrel cactus with its bulbous yellow flower buds coming in.

"We ferment them," I say.

"Impressively quaint," says Nick, standing. "Right, Vanessa?"

"Hmm?" says Vanessa. "What did you say?"

"Dad's calling for us," says Wulf.

We all follow his gaze to see Dad waving rigidly.

"We should go," I say.

We eat in Dad's building, which is where the three of us usually eat supper. While we were giving Nick and Vanessa the tour, Dad must have been putting together the meal, a mix of foods we canned a year ago and leftovers from yesterday. There's the mesquite bread I baked, hard and crumbly and starting to get stale, and cold cooked nopals. The cactus pads are stamped with sooty lines from the fire, slimy when we cut into them. We have prickly pears, green and studded with black seeds, and saguaro flesh pickled with chia sage. Dad brings out leftover jackrabbit meat and places it at the center of the table, and then brews a pot of Mormon tea in honor of our guests.

"Fantastic," says Nick after biting into a jackrabbit leg. "You've got all you need here, don't you? No need to step back into the real world for anything."

"We all have our ideas of what's real and what isn't," Dad says with a token smile.

"You know, I've never eaten meat that wasn't lab grown," says Vanessa. "It tastes so different. Though I've never eaten rabbit before, either, so that might be the real difference. It has a really interesting flavor. Like dirt, a little bit—in a good way. Earthy."

"Lab-grown meat is one thing that the outside world does that I admire," says Dad.

"There isn't much else to admire, is there?" Vanessa says.

"Some would say so," Dad says. "Tea?"

Wulf watches us eat and talk, biting into prickly pears and not saying anything.

"I'd be curious to know how you found this place," says Dad. "As you may have guessed by now, I'm a man who attributes great value to his privacy. I took pains to choose a place to live that had little information about it available. If I'm not mistaken, there aren't any records in the public nor private domain that describe this settlement's coordinates."

"Only a general location." Vanessa nods, setting her fork down on the edge of her plate. "It was research and then a lot of luck. I'm actually pretty surprised I found it myself—one of those universe-lining-up-for-you kind of things, I guess. In my free time, I've been driving around kind of blindly to see if I could find it."

"A whim I indulged," says Nick, his voice jokey. "She indulges plenty of my obsessions."

"Surely the network of charging stations isn't extensive enough to give you freedom to drive so aimlessly," says Dad. "I was under the impression that even the few in Phoenix have long since fallen into disrepair with no local government to maintain them."

"There are still some working ones," Vanessa says. "But you're right, there aren't any outside of the city. I had the car fixed up so it could run on gasoline when we moved here. It's not exactly legal, but a lot of people—well, those who can afford it—do it here. There's still gasoline on the black market, thanks to the huachicoleros."

"It still strikes me as a great deal of effort for an unlikely outcome," says Dad.

"I've justified it as time and space to mull things over," says Vanessa. "And, I mean, I have to drive for my work, too, so I was going to have to fix up the car anyway. I'm actually in the area working on a book. And it's been a bit of a headache, to be honest, so this side project has been a kind of escape for me."

Dad doesn't say anything in response or give any indication that he's heard. The table goes quiet. Wulf scrapes his plate and swallows audibly.

"What are your obsessions?" I ask Nick.

Everyone at the table looks at me, and I realize there's something unintentionally off about my question, a strange, almost sinister undercurrent swirling in it that I can't quite see but can suddenly sense all the same. I grasp for something else to say, for a way to spool it back. But Nick looks unfazed—amused, if anything.

"My obsessions?" says Nick, now studying me as though I'm a curious mineral he's picked up off the ground. "Well, let's see, what are my obsessions? They run the gamut, I guess. I was on a war-documentary kick recently. Vanessa would say I have an unnatural love for ketchup. And I've always had a thing for beautiful and interesting women, but that goes without saying."

Vanessa smiles cursorily, and Nick's eyes linger on me.

"I'm so grateful that you've welcomed us into your home," says Vanessa.

Dad nods, his expression inscrutable.

"You probably know this question is coming," she continues. "But I'd love to spend some time talking to you about how you came here and what you're doing here. Whatever you'd like to share. Even without knowing much about you yet, I have a feeling that people would be really interested in reading about your way of life and thinking about the world."

"Do you," Dad says. "I didn't think people read much anymore."

"Well, no." Vanessa laughs a little. "That's true. And I completely understand if you don't want to talk about yourself. I know it's a lot to ask already to let me hang around and do the research I wanted to do on the settlement."

"It's her pet project," says Nick.

"Don't say it like that," Vanessa says.

Nick shrugs exaggeratedly and grins at the rest of us. Vanessa's mouth tightens, and she turns her attention back to Dad. "If we could spend a week here with you, just participating in your regular life, that would be amazing. We'd try not to be too much of a bother. We have tents in the car, so we wouldn't take up a lot of space."

"There are unused buildings where you can sleep comfortably," says Dad.

Vanessa's face is lit up now, her body buzzing with the energy of an unexpected victory. "And I know you probably don't have a lot of water to spare," she says, "but we could take the car into the city and pick some up."

"I'm not concerned about our water supply," says Dad.

"Then whatever supplies that could make your life easier, we could pick those up for you. We'd be happy to do that, whatever we can do to help. I really want to show you how grateful we are for your hospitality."

"That's very kind of you, but I'm afraid it would be impossible."

Vanessa's brightness fades into uncertainty. "No, it's no problem," she says.

"The problem," says Dad calmly, "is that you no longer have a car."

"What?" says Vanessa.

"I've slashed your tires and removed them. We'll find a way to repurpose them later."

Nick stands up, his chair screeching as it scrapes the floor. "What the fuck," he says.

"This can't come as a surprise," says Dad. "Did you really think I'd let you drive off free to tell the world where I am after you found me? I have my children to protect. Our sovereignty, our privacy, our way of life. No, I'm sorry. No harm will come to you here. I meant what I said about there being space for you, about you being comfortable here, but leaving is out of the question. If you take some time to be honest with yourselves, you'll realize you already knew this was the only possible outcome of this situation. If the outcome isn't to your liking, you have nobody to blame but yourselves."

The air in the room is still and tense. Nick is still standing. I can hear Vanessa breathing, and her breathing is quick and strained, like a rabbit's. Wulf has stopped eating to stare at Nick and Vanessa, and Dad has picked up his fork again.

"I don't think anyone's tried the bread yet," he says. "Wulf?"

Wulf shakes his head.

"Georgia, please pass around the bread basket," Dad says.

I pick up the basket and offer it to Vanessa, who hesitates a moment, then takes it with a surprisingly steady hand.

2

On Nick and Vanessa's first full day with us, we hardly see them. They only join us for supper, and neither of them say much of anything, as though they've made a pact of silence. Their second day at supper, we manage continuous, though stilted, conversation with Vanessa, and Nick at least answers when directly asked a question. On the evening of their third full day with us, Dad informs them that we wake up at five to do chores before the heat sets in, and they surprise us by being prompt the next morning to breakfast. We eat in silence, and then Dad doles out responsibilities for the day. Wulf's job is to collect cactus ribs to use for repairs, which means he has to walk to the saguaro graveyard. My job is to clean the solar panels, and Nick and Vanessa are offered the option of helping me.

"I guess you guys don't drink coffee?" Nick says when Dad leaves.

Wulf scoffs, though I know he only has a vague idea of what coffee is.

"Just this tea," I say.

Nick downs what's left in his teacup, grimacing.

"I'm not sure what you're complaining about, it's not like we drink coffee regularly," Vanessa says. She turns to me and says in a friendly voice: "How did you guys get solar panels?"

I finish chewing my bread and swallow. "We've always had them," I say. I take a rag and wipe the crumbs off the table, then hang it back on its hook.

Vanessa stands up and helps me gather the plates. "How long is always?"

"I was three when we came here."

"From the Californian deadlands, right?"

"Did my dad tell you that?"

"He mentioned it," says Vanessa. "He was talking about the fires."

"Enjoy the interrogation," Wulf says on his way out.

"You don't have to tell me anything you don't want to," says Vanessa.

"Don't worry," I say. "I won't."

The solar panels are just beyond the cactus gardens, where there's never any shade to block the sun. Nick carries two buckets of gray water, and I carry a pile of rags. It's still half an hour to sunrise, but there's enough light for us to make our way to the solar panels without bumping into anything. The sky is deep blue, and everything around us—the buildings, the shrubs, the garden tools on the ground—is a dark, indistinct shape waiting to be given its shape and color back by the sun.

"You can put the buckets there," I say to Nick.

About a quarter of the water splashes out when he sets them on the ground.

"Nick," scolds Vanessa. "You can't be so careless here."

"It's okay," I say.

"It's not, though," says Vanessa.

I explain to them how I usually clean the panels. Dip the rag in the first bucket, scrub lightly, then clean the dust and dirt off the rag in the other bucket. Then return to the first bucket to dip it in clean water again, and repeat.

"Yeah, I've cleaned things before," says Nick.

"You don't have to help," says Vanessa, taking a rag from me.

"What else am I supposed to do?" Nick says. Then he grimaces. "I'm sorry," he says, and I realize a moment later he's talking to me even though he isn't looking at me. "I'm not trying to sound angry. I'm just obviously in a frustrating situation here. Do you know what your father said when I asked him exactly how long he planned to keep us prisoners here?"

I shake my head, dipping my rag in the bucket.

"He said indefinitely."

"He might come around," says Vanessa.

"I wouldn't count on it," I say quietly. I don't tell them that Dad isn't one to change his mind. If he's decided that the safest way to neutralize the threat of Nick and Vanessa is to keep them here with us, there's no sense in imagining a different future. Instead, my mind flits into the past, to when Wulf and I were children and Dad took a systematic approach to our education. To teach us animal anatomy, he would capture a cricket or a scorpion in a jar and have us study it. Nick and Vanessa seem more like crickets to me than scorpions in terms of danger. But then, I don't know enough about the outside world to be an accurate judge.

"He took our phones," says Nick, scrubbing vigorously at a caked-on mound of dirt on one of the solar panels' edges. "For a man who's so concerned about his land, his sovereignty, his whatever, he doesn't seem to have a lot of respect for other people's property."

"Do you get any kind of signal out here?" asks Vanessa. "I'm guessing you don't use phones. But what about computers? Internet?"

"We have computers," I say.

"So how does that work?"

"Satellite. But Dad wouldn't let you use them."

"No, of course not," Vanessa says, her voice bright.

We scrub in silence as light starts to rise over the distant mountains, changing from blue to pink with bluish shadows. The air is warming up, but it's still cool enough to be outside.

"These solar panels are nicer than ours," says Vanessa. "Aren't they, Nick?"

Nick gives an unenthusiastic grunt. "Not hard to find something nicer than the setup at our apartment."

"Why?" I ask, glancing up from my scrubbing.

"Because it's a shithole of an apartment," Nick says.

"What does it look like?"

Nick shifts his weight to his haunches and turns to face me, as though to observe me better. "This place is all you know, huh?" he says. "You're like a little alien who's never seen anything else. Okay, let's see what I can do to paint you a picture. It's a big complex, like a resort. Big oversize buildings with big fat architectural flourishes. Sloping roofs and balconies, big fat staircases on the outside, and they only go up three stories. Two staircases on either end of the landing of each section. It's all built out of these thick walls, pinkish-brown colored, with a texture like if someone tried to scrape off the top layer but did a really shitty job of it. We live on one of the third floors. Two bedrooms, a living room, and a kitchen. Pretty standard fare. It's in a suburb, which is technically the outskirts of the city, but it's all connected, and it's filled up with apartments like that, and massive houses, and giant buildings that used to be stores. We rent it for a steal, so that's one good thing, and barely anyone else lives there. No loud neighbors, that's another plus. No running water, either, though, so we have to go out and buy that. They truck it in. It's rationed, but if you're running low or missed your day to pick up your share, you can buy something to drink from the stores. There's always someone around peddling homemade recycled water, too, but it's best to steer clear of that. Can't always trust it."

"Can I interrupt for a second?" asks Vanessa. It seems like she's talking to Nick, but Nick acts like he doesn't hear, so I nod. "How do you wash everything else here?" she asks. "Dishes, clothes, your bodies. You must have to be careful with your water, even if you have a ground-water well. I haven't had a chance to ask Isaac yet."

"We use sand and juniper for the dishes," I say. "We take sponge baths once a week, usually with water we get from the water machine. And then, when we're finished washing, we use that water for this," I say, nodding at the buckets we're using. "Or for washing clothes. The sun disinfects them when we lay them out to dry. We keep the drinking water in the steel drums in the glass house, and that's mostly water we pump from the well."

"Impressive," says Vanessa. "It sounds like you've got it all figured out."

"We do," I say, and the pride in my voice surprises me.

"I used to play a video game that was kind of like this," Nick says. "You'd have to start your own civilization on a desert planet, and you'd have to farm and make all your own stuff and find water and all that. And then I think there were these giant alien worms you'd have to fight, because they'd burrow through everything and ruin all your work or eat you or something. What?" he says when he sees my blank expression. "You've never played a video game?"

"Probably not what they want to spend their power on," says Vanessa.

"These solar panels actually generate a lot more power than we use," I say.

"Well, then you'll have to think up a way to waste it," says Nick.

"What do you mean?" I ask. "Why?"

"Because it'll keep you from being sanctimonious."

"Don't be a dick," says Vanessa.

"I'm just saying, it seems really easy for someone to convince themselves they're a self-righteous paradigm of virtue out here." Nick shrugs. "Sanctimoniousness is a vice all the ancients warn against, so, you know, maybe we should take heed or something."

"'All the ancients'?" Vanessa cuts in, her voice biting. "Like who? Because it seems to me that *all the ancients* were more worried about having destructive, overwhelming appetites than about whatever you're talking about. Socrates, Plato, Aristotle—I can't think of anyone who *didn't* talk about the importance of controlling yourself, actually."

Nick smiles tightly, pointedly looking away from Vanessa as she stares him down.

"I've never read those people," I say, looking between them.

"Highly recommended," says Nick, his voice suddenly hearty. "I'd get you some copies, but my hands are tied. Or, to be more precise, my tires are slashed."

"Do you really think people should be wasteful?" I ask after a pause.

"Oh, we're talking seriously now," says Nick. "Okay. Let's just say I don't think it's good to always be so good. I mean, maybe it looks like a good thing for the world at large, but not on a personal level. None of us are perfect. Acting like we are goes against our nature. I just figure acting against our nature can't be the point of life, right? Do we really want to live in a make-believe, disingenuous world, everyone acting like something they aren't?"

"It sounds a lot better than a world that's burning and flooding," I say.

"You're being dramatic," says Nick. "Is that what you think it's like out there?"

I shrug, which is the only honest response I can think of.

"You've got to get out more," Nick says. He grins at me, underscoring that this is a joke.

"I think I'm done with my side here," says Vanessa, walking over to one of the buckets and wringing out her dirty rag. "Unless I missed a spot."

"No, I don't think so," I tell her. "I'm almost done too."

"I'll help Nick finish his," says Vanessa.

"Looks like I'm slacking," says Nick.

"Looks like it," says Vanessa.

When we finish washing them, the solar panels reflect the sky in perfect light-blue squares. Dawn has snapped fully into early morning, and bright clouds hang thick and low, their puffy edges as sharply defined as a drawing. I stand up slowly and stretch out my arms up toward it, my body stiff from crouching.

"How often do you have to do this?" Vanessa asks me.

"Once a month, more or less. It's been longer this time."

"Busy with other things?" asks Vanessa. She's wringing out her rag over a bucket, not looking at me as though she's not really interested in my answer, but of course she's angling for information. There's something about her subtlety, the fact that she isn't outright asking, that puts me on sudden alert. That makes me realize our conversation is less a conversation than an exchange of information, with the direction of the exchange flowing from me to Vanessa. It seems unwise to continue talking to her without direction from Dad.

"I'll show you the library now," I tell them.

The library is next to Dad's office, and it's one of the two buildings that's fully aboveground, though it still hunkers close to the earth. The roof is thick and broad, slanting slowly to the ground. The walls inside are lined with books, and a loose maze of waist-high bookshelves takes up the whole left side. On the right are three old armchairs, a small table that Dad made out of a dead saguaro, and a sideboard with a pitcher of water sitting on it.

Nick and Vanessa walk slowly along the shelves, studying the books separately. Vanessa keeps to the walls, her arms folded against her chest. She peers at the spines, turning her head to get a better look, sometimes pausing for a long time before a section. Nick plops himself on the concrete floor beside one of the smaller bookshelves. He slips out a book and flips through it until he loses interest, returns it, and picks out another.

"There's water if you're thirsty," I say.

"I'd take a cup," Nick says. "Vanessa?"

"Sure," she says distractedly. "Are they arranged in any special way? The books?"

"The ones on the walls are my dad's," I say, pulling two cups out of the sideboard. "The ones he likes or uses the most, he arranged them there. The shelves in the middle are by subject, and then alphabetical. I can help you find something, if you want."

"Don't worry about it, I'm just looking," says Vanessa. "Where are the novels? Or poetry?"

"There aren't any."

"That's a funny omission for a library."

"There used to be," I say, "but Dad burned them."

Vanessa's eyebrows shoot up. I turn away and pour water into a cup carefully.

"What I've always wondered," says Nick, frowning at the book on his knee, "is how they came up with names for prehistoric landmarks. I mean, Lake Bonneville? That's supposed to be a prehistoric lake? That sounds like the town a grandmother would be from. Was that anywhere around here, this Lake Bonneville, so called?"

"Really?" says Vanessa, turning to frown at him. "You've always wondered that?"

"I think it's further north," I say, filling the second cup with water.

"Lake Bonneville," Nick repeats, like it's the most baffling thing he's ever heard.

"Your dad has a lot of books on tech for a guy who lives so off the grid," says Vanessa.

I look up, but Vanessa's face is placid, her head tilted as she continues to read the spines. She sways back and forth lightly, her hands holding her elbows. My limbs have stiffened involuntarily, and I try to relax them. I set down the water pitcher carefully.

"My dad reads widely," I say, still facing away from her.

Vanessa only thanks me when I hand her a cup of water, but I get the sense that she noticed my reaction. That she noted it and filed it away in her head to write down later. An overreaction, I tell myself. If Dad isn't paranoid, there's no reason why I should be. Out of the corner of my eye, I watch Vanessa migrate over to another part of the bookshelf. She slides out a book about Egypt and opens it idly.

"Proto-Tethys Ocean," says Nick. "Now that's more like it."

"I'm going to leave you here," I tell them.

"You mean you want us to stay here?" asks Vanessa, looking up from the book.

"Yes," I falter. "Just for now, for a while."

"What if I need to take a shit?" asks Nick. "There isn't a toilet pit in here, is there? My stomach's still getting used to all this all-natural food."

"You can leave the library if you really need to."

"But then come back here," Vanessa says.

"That'd probably be best. You'll have something to do here."

"Something that doesn't involve, say, trying to escape," says Nick.

"It's just for now," I say again.

Vanessa laughs. "First time having captives?"

"You aren't captives."

"Oh?" says Vanessa.

"It's just not possible for you to leave," I try to explain. It seems so obvious—of course she has to do what Dad says—that I have a hard time even finding words to express it.

"All right," Vanessa says like she's taking pity on me. "We'll stay put."

Nick is watching me, the book still open on his knee. "Does Isaac keep tabs on you and Wulf like this? I guess there's nowhere for you to go, even if you wanted to. You're sort of captives, too, in a way. Do you ever feel like getting out of this place?"

"No," I say shortly. "Dad will get you for lunch."

When I close the door behind me, I take a breath and wipe my palms on my pants. I take long strides that are all the same length. The sun is high enough in the sky now to warm the top of my head, but despite that, my skin is clammy and uncomfortable.

It takes me an hour and a half to get to the saguaro graveyard, a patch of desert spotted with saguaros that used to grow taller than any other plant in the desert. The saguaros there have fallen in on themselves, and the birds have stripped them to their skeletons. When I reach Wulf, he has his arm in a dead cactus, sawing out a rib with his knife.

"Does Dad want me?" he asks without looking up.

"No. We finished washing the solar panels."

"So? Shouldn't you be keeping watch over them?" I hear a snap, and Wulf pulls himself out of the cactus's body, a rib in hand that he adds to the pile at his feet.

"I took them to the library and told them to stay there."

"You think they'll listen to you?"

"Why wouldn't they? Dad's right there."

Wulf's mouth contorts, but he doesn't argue.

I pick up one of the cactus ribs and run my palm along the smooth part of its surface, then carefully set it back down on the pile because Wulf's watching with his eyebrows furrowed, like he's worried I'll break something. "What do you think of them?" I ask.

"Nothing," he says.

"Don't tell me you haven't been thinking about them."

Wulf shrugs, his narrow shoulders rising and falling jerkily.

"They're the first strangers you've ever met," I say.

"You too. You don't remember anything from before we came here. Anyway, it doesn't matter what I think. Whatever we do with them is up to Dad."

"So that means you don't have any thoughts?"

"No," Wulf says grudgingly. He sets his sights on another cactus rib, this one slightly separated from the rest, and digs his knife into the rib at an angle, trying to turn the knife to break it. The rib doesn't give. Wulf grunts and wiggles out the knife. He uses his forearm to wipe the sweat off his face. "Do you think they'll kill themselves?" he asks abruptly.

"What? No. Why would you say that?"

"I don't know. I just thought of it. They're trapped here. Maybe they'll start feeling desperate. Or they could try to kill us if they really wanted to get away. They could try smothering us with pillows while we're sleeping."

"And go where? They can't walk all the way to Phoenix. They'd get heatstroke or get lost before they even found a road that leads there."

"If they're desperate, they wouldn't be thinking it through."

"We'd be able to fight them off," I say. "And you're a light sleeper, you'd wake up."

"It was just one idea," Wulf says. "They could think of other ways."

"They're not going to kill anyone. They're not like that."

"How do you know?" Wulf says, his voice turning bullish.

"I can just tell. Nothing about them feels threatening. Don't you think we'd feel it if they were dangerous?"

"Dad thinks they're a danger," Wulf says, frowning.

"Only if they leave and tell people about us, or about what Dad is doing here. If he thought they would hurt us, he wouldn't have had them help me with the chores this morning when no one else was around, would he?"

"So maybe they won't murder us. They could be dangerous in a different way. Maybe some way we don't see yet. But Dad does."

I open my mouth to speak, then think better of it.

"What?" Wulf says, his eyes suspicious.

"Nothing. It's just—remember years ago, when Dad was convinced he was dying? After he started getting those bad headaches all the time? And he had us memorize a whole plan for what to do when that happened? All those little details of how we'd burn and bury his body, and he'd quiz us on it to make sure we didn't forget a step. And then the headaches stopped, and it turned out he had probably been getting them because we had less water that summer, and he was getting older. I just mean—sometimes he sees danger that isn't exactly there."

"He wasn't *convinced* he was dying, he was just preparing us," Wulf says. "You think you have everything figured out about everything. Well, you don't. They're dangerous, Dad says so, and he wants us to be careful." He moves on to sawing the bottom part of the rib out of the cactus, and when he finishes, he adds it to the pile and studies the cactus again.

"I never said I had it all figured out," I say, watching him.

"What do you think is going to happen?" he says. "That we'll all live happily ever after here together? What are they even going to do here?"

I chew my lip. "I don't know. What do we do here?"

"We live the most ethical life we can," says Wulf, parroting Dad.

"Right. Everything Dad does is very ethical."

Wulf looks at me hard, and, instantly, I regret saying it.

"Let's go back," I say. "You have enough ribs now, right? I'll help you carry them."

We hardly speak while walking back, and we only stop once to examine a small half-eaten carcass. Wulf determines it's a rat, but too long dead for us to eat, and we move on. When we arrive back to the settlement, we drop off the cactus ribs by the glass house, and Wulf heads straight to Dad's office, walking quickly with long strides. But almost as soon as he's disappeared down the stairs, he's climbing back up again.

"What is it?" I ask.

Wulf scans the settlement, eyes searching.

A moment later, we hear Dad's voice, low and sonorous, coming from the library, and then a higher voice, brighter, responding enthusiastically.

3

Dad and Vanessa are sitting in the armchairs, and they both look up when we come in. Vanessa has a small black notebook resting on her knee. Dad is leaning back comfortably, his thin arms making right triangles that stick out over the armrests. His hands are folded on his stomach, and his legs are stretched out, crossed at the ankle.

"All finished, Wulf?" Dad asks.

Wulf nods stiffly.

"What's going on?" I ask.

"Vanessa and I were doing a little interview," Dad says. "Why not, I thought. With the way the situation has panned out, there's no reason to be cagey with our guests. Although perhaps *guests* isn't the most appropriate term. I do believe in the importance of proper nomenclature. Which reminds me, Georgia, I was just about to mention to Vanessa your excellent mineral and fossil collection. Perhaps you could show it to her? This might be a good time for us to wrap up here." He readjusts himself to sit up straighter in his chair.

Vanessa smiles at me apologetically. She probably realizes that Dad is politely trying to get rid of her. Wulf's expression is gloating, as he's free to stay in the library with Dad. I nod and motion for Vanessa to follow me. She trails me out of the library and across the settlement to my building.

"It's a lot cooler in here," she says when we're inside. She holds her elbows and peers around the dark space, blinking until her eyes adjust to the dark.

"It isn't like that in your building?" I ask.

"It is, I was just making conversation." She laughs self-consciously. "It actually got pretty cold at night. I had to go over to Nick's and ask him if he had extra blankets."

"You and Nick have different buildings?" I ask, looking over at her.

"Your dad said there were plenty."

"Four we don't use," I say. "Well, two now." I'm quiet for a moment. Then I ask: "Did you get the blanket? Some of the buildings we don't use might not have everything you need."

"Nick wasn't using his, so he gave it to me."

"I'll check if we have an extra stored away somewhere."

Vanessa nods. "Thanks, that'd be great."

"Why do you and Nick have different buildings?"

"We've found that it works better for us. We have different sleep schedules." She doesn't sound irritated, but her voice has a tone of finality.

"It's just in here," I say, pointing to the door of my bedroom.

The fossils are arranged on shelves nailed to my walls, rows of flat rocks with imprints of lone limbs from ancient animals, the feathery fronds of plants. There are a few pieces of turquoise, a piece of petrified wood, and a small gray meteorite. Vanessa's gaze moves to my bed and nightstand, to the blurry charcoal drawings tacked up between the shelves. They're all the same picture, all more or less the desert around the settlement. The same saguaros, the same mountains in the background, a flat expanse of dry shrubs, in different configurations.

"Those are nice," Vanessa says. "Did you draw them?"

"Dad did. He used to draw me one every year for my birthday."

"Not anymore?"

"I don't need any more," I say.

Her eyes move to my dresser, which is cluttered with more rocks and fossils, a crumbling snakeskin, a handful of stubby pencils, and my small collection of objects that I've found in and around the settlement. A cup with *IHOP* in rounded blue letters, a necklace made of jagged pieces of white coral, a lighter made of red plastic, broken and empty. A sparkly blue comb with its teeth bent, twelve empty tin cans, a jar of multicolored bottle caps, a tea tin, and a yellow sandal made of foam, the strap dangling off. A collection of small foil bags and colorful paper wrappers tied in a roll with a rubber band. Vanessa touches the snake-skin with a finger and picks up one of the tin cans. "What's all this?" she asks.

"Things I found."

Vanessa tilts the can so it catches the light coming through the window. "Pretty," she says. "Where'd you find them?"

"That one in the basement of the glass house. There's a lot of old stuff in there that isn't ours. Maybe it's from the people you're researching, the ones who built this place."

"Maybe," Vanessa says, setting down the can and picking up the comb. "What about this one?"

"It's a comb," I say unnecessarily.

Vanessa runs her fingers lightly along the teeth so they bend and spring back up. "You've got quite a collection in here. What does your dad think about all this?"

"He doesn't encourage it," I say, watching her.

"No, I wouldn't think so." Vanessa peers at the mug. "It doesn't seem like he'd like you wondering about the world. That's not his ethos."

"You just met him," I say after a confused pause.

"That's true," says Vanessa without taking her eyes off the objects on my dresser. "Maybe I'm taking too much liberty in speculating. Regardless, that's what you're doing, isn't it? Trying to piece together what it's like out there?"

I shake my head noncommittally, neither no nor yes.

Vanessa smiles brightly. "If you don't want to talk about it, no problem. Maybe we can look at those fossils Isaac wanted you to show me." She takes a few steps toward a shelf nailed to the wall and leans her face up close to the rocks. "What are these ones?"

"Trilobites. You can find them all over the place."

"Well, maybe you can," says Vanessa.

"They're really everywhere."

"Where's the good stuff, then?"

I walk to the other side of the room, to the shelves near my nightstand. "That one's interesting," I say, pointing to a fairly flat piece of rock with a thin fish head imprinted into it, its eye the size of a circle you can make with your thumb and forefinger.

"Is it a fish?" asks Vanessa, tilting her head. "It kind of looks like a swordfish."

"An ichthyosaur," I say.

Vanessa raises her eyebrows at me.

"Kind of like a fish-lizard."

"Ah, yes," says Vanessa. "The mighty fish-lizards of old."

A sound comes out of me that's trying to be a laugh, but it sounds strangled.

Vanessa examines the ichthyosaur a moment longer. Then she moves on to a collection of rocks with imprints of leaves displayed on the next shelf, humming lightly in appreciation.

"Not to harp on the outside-world thing," she says without turning to face me. "But just out of curiosity, if you don't mind me asking, what do you imagine it's like out there?"

"I don't know. Tall buildings and smog masks. People staying inside."

"You don't think people ever go outside in cities?"

"It's just not what I imagine."

"Well, you're not totally off. Usually, when it gets really bad in a city—the air, or the weather, or the natural disasters—people decamp. The Center States are still pretty livable. Life goes on pretty normally there. Stores, schools, family reunions. With some exceptions, the water's pretty safe, especially if you have a good filtration system."

"But it's not that way in Phoenix, right?"

"No, it's not. I wouldn't call it a normal life, but it's not impossible to live there. There are still long-haul trucks that bring in supplies. But everyone who can has already left, and the rest are working on scraping up the money."

"Have you always lived there?"

"No, no, we're from Ohio. The Center States. We only moved to Phoenix a year ago. It was supposed to be a temporary thing, just because of the project I was working on—a book about the Domes they're building north of here."

I blink, not sure I heard correctly. The words replay in my mind, confirming what I heard but not making logical sense. She can't be talking about the same Domes that we know—the ones Dad is bent on fighting, the ones he currently considers to be the most pressing threat from the outside world, the target he obsessively returns to via quiet keystrokes on his computers.

"Have you heard of them?" Vanessa continues, seemingly oblivious to my reaction. "They're trying to build four little cities—well, *communities* would be a better word, but I guess *cities* has a more impressive ring to it—enclosed in these huge self-sustaining Domes. Climate control, a closed water system, food grown inside. All powered by a nuclear generator they've built. Something like what Isaac's doing here, you could say, but more high-tech. And reproducible, to see if they can fill the desert with these Domes and make the deadlands livable for a significant population again. Or, at least, that's how they're pitching it. But, I mean, the generator alone is a huge giveaway that that's not the full story, right? Because why not just use solar power, if the plan is to repopulate the desert using Domes? There's plenty of that here. The fact is, they're thinking about the deadlands of the future, not the deadlands we've already given up on, like here. They don't say this, but I've talked to enough people to know that it's really a test run. Like I said, the Center States are shielded from the worst of the changes for now, but it's only a matter of time before the issues we've been seeing the world over catch up to it. Water shortages, more tornadoes than we're already seeing, bad AQI from everyone in the country crowding in. It's a deadland in the making. At the rate we're going, everywhere is. Anyway, that's what I was supposed to be working on. Obviously, I got distracted."

A brief silence falls. Vanessa's expression is placid and amiable.

"I actually wasn't expecting to live in Phoenix," she continues after a moment. "I wanted to live in the Domes themselves, or the little town they built for the workers, but they wouldn't let us, so I had to drive back and forth. I guess I'm thankful for it now. I was pretty irritated at first. You'd think they'd be more accommodating to someone who wanted to write about them, or at least sound sorry when they told me it wasn't possible."

"Why?" I ask as Vanessa walks over to examine a trilobite.

"You're only allowed to live in the Domes if you're part of the build," she says, touching her finger to the fossil. "Not enough resources yet to sustain anyone else yet. At least that's the excuse they gave me. Honestly, I think they just didn't like that I was writing about them. Asking questions about what it meant for the future instead of just blindly accepting the story they were force-feeding everyone. Two extra people wouldn't use up *that* much resources. There has to be a margin of error, some flexibility they've worked in."

"I meant, why are you thankful?"

"Oh. Turns out, it's been a nonstop headache up there. Power outages, hydraulics not working properly. Growing food has been a nightmare because of the water issues and the climate control going in and out. The system went into emergency lockdown in one of the Domes once, and some glitch made it so everyone got trapped inside for a few days with the climate control and airflow filtering failing. They were seriously worried people were going to suffocate to death in there. I think maybe a whole fourth of the team quit after that, and I don't blame them. But there wasn't a shortage of people willing to replace them—the pay is good—so the project just keeps chugging along."

I turn my attention to a fossil of a shell and adjust it carefully to center it on its shelf.

"Did you find all these here yourself?" Vanessa asks, as though the question just occurred to her. "The fossils? Or do Isaac and Wulf help you?"

I nudge the fossil back to its original location with my finger. I'm buying time, trying to decide what to tell her. But Vanessa changes tack again, veering the conversation in another direction, interrupting her own train of thought.

"Your father's right that it's not sustainable," she says. "The way the world's going about living. Even the Center States. We just keep building higher and higher, but there's only so high you can go. And there are so, so many people. They've stopped accepting refugees from other countries so they can deal with all the refugees coming in from the deadlands in other states, did you know that? And life just keeps going on as it always has. It's easy to forget the chaos happening everywhere else. We have our lawns, our movie theaters, our heating systems in the winter. But you can't blame people for wanting to live normal lives, can you?"

"Is that what you and Dad were talking about in the library?" I ask.

"No, Isaac was mostly describing all the improvements he's made to the settlement. But right before you and your brother came in? He'd been telling me about your mother, actually. You know, I lost my mother at a very young age too."

I continue watching her and don't say anything.

Vanessa smiles kindly. "We don't have to talk about it," she says.

"There's nothing to talk about," I say. "I don't remember her. All I know is what Dad told me."

"And what's that?"

"Probably the same thing that he told you. That they were really in love, and that they met while protesting a lithium mine, and that she was really smart and talented and knew something about everything. I think I—well, it doesn't matter."

34

"What?"

I shake my head, dismissing the thought. But somehow, despite my heightened awareness that I should be careful about what I say to Vanessa, I go on talking anyway. "I have this picture of her in my head," I say hurriedly, "like a memory, but I was too young to remember her before she died. So it's not really a memory, it's just how I imagine her."

"What's happening in the memory? Even if it's just in your head."

"Nothing's happening. She's just watching Wulf and me while we're trying to catch grasshoppers—they're crawling all over the ground, like there's a plague of them, but nobody's upset about it—and I can tell she's smiling, even though I can't see her well. The sun's right behind her, so she's mostly in the shadow. She's tall and has short hair. That's it."

"Huh," says Vanessa. "And this was in the Californian deadlands?"

"I guess, if any of it really happened. It looks like we're at the settlement when I picture it, but that's because I don't remember any other place. Maybe I made up the memory out of nowhere. Or maybe it's how I imagined a story Dad told me about her."

"Your dad did seem to have a lot to say," Vanessa says, her voice thoughtful. "I don't think I got the full story, but it seemed like her death was what really radicalized him. She died from the smoke, right? From the fires in the Californian deadlands? You know, not remembering someone is plenty to talk about in itself. But don't worry about it if you don't want to. I'm not here to pry into your life."

"No?" I ask.

Vanessa doesn't look startled or offended. She just looks me over, a small smile playing over her mouth. I search her face curiously. She meets my gaze, but she doesn't say anything more to explain herself. It's only when she leaves that I realize why her sentence—*I'm not here to pry into your life*—strikes me as strange. It's not that she's implying she's here for a different reason than prying into my life, or Wulf's, or Dad's—it's that she's implying she's here for a reason at all. Meaning a reason of her own, not just the simple explanation that she's here because Dad is forcing her and Nick to stay.

4

By their second week, Nick and Vanessa have adapted to our routines. If they aren't happy about living with us, they've at least become resigned to it. Vanessa joins Dad, Wulf, and me for our morning calisthenics. She starts offering to cook supper and impresses us by roasting a jackrabbit in the solar oven. She asks Dad more questions about how we came to live the way we do, and Dad looks pleased to launch into an explanation of how he taught himself to forage for food, or hunt javelina, or build chairs. Nick grimaces a lot during these conversations and seems like he takes pains to look uninterested, but he rarely says anything hostile. He takes to sauntering in and out of the library without asking Dad permission first, and Dad lets him. Every morning, he picks out a book, settles into a chair by the cactus garden with his feet up on a second chair, and spends hours alternating between reading and dozing with the book propped open on his chest. Meanwhile, Vanessa spends the hottest part of the day in the relative cool of her building. Writing, she says. Dad sometimes asks her if she wants to do an interview before supper, perhaps as a peace offering, or perhaps because he's starting to like talking to her. For reasons that aren't quite clear to me, I haven't told Dad that Vanessa had been writing about the Domes. Whenever I think about it, a hot, sharp pain settles in my stomach, and my mind leaps away as though scorched. I decide to pretend I forgot the conversation, to keep my distance from Vanessa so I don't get weighed down with whatever else she tells me.

One day, Nick calls out my name when I'm walking by with an empty tin pan. "What are you up to right now?" he asks.

"Harvesting the mealworms," I say, slowing my pace.

"Oh yeah?" He lowers his feet off the second chair and sits up. "Mind if I join you? Reading and sunning myself just isn't cutting it for entertainment today."

"Sure," I say, watching him cautiously.

He hops out of his chair, and I lead us to the ramada, where we keep the mealworm farm in the shade. It's a four-level container, about half as tall as I am. I explain the four levels to Nick and pull out the drawers one by one to show him the eggs, then mealworms, then pupae, then black beetles wriggling and crawling over each other.

"So, these little guys are just babies," says Nick, picking up a golden-brown worm when I open the second drawer again. "I thought mealworms were just mealworms, but they're beetles in training, huh? Who would have thought?"

"We harvest them at three months, when they're in the larval stage," I say.

"Little three-month-old worm babies."

"Do you still want to help?"

He drops the worm back into the container and grins. "All right, no more fun and games."

"I didn't mean it like that."

Nick gestures with his hand, telling me to move along, a grin still plastered on his face.

I point to the open drawer. "We'll harvest about half of them and put them in the tin. If it's not moving, leave it be. It might've already gone to the pupa stage. We need those to turn into beetles so they lay more eggs."

"All righty then," says Nick, and starts plucking out the wriggling worms one by one and dropping them into the pan. When we finish, we transfer the pupae we find to the third drawer, move a handful of new larvae from the drawer with the eggs to the mealworm section, and remove the bugs' excrement, which I tell Nick is what looks like flecks of dirt.

"What's next?" asks Nick. "Do we just put them in the sun to sizzle?"

"We use the solar oven. It goes quicker."

"The things I'm learning," says Nick.

The mealworms take just under ten minutes on the solar oven to stop wriggling, but I tell Nick we'll leave them on for a while longer, until they turn crispy. We should still stand by, I tell him, so that the birds don't eat them. Nick shakes his head and says that never before in his life has he had to compete for food with birds, and I tell him that he has, that he's been competing with everything else that's alive in the world whenever he's eaten anything. But he scoffs and says it isn't even a bit the same when it's just abstract.

"We're pretty concrete here," I say.

"Did I just hear a pun on the dominant building material used in your settlement?" Nick says, his eyes widening in mock awe.

"It was unintentional," I say after I realize what he's talking about.

"Nothing is an accident, some people say. What do you say to that?"

"You mean, do I agree?"

"That's exactly what I mean. What do you think? Is there a great cosmic plan we're all a part of, or are we flailing around in a meaningless void?"

"Are those my only two options?"

"Are you saying you want nuance and gray area?"

"That might be nice."

Nick grins at me, the corners of his eyes creasing. "You know, I like you," he says. "I don't like this situation I'm in, being restrained against my will and kept under surveillance. But I had a feeling we'd get along when I first met you. You know, it'd be nice to get to know you better."

I nod with a vague sense of not knowing what I'm agreeing to. "How's Vanessa's writing going?" I ask after a few moments of us both watching the mealworms toast to a darker brown.

"You're better off asking Vanessa that," Nick says, smiling placidly.

"Okay." I fumble for something else to ask. "What were you reading earlier?"

Nick waves his hand. "A textbook about electrical engineering. I was just flipping through the pages. What are you doing after this?"

"After this? I'll grind up the mealworms into flour. And then I'll go walking or read."

"You know what I'd like to do?" says Nick.

I shake my head.

"See that funny piece of metal you found out there, out where we first found you."

"The container?"

"That's what you're calling it, huh? Well, how about we go see The Container?" He says this in a deep, slow voice, as though it's some otherworldly creature he's announcing to an audience. I can't tell whether he's mocking me and, if he is, whether I should laugh.

It's strange to see myself watching myself this way, thinking about how I should or shouldn't react to another person. I think back to when I told Wulf I didn't think Nick or Vanessa were a danger. Suddenly, this doesn't quite ring true. There is a hint of danger, just not the kind that Wulf meant. I'm not sure how to act around Nick, and I'm not sure why. And that uncertainty feels like standing on a cliff's edge—destabilizing and precarious.

"I don't think so," I say.

"What else do you have going on?"

"It's just that it's a little far."

"What's some sightseeing that's nearer, then?"

I shake my head again.

"Well, where were you going to walk to?"

"Nowhere special. I just walk sometimes."

39

"No particular destination in mind?"

"No."

"What are you looking for out there?"

"Nothing," I say, and I can hear my voice sounding defensive.

"All right," Nick says, and there's a glint of triumph in his eyes, like he thinks he's caught me out on something. "But if you ever want to admit you're scouting for your own escape—not saying that's what you've been doing, just saying if—I'll happily lend an ear."

I shake my head firmly. "That won't happen."

"Also, I wouldn't be opposed to taking a walk with the intention of finding nothing, you know. I don't know why I didn't bug you to let me tag along sooner. This is a lot better than sitting around and pretending to read to keep myself busy."

"I should finish with the mealworms," I say.

"All right, well, another day then," Nick says. He gives me a kind of parting salute, and then starts heading back to his chair before pivoting and walking to his building instead.

It doesn't take me long to finish the mealworms. I pull half off the oven and pour them whole into a jar. I let the other half bake a few minutes longer so they're easier to desiccate. When they look close to burning, I gather them up and grind them with a mortar and pestle and pour the resulting flour into a second jar. Then I take them to Dad's house to store in the pantry. It's always empty at this time of day, so I don't knock. But when I open the door, there's Dad, sitting alone at the kitchen table, his body leaning forward like he's falling asleep, his eyes closed. A pad of paper on the table is open to an unfinished sketch of a settlement similar to ours, but with more buildings, with people milling around that are presently just their component shapes. His eyes flash open when I enter. "Georgia," he says, sitting up straighter.

"I'm just putting these away," I say, holding up the jars.

He nods and rubs his face with his hand.

"Are you okay?" I ask.

"Just a little tired," Dad says. "I've been having trouble sleeping."

His candor surprises me; it's unlike Dad to admit a weakness, even a temporary physical failing. "Can I get you anything?" I ask.

"No, no. But since you're here, let me ask you something."

I set the jars down in the pantry and obediently sit down on the edge of a chair.

"Have you noticed anything unusual in the desert in recent weeks? Anything different? Apart from the arrival of our guests—I'm not referring to that. I'm speaking more broadly. Anything that caught your attention."

I run the last few weeks over in my head. It's a montage of cooking food and harvesting water, one-off tasks like washing windows and replenishing our stash of mesquite flour. Of calisthenics in the morning, then Dad and Wulf disappearing into Dad's office and me retreating into the library or my building, walking for hours through the cacti and chaparral.

"Anything," says Dad.

"I haven't," I say, and I can't help feeling like I've failed a test.

Dad looks past me, like he's trying to figure out something that he can't quite see or put together, something that's just behind me. "Yesterday I came across a family of dead quail," he says. "One adult and three chicks, just outside the settlement. At first, I thought to myself, maybe the dog's come back, but when I looked closely at the birds, there were no bite marks, no blood on the feathers. No sign of any kind of physical altercation. Not to mention, no sign of the dog anywhere. Now, what could make a family of quail just fall down dead? I don't know if I've ever seen a whole family of them dead on the ground like that for no discernible reason."

"It's been dry," I venture. "Maybe they couldn't find water."

"They've been able to adapt up to this point. They're resourceful creatures. I can't think of a reason why they'd suddenly find themselves unfit for their habitat."

"Maybe they were sick," I say.

"You know, Georgia," Dad says, and from his voice I immediately know I've hit upon what he wanted to hear. "That's exactly what I was thinking through myself. Four quail in and of themselves aren't necessarily worth mourning or mention, but if it's indicative of a larger problem, if it's a warning sign of a greater truth, then that's something we need to keep our eyes on. We'll have to keep observing."

"I'll keep an eye out."

"Good," he says, standing. "Is there anything else you need here, Georgia?" I shake my head. "Back to work, then." He gestures at the front door, ushers me outside, and shuts the door behind us. Then he heads to his office, his strides long and quick.

It's only midmorning, and the temperature's still okay for walking. I think about Nick asking me what I'm looking for out there, and I let the question rest lightly on my mind and then float away like sand combed by wind without unearthing anything.

I pick my way across shrubs and around cacti and clusters of rocks too big to climb over. It's easy to focus on my steps and the growing plants around me and the dirt. I pause to rub creosote between my fingers, releasing the scent of rain. The sun's heat is growing steadily, and I walk slowly so my body doesn't overheat from exertion. The ground becomes rockier, less sand and more stone, until I'm stepping from rock to rock, keeping an eye out for snakes.

Idly, I wonder what Nick and I would be talking about right now if he were walking beside me, like he'd suggested, but I haven't spoken to him enough to imagine a conversation. Vanessa is easier to predict. She'd be asking me the kinds of questions she's asking Dad now: what's this plant called and is it edible, how we cut our hair, how deep our well is.

An hour later, the only animal I've seen is a small tarantula scuttling to hide from the sound of me coming closer. I spot a rock with what looks like an imprint and pick it up, but it's only a rock with a funny shape, and I place it carefully back where I found it. When cacti start to poke up from the rocks more insistently, I know I'm close. Most of the cacti are stubby here, small barrel cacti and stunted ocotillo no taller than my knees, but I pass a saguaro, and yucca and cholla start popping up here and there. The landscape flattens. There's more rock and looser sand. I check a shrub for soapberries, but there are none, just leaves smaller than my fingernails. When I find a cholla with little light-green buds, the spines weak and sparse, I pull out a cloth bag from my pocket and pluck off most of them. Later, I'll pull off the spines with tweezers, extracting them one by one, and then we'll eat them with tepary beans, or can them.

My eyes wander across the stones to see if I can find anything, a crumpled piece of foil, an abandoned bucket, a piece of plastic poking through the sand. Sometimes, the desert holds them back, hides them behind a shrub or a shadow, keeps them covered up with dirt. There's nothing, though. For a long time, all I see is stone and plants. Later, a thin line of ants crossing the ground jaggedly.

5

By the time I arrive back to the settlement, it's too hot to stay outside any longer. My head is pounding, and my skin prickles with dried sweat. I drop off the cholla buds in the dehydrator. The settlement is quiet and empty, nobody outside to ask where anybody is. Inside my building, I strip off my clothes and lie on the floor where there aren't any rugs over it, my naked back pressed against the cool cement. I adjust so my spine is flush against it. I turn one cheek to touch the floor, then the other, then roll onto my stomach and lay my head on my arms. The curtains are drawn, and the darkness feels good against my eyes, almost a substitute for cold itself. I breathe deeply and evenly, imagining breathing out the heat and the heat dissipating. I end up falling asleep there, dreaming fitfully through the afternoon, images and scenes flitting in and out of my mind, none sticking.

It's a knock that wakes me. I pull myself off the floor to sit up, my limbs tight and aching, and rub my face with my hands. Blistering orange light is streaming through the curtains like a wasp intent on getting in. The knocking repeats, loud and insistent.

"It's Wulf," Wulf's voice calls. "Dad wants you."

"Just a minute," I call back, my voice groggy.

I heave myself off the floor and pull my clothes back on, then hurry outside, my head spinning, the edges of my vision darkening briefly from standing up and moving so fast. The light and heat stab my eyes when I open the door, and I flinch.

"What does he want me for?" I ask, squinting up at Wulf.

Wulf studies me critically from the top of the stairs.

"What does Dad want me for?" I ask again, climbing up and into the full sun.

"He wants to talk to both of us together."

"About Nick and Vanessa?"

"Don't know," Wulf says.

Dad's office looks similar to the other buildings except there's no furniture when you enter, and there's a set of stairs that leads down to an even lower level, a basement. The basement is a single room, the walls lined with a flat board for a desk and two straight-backed chairs placed at different computers. There are two desktops and three laptops, all different sizes and slightly different shapes. One of each doesn't work, and they're harvested for parts for the others. They're like bodies in the middle of a vivisection, opened up and missing pieces, various bits of metal and plastic with wires spilling out lying on the desk's surface next to them. The lights are dim, and the computers are off, their screens black. There's nothing on the mudbrick walls except remains of clinging cobwebs at the corners, heavy with dust and age.

Dad's sitting in one of the chairs, leaning back with his hands folded in his lap, waiting. Wulf moves as though to sit in the other, but Dad shakes his head, and Wulf starts to scowl before remembering himself and taking his place standing beside me.

"I wanted to talk to the two of you in private about our guests," Dad says. He pauses and examines us briefly, as though to glean our responses. I keep my face empty, a receptive blank. Dad says: "I realize it's an adjustment for the two of you, sharing our space with others. I'd like to thank you for your hospitality to them. It's an unexpected intrusion, but I suppose it was bound to happen one of these days. People get curious, nose around. Herm and Eduardo were always warning me something like this could happen. We're lucky our visitors appear relatively harmless. Regardless, I should tell you, so that there's no misunderstanding, that you should keep them at a distance. Even if they're here permanently, a part of our settlement now, it's best to introduce them to our life slowly. They learn what they need to know when they need to know it. Is that understood?" Wulf and I say yes. Dad's gaze rests on me for a moment. "Good," he says, moving his eyes away. "We'll move on to a related matter. I'd like to know, from your perspectives, how you believe our guests to be settling in. Wulf, let's begin with you."

Wulf looks stricken by the question.

"I realize that you haven't interacted much with them," says Dad. "I'm looking for an answer that takes that into account. Only an impression from afar."

"They haven't been to their car," Wulf says finally.

"Yes," Dad says, nodding. "It's a good observation. I've noticed that as well. Although we have to be careful not to take that as incontrovertibly signifying the meaning we assign to it. Our guests may be thinking about leaving all the time and consciously avoiding their vehicle because they'd like us to think exactly as we're inclined to—that their desire to leave is seeping away or has already left them. Georgia, you've had conversations with them. What have you talked about with them?"

"Vanessa's been asking questions," I say.

"What has she asked you?"

"Just about what life is like here."

"And Nick? Does he ask you questions?"

"He asked to help with the mealworms today."

"So he's beginning to participate. That's good to hear. A positive sign that he's adjusting. I'd ask you to encourage that attitude, if the occasion allows."

I nod, keeping my face expressionless.

"Encourage it slowly, of course, taking what I said earlier into account," says Dad. "We need to keep them at a distance while still encouraging them to feel more comfortable, more welcome. That seems to be the best compromise, the best way to ensure everything stays the way it's been as much as possible. Is that understood? Good. That's all for now. Georgia, you can start on supper. Wulf, you can pump some water from the well and prepare the water machine for harvesting. Thank you both for your attention."

When we climb out of the office, Wulf says: "That was for you. Dad telling us to not get too close. He's telling you to be careful."

"He's not telling me any more than he's telling you."

"You're the one who talks to them."

"So what? What's wrong with that?" I can hear myself sounding defensive, and maybe it is because I feel some guilt about the pull I feel toward Nick and Vanessa. Maybe I should force myself to be more like Wulf and try harder to avoid them. Even as I think this, I know it's impossible. And so I double down on my obstinance.

"I'm just saying, you've got to be careful," Wulf is saying. "We can't trust them and just say whatever to them. You might be talking, and let something slip, and—"

"Talking to them doesn't mean I trust them," I interrupt, my tone sharp. "And it doesn't mean I'm not careful. You know what it does mean? That I can answer Dad's questions. I'm the one who was useful in that conversation."

"I was too," Wulf says with a wounded expression.

"I'm going to make supper," I say, not letting myself sound repentant. "You should mind your own business, Wulf. You're not the spokesperson for Dad." Wulf glares at me silently, the aggrieved hurt on his face making him look like a child. I turn on my heel and walk to Dad's building.

It's dark inside, the curtains drawn against the heat. I scan the kitchen in the dim light. We still have some rabbit jerky from last night, but no more mesquite bread. My eyes move to the shelf and alight on a jar of mealworm flour and a jar of mesquite flour. For the next half hour, I busy myself making pancakes. I mix the two flours with salt and water from the pitcher. I flip on the stove and wait for the burner to start emanating heat. When it does, I drop thick dollops of the paste onto the pan and wait until they set before flipping them over and waiting again until the bottom turns dark brown. The heat is weak, so it takes a long time.

The door creaks open just when I'm transferring the second batch of pancakes to a plate. "Oh," Vanessa says, opening the door fully and letting the light rush in. "I'm sorry. I thought Isaac would be here. We usually talk around this time." She scans the room as though expecting Dad to still be inside, sitting in the shadows somewhere.

"He's in his office," I say.

"Want some help?" she asks, coming closer. "What are you making?"

"Mealworm pancakes."

She eyes the pile on the plate dubiously.

"You can't taste the mealworms," I say. "They just taste like salt."

"Isaac doesn't like anyone bothering him when he's in his office, does he?" Vanessa says, seeming to forget her interest in the food or helping. "I'll just wait outside for him."

"I'll come with you," I say, gathering up the dishes I dirtied.

When we climb back outside, squinting at the sunlight, it turns out that Dad's not in his office after all. He's by the water machine with Wulf, about to harvest the water the machine's pulled from the air. Without saying anything, Vanessa starts walking toward them.

"I'm just going to wash these," I say, but she doesn't hear me.

I walk to the edge of the settlement and scrub the bowl and pan with sand. I keep my eye on Vanessa as she gesticulates enthusiastically at the machine. She walks in a circle to examine it, bending down to study the metallic box. The murmur of their conversation drifts toward me in words and phrases. Wulf's chest expands, his height growing a visible centimeter, however curtly he answers Vanessa's questions. Dad enters into a technical explanation of how the machine pulls water from the scant moisture in the air, as well as the improvements he's made. I leave the dishes to the sun and walk over to join them.

"Supper's ready when we want it," I say.

"Thank you, Georgia," Dad says.

"Is it different between the seasons, the amount of water you can collect?" Vanessa asks.

I nudge a rock out of the dirt with the toe of my shoe, waiting.

"It varies," says Dad. "But with careful planning, we have a steady supply year-round to supplement the well water. We collect a surplus during our July monsoon months, and that keeps us going during the dry summer months. Although, I concede, it does tend to taste stale."

"Where's Nick?" I ask.

"Probably in his building," Vanessa says. She walks over to the other side of the water machine, where the motor is. "Does it taste the same as rainwater?" she asks.

"Should I get him?" I ask.

"Please do, Georgia," says Dad.

When I knock on the door to Nick's building, there's no answer. I call his name a few times, and nothing. Then I check the library and the spot where he sits in the mornings.

"He's not there," I say when I return.

Everyone turns to look at me, then Dad and Vanessa slowly look around the settlement in tandem, scanning it. Wulf continues filling glass bottles with water, making out like he's uninterested, but briefly glances around as well. It seems as though everybody thought Nick had been with someone else all afternoon, and this is the first time we've realized collectively that none of us has seen him since morning.

"I'll check again," Vanessa says. We watch her stride over to his building and disappear inside it, then check her building and the library. When she returns, she's shaking her head. "He's probably out for a walk," she says with what sounds like forced confidence.

"He'll be back," says Dad.

"Of course he will," says Vanessa.

"Unless he gets lost," says Dad. "Or bitten by something."

"He's always had a good sense of direction," says Vanessa.

"Good," says Dad. "Naturally, we'd look for him if the situation called for it, but it's something of a strain on our time and resources if we're forced to play search party."

"He'll be back by sundown," says Vanessa firmly, as though trying to convince herself.

6

Vanessa is right, Nick does return by sundown, but he comes back hobbling. We're outside, finally eating cold mealworm pancakes and rabbit jerky in the last of the day's light, and when he appears in my peripheral vision, suddenly everyone seems to see him at once.

"Got bit," Nick calls out when he's close enough.

Even in the dimming light, we can see his injury. His foot, strapped into his sandal, is an angry, swollen red, and there's a distended bulge by the heel.

"What did it?" asks Dad. He bends down to examine the foot, then straightens up again, unalarmed, in no apparent hurry.

"Scorpion," says Nick. He uses the back of his hand to wipe sweat from his face.

"Stung," says Dad.

"What?" says Nick.

"You were stung, not bitten," says Dad. "Common linguistic mistake. It's a shame how little most people know about scorpions. What many don't realize is that they've hardly evolved in the four hundred or so million years they've been on this earth. We could call them a living prehistoric relic."

"Okay," says Nick, blinking hard like he's trying to rouse his brain into grasping these facts' relevance. His skin is pale and clammy, signs of dehydration.

"What period were we in four hundred million years ago? Georgia? Wulf?" asks Dad.

Wulf's brow creases, and he stares hard at the ground, his mouth moving silently, like he's counting to himself.

"Anybody?" Dad says.

"Devonian," I say, trying to tamp down the irritation in my voice.

"Correct," says Dad. He turns his attention back to Nick. "What color was the scorpion?"

"Brown or orange. Didn't get a good look."

"More brown or more orange?"

"More brown, maybe."

"My guess is that it was a bark scorpion," says Dad. "Most dangerous one we've got out here, and the most common. You're not frothing at the mouth, so you should be fine. Fatalities are rare. Your foot's likely so swollen because of the constriction from your sandal straps and the pressure you've been putting on it by walking in combination with the venom."

Nick's throat bulges as he swallows dryly.

"We should give him water," I say.

Vanessa picks up the cup she's been drinking out of and gives it to Nick. We watch as he tries to grasp it, but his hands are shaking, possibly from mild shock and heat exhaustion. Finally, Vanessa brings the cup to Nick's lips instead, and he takes a small sip, sputtering.

"Slow sips," says Dad.

Vanessa looks alarmed and surveys Nick's face intently, peering at his pupils.

"You won't want to do much more walking tonight if you want the swelling to go down," says Dad. "Georgia can get you some salve for the pain."

"We have ibuprofen in the car," says Vanessa.

"Fine," says Dad. "But the faster you wean off artificial medicine, the better. We have a stash of mild painkillers, but we use it for emergencies only, and that rule's going to apply to you, too, once your supply runs out."

"What constitutes an emergency?" asks Vanessa, her voice tight.

"I'll tell you when I see one," says Dad, and he turns to Nick. "That's all the doctor I've got in me for tonight. I don't know whether you made the imbecilic decision to explore in the middle of the day or whether you were trying to walk your way home. Either way is a fool's errand and only makes the lives of those around you more difficult. I've opened my house to you and welcomed you to break bread with me. I sincerely hope that you'll start appreciating that hospitality instead of continuing to disrespect my time by wasting it." Dad sweeps his gaze across all of us, as though we're equally culpable. "Wulf, you can do the clearing up today," he says.

Wulf murmurs his assent, like he's got something to be sorry about. The four of us watch Dad's wiry body blend into the dusk as he walks away. A moment later, Wulf collects everyone's dishes and follows Dad without speaking.

Nick slurps some more water noisily. "If I were him, I'd welcome the diversion."

"You're looking a little better," says Vanessa, peering into Nick's eyes again.

"The water," says Nick, raising his cup to me. "What do you think, Georgia? It must get boring doing the same chores and seeing the same people day after day. A scorpion bite spices things up a little, right?"

"Sting," corrects Vanessa, as though automatically.

"Or have Vanessa and I spiced things up enough already?" Nick asks, ignoring her.

I shrug, uncomfortable. "Nobody wants you to get hurt."

Nick sighs like I'm being tedious. "I know, I know," he says.

"So what were you doing out there?" asks Vanessa.

"Oh, you know," Nick says. "Seeing the sights."

"What was your intention, exactly?"

Nick eyes her. "Being stupid," he admits. The look he gives her is sincere, apologetic.

"We know that much," says Vanessa.

An unspoken exchange seems to pass between them, a petition for forgiveness submitted and only partly granted, a whole conversation I'm not privy to.

"Do you want that salve?" I ask Nick, standing.

"Hmm?" Nick asks. He turns to me, disoriented, like he's startled to still see me here. Then he glances down at his foot, which is the same throbbing red. "Oh, right," he says. "Sure, that would be good. Can't hurt, probably. Thanks."

The salve is in the basement of the glass house. The light flickers when I turn it on at the top of the stairs, and there's a cold, earthy smell inside. We rarely touch the poultices and salves stored here because we're careful. Wulf and I know how to get along with the desert, how to tread lightly on its dry, prickly skin, how to avoid bothering the animals. After smelling a few glass jars and reused plastic containers, I find the one I'm looking for. Nick and Vanessa have gone inside by the time I return, but the lights are on in Nick's building. I waver for a moment, and then remember it's Dad who wanted me to give Nick the salve in the first place. My knock is noncommittal, faint. "Come on in," Nick's voice says.

I slip inside soundlessly, trying to shake off the sense that I shouldn't be here. Nick's building looks nearly the same as it did when it was empty. There's only a heavy-duty flashlight that isn't ours on one of the shelves, and a woven blanket hanging over a chair that I remember seeing draped over the back seat of their car. On the wood table there's a small first aid kit Vanessa must have brought over while I was getting the salve. Automatically, I look around for other signs of Vanessa, but it's just Nick here in the building, standing barefoot on one foot, steadying himself with his hand against the doorframe to his bedroom.

"So that's it?" Nick asks, nodding to the plastic container in my hand.

"The salve," I say, nodding.

"I'm guessing there's no instructions for how to use it on the side of that jar."

"It's a peanut butter jar," I say.

"A peanut butter jar? How did a peanut butter jar wind up all the way out here?"

"There's a lot of stuff like that around here. Empty jars and cans and broken stuff left over from the people who used to live here. Vanessa didn't tell you?"

"Tell me what?"

"That I collect it," I say. The words sound immediately ridiculous to me, but Nick doesn't seem to notice my embarrassment.

"Oh," he says. "No, she didn't mention it. You must be good at gathering it up because I haven't seen any lying around. What do you collect it for?"

I shrug and turn my attention to the jar. I unscrew the lid slightly, then retighten it.

"Yeah, you're right, stupid question. Why does anyone collect anything? I used to have a rock collection when I was a kid. My dad used to collect coins and paper money. Why not, right?"

"Right," I say awkwardly. "Do you want the salve now? It takes a while to soak into your skin, so you should rub it on and then keep your foot elevated. I'd try to wait until it soaks in fully before going to sleep. It'll work better that way."

"You mean I have to put off my beauty rest?" Nick says.

"You can sleep as long as you want tomorrow morning."

"Oh, I plan to. Vanessa gave me one of her sleeping pills when she came over with some ibuprofen, and when that stuff hits, it makes you sleep like a baby in a coma."

"Like a—what?"

"It's a figure of speech. Anyway, it hasn't hit yet, so I'm all right to stay awake until this salve stuff soaks in. Want to keep me company until then?"

I hesitate for a second, frozen in indecision, too many thoughts competing for attention in my head—the absence of Vanessa, and her concern for Nick earlier; Dad's admonitions to keep a certain distance; and then the pull of Nick's invitation, the fact that he's suggesting that I stay. But Nick is already hobbling back into his bedroom, waving his hand for me to follow, and I pause all the thoughts and do just that, plunging into a decision half-made.

Nick situates himself on the side of the bed and arranges a chair next to it to prop up his foot on. I sit down gingerly at the foot of the bed. Both of us stare at his swollen foot like we're examining a new species of plant or animal. I hand Nick the jar, and he opens it and sniffs it.

"Medicinal," he says. "I guess I should ask you what's in it before slathering it onto my skin."

"California poppy and banana yucca," I say.

"Uh-huh," says Nick. "Plant names mean nothing to me, but let the record show that I did my due diligence." He dabs the yellowish cream onto his foot and sloppily spreads it around. "Good enough?" he asks when most of his foot is covered.

"I think so."

"So, what do you think, a half hour to let it soak in should do it?"

"Probably."

"You're not inspiring a huge amount of confidence here. Does your dad make these?"

"Yes, but he didn't make up the recipe himself. It's from a book of plant medicine."

"What does he have against modern medicine?"

"Nothing. He just doesn't want us to rely on it. We don't have a lot of it here."

"Mmm," says Nick. "But then he has to realize that oils and salves only get you so far. What happens when one of you gets really sick?"

"We've always managed. We probably have an easier time of it than you do."

"What's that supposed to mean?"

I gesture vaguely. "All that pollution you live with over there."

"Georgia," he says, and shakes his head. "I don't know how you picture the world outside walking distance from here, but it's really not that bad. Not everywhere."

"Where did you go?" I ask after a beat passes.

Nick is studying his foot, apparently checking if he can still wiggle his toes. Some he can, the others just manage to look like they spasm momentarily.

"Were you trying to leave?" I ask.

Nick's mouth twitches. "I'm not that much of an idiot," he says.

"Only enough of an idiot to get stung by a scorpion." It sounds like something Nick would say, the kind of teasing, familiar reply he'd make, and instantly I feel ashamed for mimicking his familiarity. But Nick just winks at me.

"Exactly," he says. "See, I told you I knew we were going to get along. I was just trying to get the lay of the land. A better idea of what's around here. I underestimated how similar everything looks, so I got turned around. That distracted me from watching where I stepped, and here we are." He lifts his foot a fraction off the chair.

"What did you think was around here?" I ask.

"I try not to live my life with too many preconceptions," says Nick.

"Were you looking for other people?" I press.

"The thought may have crossed my mind."

"There aren't any other people around here. You could have just asked."

"I could have, but I have a bad habit of wanting to check things out for myself."

"You mean you wouldn't have believed what I'd have told you."

"Don't take it personally. Not believing you isn't the same thing as disbelieving you."

"No preconceptions," I say.

"Exactly," Nick says again and grins at me. Then he squints his eyes shut and rubs them with his fingers. "That sleeping pill is starting to kick in," he says.

"Do you want me to go?"

"No, no, stay," he says, flashing his eyes open.

There's a beat of silence.

"Do you have a conception of us?" I ask.

"Of you and me?" asks Nick.

"No," I say hastily. "Of me and Wulf and Dad."

"Hmm," says Nick, opening his eyes wider, as though to stay awake. "I've got some initial impressions. I think Isaac shows megalomaniac tendencies, though Vanessa seems to think he's just as interesting as he thinks he is, so maybe I'm wrong there. Wulf seems like a very devout acolyte, natural for an isolated young man. What, am I far out in left field?"

"Dad isn't a megalomaniac," I say automatically.

"You wouldn't call him obsessed with power and control? Because it sure seems like it to me. His word is law in this little world he's made, and the rest of us have to do whatever he says. He thinks he's got everything figured out, and he has an answer for everything."

"But he does have a lot figured out," I say. "He's figured out how to live out here in the desert, even when the rest of the world thinks it's impossible unless you build a bubble to hide away in. He's learned how to work with the situation here, instead of against it. Even when the outside world's made it hard for him with everything it's doing to destroy itself."

"Well, now you're sounding like quite the devout acolyte yourself."

"You're making us sound like we're a cult," I say, frowning. "It's not like anything I'm saying is delusional. They're just the facts."

"Don't worry," Nick says, "I don't think you're a cult." He pats my hand, which is resting on the bed. His hand lingers over mine, pressing down lightly on it.

"I'm not worried," I say, just to say something. Suddenly—unnervingly—my train of thought about Dad and our lives here evaporates, and all that I'm aware of is the weight of Nick's hand on mine, the strangeness of his physical presence beside me.

"Do you want to know what I think of you?" he asks, the words slightly blurred, elongated by drowsiness.

"Sure," I say skittishly.

"What I think is that you're a curious person. I think you're curious about what you haven't seen or experienced and you're desperate to see and experience more of it. Am I right? Have I hit the nail on the head? It's a good quality to have as a person. But you can't do much of that here, in the middle of the desert, can you?"

"No," I say after a short pause.

"No, you're not curious, or no, you can do that here in the desert?"

"It's pretty late," I say, standing. "You should sleep. Dad says sleep is the best medicine."

"Debatable," says Nick. "But point taken."

"There is no point," I say.

"No?" Nick smiles. "You're not trying to get away from me?"

"No," I say, my pulse thundering in my ears.

"Well, that's good," says Nick. "That's nice to hear."

"It was nice," I say.

"It's always nice talking to you, Georgia."

"Okay," I say awkwardly. "Well, I guess I'll see you tomorrow then."

The air outside is cooling down, smelling of rain that won't come. I walk quickly to my building, head down and arms hugging myself. I have a hard time falling asleep, and when I do finally fall asleep, the sleep is light, on and off, like I have things to think through even though my mind is a tired blank.

7

It's just me and Vanessa outside the next morning. Wulf and Dad disappeared into Dad's office early, and Nick is apparently still resting. We're weeding the small tepary bean field while Vanessa chatters about the connections between what she calls the farming industry, the military-industrial complex, and the banking industry and says that if I can't follow what she's saying because it sounds complicated and illogical, that's because it is. I get the sense that she doesn't want to dwell on last night's events.

"What's Ohio like?" I ask her after we fall into silence.

"What do you want to know?" she asks.

"More about how it's different than Phoenix, maybe."

"It's a lot more crowded," she answers after a pause. "People everywhere. Well, in the city, at least, but that's the only place you can live, really. In Columbus."

"Why can't you live outside the city?"

"You could live off the grid, in theory, but you wouldn't have access to public services or functional roads. Plus, no tornado shelters. It's mandated that all buildings in the city have those, but all bets are off if you're outside the city limits. So most people crowd into Columbus. We're demolishing the old suburbs and building upward to fit all of them, and then expanding outward."

I nod, trying to imagine it. The only pictures I've seen of cities in the Center States are over a hundred years old. The encyclopedias in the library show flat buildings that spread out like an oil spill, trying to cover as much ground as they can. Only a few skyscrapers poke into the sky in the pictures. I try to superimpose what Vanessa's saying onto them, on top of everything I've heard from Dad, but the image in my head just comes out a mess.

"Are you still writing about the people who built this place?" I ask Vanessa.

"Mmm," Vanessa says, adding a clump of dried weeds to our pile. "I've put that on the back burner for now. It's a little difficult thinking about working on a project like that when you don't even know if you'll ever see civilization again. And, to be honest, I've become more interested in the people who live here now. You and Wulf and Isaac." She smiles ruefully. "Getting distracted seems to be my way of working, doesn't it?"

"There are some folders I can show you in the library with some old records," I say.

"Records of—oh, from the people who built this place?"

"They have people's names and dates of birth and building plans for what looks like our settlement. And then there's all their old objects I've found. I didn't show you all of them when I showed you my fossils, but I can if you want, if it could help."

"Sure," says Vanessa, but there's no enthusiasm in her voice.

I study her out of the corner of my eye as I work a tough, rope-like weed out of the dirt. Even though Vanessa is friendly and always willing to have a conversation, it's difficult talking to her. It feels like walking around huge, mysterious shapes, knocking into and stumbling my way around them, and never arriving anywhere. Dad doesn't seem to feel that way, since he's been talking to Vanessa for at least an hour every day. He even seems to enjoy it, looking genuinely pleased after their conversations. I let our conversation hang there in case Vanessa says something else about her projects, but we just end up working for a while longer in silence, the pile of dry and shriveled grasses between us growing larger. We weed until we notice Dad strolling over to us, carrying a water bottle in one hand and lugging three folding chairs under his other arm.

"Guten morgen!" he calls.

"Morning," Vanessa replies brightly. She rises to her knees and uses her hand to shield her eyes from the sun.

Dad arranges the chairs at the edge of the field before settling himself into one of them. "Looking to be a great day," he says. "Not too hot today."

I slow down picking off the dead leaves of a small plant and peer at him discreetly. The bags under his eyes are more pronounced, which makes me think he was awake late into the night. His eyes have an exuberant glint to them that tells me something good has happened.

"Take a break," he says to me and Vanessa.

We wipe our dirty hands on our pants and settle into the two other chairs. Dad hands me the bottle of water, indicating that Vanessa and I should share it. I take a few large gulps, then pass it to Vanessa, who does the same.

"How are things coming along here?" he says. "How's the weeding progressing?"

"It's getting there," I say.

Dad nods, rocking forward and back lightly with the movement of his head. "And how are you getting along here, Vanessa?" he asks, turning to her.

"With the weeding?" Vanessa asks.

"With everything," says Dad. "We've talked a lot about me over the past few weeks. It occurred to me this morning that I haven't had a chance to ask you: How are you doing yourself? Would you say you're adjusting to our life here? From what I've seen myself, I'd venture to guess yes, but I'd like to hear your perspective. Are you missing anyone or anything in particular? Having any feelings of alienation or disconnection?"

Vanessa hesitates, watching Dad's face, as though trying to deduce where this conversation is headed and how she can guide it, whether to nudge it in this or that direction. "Not too often," she says lightly. "It is still pretty surreal, being here, and these past few weeks. But it hasn't been as hard of an adjustment as I might have expected, surprisingly."

"Is there anything that you miss?" Dad asks.

"Maybe more frequent showers and air-conditioning." Vanessa smiles tepidly. She fiddles with the water bottle lid, running her fingers along the ridges.

"Do you miss knowing what's going on in the world?"

"You mean the news? Do I miss the news?"

"I read some today that might interest you," Dad says, his face inscrutable.

"What was it?" Vanessa's fingers still, then start fidgeting with the lid again.

"A power failure at the Domes again," says Dad, his gaze steady on the reedy bean plants. "I thought you might be interested, if I remember correctly that you had been writing about them."

So she's told him, too, I realize with a start. And then I think: of course she has.

"That's right," Vanessa is saying. "Thanks for the update. And for thinking of me. It's nice to get some news from the world out there."

Dad nods, accepting her thanks. For a moment, he seems unsure of how to proceed. Then he says: "Seems like there's been a lot of failures with their little project. More and more, lately. I can't help feeling some concern about the continual failures, especially in light of their construction of a nuclear reactor. Power failures are one thing, but a reactor accident is a different level of concern."

"Well, nuclear's pretty safe these days," says Vanessa, tilting her head.

"Says who?" says Dad. "The ever-trustworthy state?"

"Scientists," says Vanessa.

"I'm a scientist," says Dad. "And I beg to differ. Isn't it true that in the last twelve years alone, there have been four serious nuclear accidents around the globe, three of which have rendered entire cities unusable for any foreseeable future? That's what we're calling 'pretty safe'?"

"I do see where you're coming from," Vanessa says, nodding with practiced composure, like this is a conversation she's had before. "But those were all really old, obsolete plants. They should have been decommissioned long before those accidents, everyone in the industry knew that. That's not what they're building at the Domes. They use liquid metal for cooling, not water. We haven't had an accident at one of these new reactors in decades."

"Luck," says Dad, disparagingly. "Luck that leads to complacency in construction and upkeep. I don't put it past anyone to not cut corners when it'll save them a dollar or two. It's human nature. Especially when you don't have to live directly with the consequences. I don't see the government sending its own people to work on the Domes. It's all contractors. They're sending guinea pigs disguised as workers. Test subjects for an unrealistic future they're imagining in their little isolated government buildings, planning it out with markers on a smart screen. I expect they imagine, in a few years' time, everyone still living in the western deadlands is going to crowd into those Domes? While temperatures continue to rise and fires blaze right outside, scorching their protective screens? That's how we're going to continue to exist on this world when the entire planet becomes a deadland? Is that their vision for the future of this country? Of the world? They're no different from the idiots who used to pontificate smugly about how the solution to our environmental crises was for everyone to stop reproducing. How the fact that environmental contaminants had rendered a significant portion of our population infertile was, in fact, a boon for civilization. As though the solution to ensuring the continuation of the human species was to eliminate the human species altogether. As though their aversion to caring for anybody but themselves wasn't rooted in the same drive that led to the rampant materialism and consumerism that caused our problems, to our stripping of all the oil and rare metals from the earth—the worship of convenience, the abdication of responsibility, the capitulation to base selfishness. We humans are true masters at deluding ourselves."

I'm volleying my gaze between Vanessa and Dad. If Vanessa told Dad that she was writing about the Domes, the same thought must have occurred to Dad that had occurred to me—that it's a strange coincidence that she ended up here, with us, that her side project writing about our settlement happened to lead her to a link pointing back to start—to her project writing about the Domes. Either it's a strange coincidence, or it isn't a coincidence at all but the opposite—planned. I can't tell what Dad is thinking, and Vanessa's face is a practiced blank. There's so much that I don't know, and it's infuriating, mesmerizing. The conversation shimmers like sharp reflecting glass, a prism turning.

"But it's just a start," Vanessa is saying. "It's just one idea."

"An idea that encroaches on my territory," says Dad.

Vanessa opens her mouth to answer.

"You're going to say I don't own it," says Dad before she can. "That it's not my land. Well, I say that I have more claim to it than anyone else does. Who stayed here when everyone else left? Who's tamed this desert as well as I have? Who knows it better than I do? It's taken me years—it's taken mistakes, it's taken tragedy—to get to where I am. To arrive at what you see today, the fruits of our labor you can enjoy by living here. Can I not call that a claim? Surely it's more legitimately defensible than the right of conquest, or the principle of first possession."

"Sure, that's fine," says Vanessa, watching Dad closely. "I wasn't going to argue with your claim. I was just going to say that you're pretty far from the Domes here. If you're worried about fallout from an accident, I think they'd have it contained before it reached you here. Their protocols for emergency response are really well developed."

"I wouldn't be so sure," Dad says brusquely. "Regardless, it's not only my personal safety that I'm concerned about. That may have been the seed for my opposition, I'll allow that possibility. But there are more important matters at stake. Put bluntly, this project is a continuation of everything we're doing incorrectly. It's not a solution, but yet another temporary lease, a misguided extension. What humanity needs to do to survive is learn how to control itself. Control, restraint, sacrifice—those are the answers. Not sequestered cities under Domes. Not hiding away from the inhospitable planet we've created and limiting our goals to hoping that we're safe enough inside to survive another day, another year. Do you see what I'm saying?"

"I do," says Vanessa. "I really do see where you're coming from."

"You're just starting to realize," says Dad, his tone satisfied. He leans back in his chair. Then, almost immediately, he sits up again. "I'd like you to come with me this morning," he says.

"Where?" Vanessa says when he doesn't elaborate.

"The dog is lost," Dad says.

Vanessa looks to me for an answer.

I nod slowly in confirmation. "Moonpie," I say. "Our dog."

Dad says: "Sometimes she leaves for a week or so, but it's been about a month now. Historically, she's been able to take care of herself, but she's getting along in years. You can't outrun coyotes forever. This compounded with the fact that some unexplained events are causing me to worry. Some patterns that have been weighing on my mind lately. I don't know if the dog is involved or related, but it won't hurt to take a little walk, to search."

"You've never mentioned a dog," says Vanessa.

"No, I don't think we have," says Dad.

"Anything else I should know about?"

"Not presently."

"Right," says Vanessa.

"Should I come too?" I ask, and I realize that I'm clinging to the hope that he'll say yes. Take me with you, I think fervently. The thought surprises me, indecipherable and menacing.

But Dad shakes his head. "Wulf will be occupied in the office. I need you here to keep an eye on our patient, Georgia."

"Sure," I say, my stomach sinking.

"Seems like there's a lot of getting lost around here lately," says Vanessa.

"Your husband is what made me think of the dog," says Dad.

Something flickers in Vanessa's face, amusement or distaste.

They leave to fill their water bottles, and I watch them walk into the desert before pulling myself out of the folding chair and kneeling in the tepary bean field again. I tug out a clump of dry grass, combing the roots to shake out the earth. I work my way down the row, then pull myself into a crouch and look around the settlement. Wulf is in Dad's office, and I know he won't leave until late in the day. Nick hasn't left his building, either, and I wonder if he's still in pain, or sleeping. I know it's inevitable that sooner or later I'll walk over to his building and fall into the trap of conversation. I try to work in the bean field longer, but there's not much dried grass left to pull. I give the rows of plants a final glance, then rouse myself to take the weed pile to the compost pit and put away the folding chairs.

Nick calls me to come in as soon as I knock. He's at the table, nothing in front of him, as though he'd just been sitting there and staring into space.

"I thought I'd check on you," I say, closing the door behind me.

"That's nice of you," he says.

"Are you feeling better?"

He lifts his bare foot a few inches off the floor, and I see that the swelling has gone down around the bump, though there's a patch of skin that's still an angry red. "I'll live," Nick says. "Keep me company again?"

I nod and sit down stiffly across from him at the table. Nick lifts his leg to prop it up on another chair and then settles himself comfortably again. I'm uneasily aware of how straight my posture is, how tightly my hands are folded on the table.

Nick says: "I'd offer you something to eat or drink, but . . ."

"You haven't had breakfast," I say, and abruptly, irrationally, move to stand.

"No, it's fine," he says, lifting his hand. "I have."

He doesn't elaborate, but I realize Vanessa must have brought him something earlier. Awkwardly, I scoot my chair in toward the table again.

"What should we talk about?" asks Nick. Then, without waiting for me to answer, he says: "How about you tell me more about what it's like living here?"

"Tell you what? You live here now too."

"Good point. How about you tell me about your life before you came here, then?"

"I don't remember that."

"You don't remember anything?"

"Maybe a little, but I don't know what's real and what I made up or imagined."

"Well, I won't know the difference," says Nick. "That happens to all of us. I spent a good portion of my life convinced I'd been to Canada with my family as a kid only to have my sister tell me that no one in our family had ever been to Canada except my dad, who'd been once, briefly, for a conference. I only believed her after she pointed out that I'd only gotten my first passport when I was twenty-three."

"Where did you go with the passport?" I ask.

"Mexico City."

"Why there?"

"My college best friend's family was from there. Super rich family. They owned some kind of mining empire. He was going back for a visit after we graduated, and I got my parents to cough up enough money to let me tag along because I thought I'd never been anywhere except Canada. They weren't too keen on funding my whims at this point, so this was a pretty impressive achievement. I don't know if you know this, but air travel is insanely expensive. That's how they're trying to restrict it, to reduce the pollution and ration the fuel, by making it almost impossible to afford. But it just ends up being something only the super rich can do, like my friend. And then there are idiots like me, who just pay an arm and a leg anyway."

"Was it nice? Mexico City?"

"Oh, yeah. They've got these really nice parks all over the place, and people still walk around in them. They walk their dogs, they talk, they sit on benches. AQI was bad, though. Level purple almost every day. Trees can only do so much when you're surrounded by an industrial wasteland. I had to buy one of those heavy-duty smog masks that make you look like a robot from a vendor outside the airport. That was a pain, wearing that, but still, best city I've been to in my life. Not that I've been to many. But I can't imagine any city beating that one."

"What was being in a plane like?" I ask.

Nick squints slightly, like he's trying to see into the past. "I don't remember it much. We got a flight in the middle of the night, and you couldn't see anything out the windows except blackness, so I slept. The plane started shaking at one point—shook me awake. Really bad turbulence. It was fine, but people started praying, there was some screaming. And about half the plane threw up from motion sickness. That smell's cemented in my memory forever." Nick's eyes find me, and his expression changes slightly, becomes more alert. "You think you'd get motion sickness on a plane?" he asks with a kind of studied nonchalance.

I shrug. "I'm not sure."

"Do you get carsick? Do you remember?"

"You mean when in the car with you and Vanessa?"

"No, I mean earlier, when you came here. Isaac must have used a car to get here."

"I don't know," I say, stiffly now. "I don't remember."

"Where's the car now?" asks Nick.

"We don't have a car."

"Not here," says Nick smoothly.

It's true that there's no car here for Nick to find, no truth he's wheedled out of me, but a rush of fear leaps into my throat anyway. What am I doing here? I ask myself, and the question repeats itself in my head to the beat of my pulse. I can feel myself losing grip over the conversation, its currents and undercurrents moving too quickly for me to grasp, flowing forward and away from me.

"You know what crazy image just popped into my head?" says Nick. "You and me on a car ride together, like in an old movie. Have you ever seen a movie? I'm picturing you wearing big sunglasses and one of those silk scarves over your head to keep your hair from flying all over your face." He sits up and reaches across the table to tug a piece of my hair. His thumb brushes my cheek, and then he leans back in his chair again, grinning, like he's just said something and is waiting for an answer. My skin prickles like it's brushed against tiny cactus spines. "Windows down, speeding off into the horizon," says Nick. "What do you think of that?"

"I don't know," I say, my voice a few pitches higher.

"It's fun to imagine sometimes," Nick says.

He leans back in his chair again. He's watching me like I'm a curiosity he's considering, an interesting rodent he's come across that he's decided is harmless, cute even, the way it stares back at him, deciding whether it's better to make a run for it or stay frozen. There's a stillness in the room, and my heart rate starts to slow, to slip back into the lull of homeostasis.

"You don't seem so upset anymore," I venture, my voice now steady. "About being here."

"You know, it was a shock at first," Nick says. "But I'd say I've gotten used to it."

"To being here?"

"To waiting."

From the goading way he grins at me, it seems like he's expecting me to ask what he's waiting for. I don't ask him. I just make a noise to let him know I heard and then—trying not to flinch from the knife-edge of danger, from the metallic chill of it—I change the topic of the conversation.

8

Vanessa and Dad don't find Moonpie that day, but it becomes a routine of theirs to walk into the desert in the early morning or late afternoon, ostensibly looking for the dog. "Sounds like code," Nick says archly, and he asks me whether there really is a dog. There is, I tell him, but we're used to Moonpie leaving for long stretches. I don't tell Nick, but my guess is that Dad is looking for something else, and Vanessa is willing to tag along, to play witness. It seems like she passed some test while I wasn't looking and suddenly became initiated into Dad's confidence. Sometimes, when they return, Dad's expression is stern, deep in thought. Other times, he's talking enthusiastically with Vanessa, their voices bright and carrying.

Nick's foot isn't well enough to let him walk much yet, but he keeps himself busy around the settlement. We team up on chores and finish them in half the time they would take one person, even with Nick limping. He waves me off when I say his foot seems to be taking longer to heal than it should. We carry wood and dead grass to the composting toilet pits and harvest nopals from the nopal field. We shoo black widow spiders from the corners of the unused buildings, tearing their webs with a long stick.

When Nick knocks on my door one day, I show him the objects in my bedroom, the ones I showed Vanessa, and Nick explains them to me. He tells me about diners and canned food and islands of trash in the ocean, coloring in the clues of what's outside the settlement, gifting me details. Impulsively, I show him a stash of books I have hidden under my mattress—*The Tempest*, three yellowed Westerns, an anthology of poetry, *Moby-Dick*, and a clothbound book of fairy tales Wulf and I used to read together—and Nick rummages through them impassively, only noting which he's read and which he hasn't. When we leave my building, Nick motions for me to go first. He puts his hand lightly on my back, halfway down my spine, and rearranges us so he's standing just behind me. The light outside is soft, the sky white with a false promise of rain. Vanessa's walking past just then. She turns her head and gives us a strange look, searching but unfocused, like she's deciding whether to return home for something she's realized she's forgotten. Then Dad calls her name, and her attention shifts. She gives us a quick smile, like she's only just noticed us, and quickens her pace to catch up with Dad. For a few days afterward, Nick avoids touching me at all. It catches me off guard, how much this bothers me. How often my mind returns to it, this lack of touch. I all but fixate on it, nursing a childish sense of injury. But soon enough Nick's hand returns to touching my back when we're walking together, to touching my arm when he makes a joke or an observation.

It isn't long before Nick says he's getting restless. It's starting to get to him, he says, how long he's spent trapped in the settlement. It's been a week and a half of coddling his foot, and he decides it's well enough to walk somewhere. I ask him where he wants to go, and he asks if I remember where the container I found is buried. "That's where you want to go?" I ask. He says he's open to other recommendations, but so far, I haven't come up with any. After some hesitation, I agree. Even with Nick walking slowly, it shouldn't take us more than a couple of hours to walk to the container, and Nick does seem to be doing mostly better. The chores are done, and Dad and Vanessa have gone on another reconnaissance mission, and Wulf has sequestered himself away to tinker with a broken solar battery.

The desert is languid, a hushed, sleepy warmth. Gauzy clouds float like torn sheets across the sun. For a while, the only sound we make is the crunch of our shoes over rocks and dried weeds. Cactus wrens cry out some distance away. Nick startles when we hear a rattle, but I tell him it's a plant, a dried husk with seeds and the mute, hot wind shaking it.

"Hey, Isaac isn't the serial-killer type, is he?" Nick asks.

I frown at him, trying to make out what he means.

"He's not taking Vanessa on these walks in the desert with the plan of eventually murdering her, right?"

"No. Does Vanessa think that?"

"I have no idea what Vanessa thinks," Nick says.

We walk a little longer before either of us speaks again. I use the back of my hand to wipe off beads of sweat forming at the edge of my hairline. Nick readjusts his hat, a bucket shape with a flap that covers his neck. Despite his efforts and the sunscreen he says he's wearing, his nose and arms are turning pink.

"Are you and Vanessa fighting?" I ask.

Nick's mouth contorts. "It's that obvious that we're not on the best of terms, huh?" he says. "I wouldn't call it fighting, exactly. There was a culmination of things, and then there was an incident a while ago, and Vanessa is still upset with me about it. Frankly, it should be water under the bridge by now, but I guess she doesn't think I've been punished enough."

We walk past a pile of rocks, and my eye falls on a lizard sleepily sunning itself on one of them. Impulsively, I stoop down to pluck it up by its tail. The lizard jerks to life, but, by that time, I'm holding it upside down by two fingers, showing its light-blue belly to Nick.

"Looks poisonous," he says.

"It isn't. It's a fence lizard."

"I don't see a lot of fences around here."

"That's just what they're called."

"Do you ever eat those things?" he asks.

The lizard's small hands and feet pedal frantically, as though it's understood Nick's words. I cup my hand around it, and it calms down, shrinking into the dark cave I've created.

"No," I say, "not lizards. We eat snake when we have it, but that isn't often. There aren't many you find dead, and it's not worth the risk to catch them. Sometimes you find one that was just killed by something like a hawk and the hawk got spooked by something else and left it. But it's hard to eat it. There's a lot of little bones to pick out."

"I've eaten snake," says Nick. "Snake fillet."

The lizard starts struggling again in my cupped hand, so I bend down to drop it back on the ground, and it darts into a cluster of rocks. "Where?" I ask, watching the lizard.

"A novelty restaurant in Ohio that I went to when I was a kid. Their thing was meats from all around the world. Snake, wombat, whale, kangaroo, tarantula, camel—if anyone at any point in history ate it regularly, they served it. I think I had snake and wombat. It was all grown in a meat lab across the city, and not one of the better ones, so everything tasted pretty much the same, kind of antiseptic-y. But I still loved it. My parents took me for my birthday. And the restaurant was built like a replica of an igloo, so that was a fun bonus for a kid."

"In Ohio?"

"That's where we lived," Nick says.

"But why a replica of an igloo in Ohio?"

"I don't know, it was some rich guy's pet project. I guess he liked igloos and meat."

"Weird," I say.

"Yeah, well." Nick shrugs. "If you've got the money, why not, right? Maybe I'd do the same thing if I were rich and already had everything else I wanted. Not the restaurant part, though. That sounds like a lot of work. The replica part."

"What would you build a replica of?"

"I don't know, maybe a pirate ship."

"On dry land?"

"I figure I'd have an oceanfront property if I were rich."

I look at him skeptically.

"I'd keep an eye on the weather," Nick says reassuringly. "They know when a hurricane's coming, the meteorology people. And even if something happened to my oceanfront property or my ship replica, it wouldn't matter. I could just get another. I'd be rich, remember? Come to think of it, I'd probably get a normal ship, not a replica. A yacht run on the last dregs of oil available. Or no, scratch that. Actually, if I were rich, I'd get on one of those spaceships the billionaires are trying to build. The really rich aren't wasting their time with replicas. They're thinking about long-term survival. About how to pass on their rich-people genes. I'd get on one of their spaceships, or rockets, or whatever, and say adios to this earthen wasteland, waving goodbye to all the poor suckers left behind from my little rocket window."

"Why would you do that?" I ask, slowing to study his face.

"Because I'm a hideously rich billionaire who's only out for himself."

"But that's the whole problem, people thinking like that. That's why we even have deadlands. You'd really want to be a part of that?"

"You're sounding a lot like Isaac," says Nick, his tone making it clear that this isn't a compliment. "I didn't say I wanted to be a part of anything. In this scenario, I've already been morally corrupted by my riches. I'm just imagining realistically."

We fall into a silence. The terrain gets rockier, more elevated, studded with chollas as tall as we are. Sometimes we see dry shrubs with long-stemmed yellow flowers poking out of them. The sun warms one side of my face comfortably until the heat starts to hurt. My head starts to throb on and off, a dull pendulum beat behind my right eye. Finally, we arrive at the container. I crouch down and brush aside loose sand that's blown over the metal. It's buried deeper than it was when we were here last, the desert reclaiming the object as its own the best it can in the time it had without us. I brought two hand trowels with me, bent and the metal crumbling. I take them out of my pocket and hand one to Nick.

Soon, we've settled ourselves into a rhythm of stabbing the dirt with our trowels on opposite sides of the container. After some easy scoops of loose sand, the earth only comes out in small, dense chips, as though it's trying to hold on to its shape and wholeness. The side I'm working on seems to be the top, a part of a round lid dipping into the ground at an angle. I've unearthed nearly half of it, the surface glinting like a dusty half-moon, and I move to the side. Sometimes Nick's trowel strikes the container, and a hollow sound of metal striking metal clangs out. It's becoming clear that we're only seeing a small fraction of it.

The sun is just past its peak in the deep-blue sky now, ushering in the hottest part of the day. All the sand and rocks and vegetation have absorbed its rays and are holding on to them, cradling them within their bodies like they're something precious, like the same sun isn't going to come up the exact same way tomorrow.

I take my bandanna off from around my neck and wipe my face with it. Consciously or unconsciously, Nick sets down his trowel and does the same.

"So, those books you showed me," he says. "The ones under your mattress. You're not supposed to have those, are you? I didn't realize they were such forbidden knowledge. Vanessa told me she'd weaseled it out of Isaac why there aren't any novels in the library. She said he admitted to her that he'd burned them."

I nod. "A few years ago."

"What, did literature make exceptionally good fire starter or something?"

"It was my fault," I say slowly, picking through how much I want to tell Nick. "I started to get curious about things. About what was outside the settlement, and how people live differently than us out there. I started reading a lot—too much, Dad said—and asking questions about the outside world. I was spending a lot of time walking around, looking for clues about the people who built this place or anyone else who lived here, thinking that could tell me a little more about what other people's lives were like. I even tried to look things up on the computers that I knew Dad wouldn't like—just some pictures of buildings and streets in Phoenix, really. But Dad got convinced I was trying to figure out how to leave the settlement. I wasn't—I only wanted to know what the city looked like—but that's the idea he got in his head, and he couldn't let it go."

"And he burned your books because of that?" asks Nick, incredulous.

"Yes. As punishment. And I wasn't allowed to use the computers anymore."

Nick raises his eyebrows. "Seems extreme."

"It's my fault," I say again. "I knew what I was doing, and I knew how Dad would react."

"What were you doing?"

"Distancing myself. Telling Dad and Wulf that I didn't want to help them anymore."

"What do you mean? Help them with what?"

I study him. "You don't know?" I ask.

"Know what?"

I pick up my trowel and scrape the tip against the dirt. The silver metal catches the sun, flashes blinding light into my eyes. It feels like we're miles and miles away from the settlement here, just the two of us, and I'm flowing forward on a deep river, strangely calm, coursing toward the inevitable. Didn't I know that this is where the conversation would eventually arrive? That Nick was going to ask? That I was going to tell him?

"They're attacking the Domes," I hear myself say.

"The Domes?" Nick furrows his brow. "Hold on, the ones Vanessa's supposed to be writing about? They're attacking—Isaac's the one causing all those malfunctions? All those power outages and systems failures?"

I incline my head, my eyes trained on the dirt, the glint of metal.

"How—hacking in? That's what Isaac's doing down there in his creepy basement?"

I nod shortly again.

"Holy shit. Why?"

76

"Because he thinks the Domes are a dangerous idea. That it's the outside world going about trying to solve its deadlands crisis the wrong way, and that it's going to make the world a lot worse if they succeed. It'll just be Domes everywhere for a while until those are unlivable, too, and then it'll be over for humanity. That's his reasoning, anyway."

"So basically he's some kind of ecoterrorist? Is that what you're saying?"

I frown. "I didn't say that."

"Well, not in those words. But that's sure what it sounds like to me."

"You really didn't know what he's been doing?" I ask, studying him. "Vanessa knows, doesn't she?"

"What makes you think that?"

"Did you know, or didn't you?"

"Look," Nick says with a small impatient hand gesture. "Don't go thinking that Vanessa and I are working as a team or even on the same page. If you want to know what Vanessa knows, you should ask her. And then tell me, while you're at it. Whatever she knows, I'm not in on it."

I consider him for a moment. "Okay," I say.

"All I know is that she's been working on this side project of hers, researching this old settlement place, searching for it," Nick says.

"It seems like she's lost interest in it now," I say.

"Well, no surprise there. Things didn't exactly pan out as she expected."

I shake my head, skeptical.

"Maybe she knows," says Nick. "Well, does Isaac think she does?"

"I think he has an idea. I think he's trying to figure her out."

Nick sighs like he's tired of thinking about it. He shifts position so he's sitting with his legs more loosely crossed. "You know," he says, "I wasn't even supposed to come on this trip with Vanessa. I had other plans that day. We'd gotten into an argument that morning, and I told her that she was never home, either, and who knew what she was doing on these trips she was taking, while I'd had nothing to do all day ever since I'd agreed to come with her to the godforsaken deadlands. So she told me to come with her. It wasn't an invitation, she was just angry. And I said fine, which I think she didn't expect."

"Or maybe she did," I say.

"Maybe," says Nick. "She's a careful planner, but there's a limit. I won't say any of this couldn't have been planned, but all of it couldn't have been. You know what I mean? You can't plan everything. Sometimes unexpected things happen that surprise you."

"Like what?" I ask.

"Like you being here. Like me meeting you here in this desert."

He stretches his legs out in front of him, and we both look at them. They're covered in loose gray pants made out of a thin synthetic material. He crab-walks over to me, and suddenly he's so close that I can smell his sweat, salty and metallic. I sense him searching my face, like he's trying to catch my eye, but I know instinctively not to make eye contact. It's the same way I know not to stare straight into the sun. He dips his head, and I stare intently at the ground, my mind as blank as the white-hot sky of a monsoon day. Nick moves his hand to my back, reaching for the skin under my shirt. His fingers rest against my spine, sticky from sweat and grimy, then tap it lightly, like he's counting the vertebrae. I turn my head, and then, as though this is the sign he was waiting for, Nick's mouth is over mine, and moving. His lips are large and cracked, but soft. When they press against mine, I picture a pair of larvae. A part of me is repulsed, and a part is roiling through a choppy sea, and a part is wondering confusedly if this is what motion sickness feels like on a ship or on a plane.

"Like that, too," Nick says blithely, breaking away. "That was unexpected."

I stare at him. I want to ask—was it? But I don't say anything.

Nick scoots back to his side of the container and starts chipping away at the dirt again. His trowel bangs against the metal repeatedly, making a surreal clicking sound, like a bell ringing rhythmically. I blink, trying to force the world into looking real again. I pick up my trowel and scrape it against the corner where the metal sinks into the dirt. We do that for minutes or hours. I slip into a timeless space, every second new and endless. When I dig my trowel into a chunk of dirt and pry it out, it's like I'm watching someone else do it.

"Maybe it's a time capsule," Nick says finally.

"What?" I say.

Nick points his tool at the container, which is only slightly more unearthed than it was when we arrived. "This thing," he says. "Maybe it's a time capsule. Do you know what that is? People put a bunch of things in a box, like photographs and electronics and the newspaper, and bury it so people can find it hundreds of years later and know what life was like way back when. Maybe there'll be things in here a museum will want." When I don't answer, he looks up. "Do you know what a museum is?" he asks.

"I know what it is," I say.

"It's hard to know what you know and don't know sometimes."

"Just because I've never seen something doesn't mean I don't know what it is."

"Sure, sorry. I know that."

"You don't have to apologize."

Nick makes eye contact with me, and I look back at him levelly, a fear of blinking gripping me. My eyes start to sting from the dryness, but I manage to keep my face blank.

"Okay, then," says Nick, and he smiles.

"Do you think a museum in Ohio would want it, if it was a time capsule?" I say, to rein back in the conversation.

"Only one way to find out."

"That's pretty far away, isn't it?"

"We'll make a road trip of it."

I try to imagine this—Nick and me in a car, driving to Ohio together. It's an incongruous image, one that can't make sense no matter which way I turn it. I know that he's only talking, not meaning anything by what he's saying. And yet, despite knowing that, a flicker of pleasure pulls at me at hearing Nick refer to the two of us outside the settlement, at knowing that he can picture me there with him. What else do you see? I want to say.

"And then?" I say out loud, keeping my voice neutral, my face blank.

"They'd probably put it in storage. That's what they do with most of their things."

"Really?" I ask, momentarily distracted. "They have that much?"

"Oh, yeah, they all do. History museums, art museums, archaeology museums. And it's just going to keep piling up. They'll be drowning in crap that supposedly represents our lives but that none of us ever thought was very interesting or important. Can you imagine a museum hundreds of years from now? They'll have to figure out what to do about that."

"Optimistic of you, assuming the world will still exist then."

Nick grins. "Got to keep my chin up," he says.

"What would we do then? After we went to this museum."

"Well, what would you like to do?" he asks after a pause, watching me.

I pick up a craggy pebble and examine it. "What's there to see in Ohio?"

"Not much. There used to be some forest when I was a kid, but they've had to develop most of that land for all the new people coming in. Not that I think that's a bad thing, obviously. I like people more than I like trees, so if one of them has got to go, I volunteer the vegetation. There's a river too. Just brown sludge, but it's kind of nice how it runs through the city."

In my mind, I graft the place Nick is describing onto the descriptions Vanessa gave me. I can see the river and buildings rising tall into the air. If I try harder, I can imagine people, a few scuttling around at first, like they're afraid of a monster about to arrive, and then crowds of them, shoulder to shoulder, moving through a world they know instinctively.

"Were you planning on going back?" I ask.

"To Ohio? Eventually, probably. Did Vanessa happen to tell you why we left?"

"She said she was writing her book about the Domes."

"Well, that's how we ended up in the deadlands. But not exactly why we left Ohio."

"Do you want me to ask you why?"

Nick makes a sheepish face. "Maybe I do," he says. "Not sure why. It's not too interesting—oldest story in the book. I had sex with someone that wasn't her, without her knowledge, obviously. One thing led to another, and it got me into trouble at work, and then everything kind of exploded on me. It was stupid, to be honest, which is what got Vanessa so mad. So that's what got her to suggest we move to the Arizonan deadlands, where she could pursue this Domes story. This must all sound completely out of context to you, I'm sorry. I'm not sure why I'm rambling about it."

"It's not out of context," I say.

Nick raises his eyebrows at me.

"I mean, I understand what you're talking about."

"Do you?"

"I know what sex is."

Nick laughs, a sudden, ebullient sound that spooks a bird in prickly shrub nearby. It explodes out of the branches and flies off, squawking.

A stupid thing to say, I think wretchedly, humiliation pulsing hot and angry through my body. My mind whirs frantically to figure out how to coerce the conversation forward, to take a step back from what feels like a cliff.

"Anyway," Nick says, "Vanessa and I are like roommates at this point. Not even that now. I guess we've lived for so long together that neither of us can imagine anything else. I don't know what I'm trying to tell you. Maybe that Vanessa and I have something of an understanding. I don't want you to think that I'm a horrible person."

"I wasn't thinking that."

"No, you wouldn't," he says, and there's relief and appreciation in his voice, a trust that feels almost dangerous, like a snake I'm not sure I should be handling.

"I don't know what I'd do in Ohio," I say.

Nick gives me a puzzled look.

"When we were talking about the museum," I say cumbersomely, lurching over the words. "We were talking about going to a museum in Ohio. But, I mean, if I left here, in general. I wouldn't know what to do out there."

He waves his hand. "You'd figure it out."

Something like disappointment fills me, indistinct and irrational. I swallow and train my eyes on the ground. We start digging again, our trowels dully clinking.

It's late afternoon by the time we come to a mutual silent agreement to stop, both of us standing up and stretching our bodies for a few minutes before starting the trek back home. The sun is at its peak, but it doesn't feel oppressive, it just makes me sleepy. I feel peaceable and warm and tired from the work and heat. Nick jumps when he startles a group of cactus wrens, and both of us laugh more than the situation merits, unspooling a tension.

"Hey," says Nick, turning to me just as we see the buildings of the settlement show up ahead of us through the scraggly mesquite trees. He slows down, and I match his step. "How are you doing?" he says, looking at me intently, his forehead creased.

"Great," I say, fighting the urge to walk faster.

"I don't know if that was such a good idea, all that back there." He rubs at his forehead with the tips of his fingers. "We should probably keep it between ourselves."

"Who would I tell?" I say.

Nick exhales, smiling thinly. He shakes his head to himself.

When we return, Wulf and Dad are dragging our old solar dehydrator out of the glass house, likely to strip it for parts. Dad stops and waves when he sees us, handing off the contraption to Wulf. Wulf stares across the distance at us, his arms grasping the bulky piece of machinery, his muscles straining. I look over at Nick and see that he's scanning the buildings and gardens, his eyes moving rapidly.

"Vanessa's making supper," Dad calls to us.

For a fleeting, irrational moment, I'm certain that he knows exactly what Nick and I have been doing these past few hours, that he saw us and heard our entire conversation. But as Dad strides closer, I see his face is placid and distracted, even making an effort to seem friendly. He nods amiably at Nick, who seems surprised, but nods back, a delayed greeting. Dad doesn't even look at me, and I realize with relief that I'm safely beyond his notice presently.

"Find the dog today?" Nick asks.

"No," says Dad, curt but congenial. "We shot a javelina. It should last us for supper about a week. How's the foot getting along?"

"Fine and dandy," says Nick.

"No sharp pain?"

"Nothing to worry about."

"Okay, then," Dad says, turning his head to Wulf. "We're just going to finish up here, and then we'll all eat together. It'll be the javelina meat."

Wulf hasn't taken his eyes off me and Nick. His face is shadowed by the sun setting behind him. The horizon is a bright orange, the clouds bubbling in violent pinks and crimson, and Wulf's figure is darkening rapidly, his face losing its contour along with the trees and buildings, everything except for the brilliant sky flattening and dimming. The dusk smudges away my brother, turns him forbidding as a rare approaching storm: wind gusts building up, a wall of sepia clouds, the desert dirt primed to be swept into a frenzy.

9

Maybe it's because Dad's mind is occupied elsewhere—with his walks with Vanessa, with their steadily lengthening conversations, with the brooding mood he's taken to slipping into—that he doesn't ask where Nick and I go when we start trekking into the desert regularly ourselves. It's slow work, unearthing the container. The dirt is packed tight around it, as though the minerals from the metal have mixed with the minerals from the earth, welding the container and the ground together. It's a few trips before we start to get an accurate picture of its shape: a cylinder three feet long and two feet in diameter, buried at a forty-five-degree angle from the ground's surface, its lidded top pointing downward. Even after figuring out the shape, the surface is so corroded, its grooves worn down, that it takes me even longer to realize it's a shape I've seen before. When I do, the knowledge comes quick as monsoon rain, the shape taking on form and meaning all at once, torrentially. It's one of the steel drums we use to store our water at the settlement. I put down my trowel and lean back on my heels to get a better look at its entirety. Nick stops, too, and looks over at me. "What?" he says, and I tell him.

"I don't get it," he says, following my gaze to the container. "Someone buried some water?"

I put my hand on the drum and scrape off some caked-on dirt with the back of my nail. The exposed streak of black metal gleams poison-ously. "It doesn't have to be water," I say. "That's what we use the drums for, but I don't know what the people who brought them here did with them. They could have used this one to bury anything."

"Maybe toxic waste," Nick says good-humoredly.

I frown at the container, considering this.

"I'm only joking," Nick says.

"But it's a good point, you're right. It might be old objects with chemicals like mercury or lead or arsenic in them. Someone might have sealed them off and buried them so they wouldn't contaminate the area."

"I'm probably wrong," Nick says in a tone implying he wants to move on.

"Why do you say that?"

Nick laughs lightly. "I just usually am."

"Maybe we should stop," I say, prodding the metal dubiously with my trowel.

"What, digging it up? How else are we going to occupy ourselves?"

"It's buried for a reason. If it's toxic waste—"

Nick waves his hand. "If anything, it'll be regular waste. We're probably digging up someone's toilet or something."

"You should take this more seriously."

"No, I really don't think I should." He brushes the dirt off his hands and wipes his forehead. "Are you tired? I'm tired. Maybe we should call it a day."

I give the container one last look. "All right."

We pack up and start walking. The desert is unforgiving today—the air dry and crackling, the sun beating down on our skin with what feels like malice. Nick swats at something near his face, irritated, and an insect zooms away from him, emitting a whir that sounds equally vexed. My arm scrapes against a shriveled, prickly bush, its long thorns tugging at my skin, nagging and painful, drawing a small amount of blood. I suck in my breath sharply.

"Careful," Nick says, glancing in my direction.

"It's fine." I wipe the dots of blood off my arm with my hand.

"I could go for a Coca-Cola right about now," says Nick. "Cold, and sweet, and so fizzy it hurts to drink. That's the desert mirage I want to appear right here, right in front of me."

"That'd be nice," I say, absent minded.

Nick looks over at me, this time studying me with his full attention. The world snaps back into focus, ringing shrilly, the sun beaming down white and hot, illuminating every spiny plant, stripping them of shadow. The rocks crunching under my feet crackle like a fire. Out of the corner of my eye, I can see Nick's eyes still latched on to me. He says: "So, you've had a Coke before, huh? How'd you manage that?"

"No," I say. "I didn't say that."

"Come on," he says in a chummy tone. "Tell me."

"I just meant that a cold drink sounds nice."

"Maybe you did. Or maybe you're not as isolated here as you would have us believe."

"What do you mean?" I ask after a pause.

"I've just been thinking," Nick says, his voice pleasant. "All that preserved food we eat—the rabbit jerky, the canned tepary beans—sure, you make it yourselves, but you know what I realized you need to preserve food? Salt. You need salt to preserve things."

"All right, I've had a soda," I say. Suddenly, it doesn't feel quite real, this conversation. As though I could say anything and the words would just be bleached clean by the sun, the sound waves broken into little pieces nobody would ever find.

"That's it?" says Nick, his smile wheedling. "You're really not going to tell me? Maybe you just found a Coke, like you find everything. A Platonic two-liter plastic bottle, glossy red-and-white label, just lying there unopened in the desert. Right next to a big old bag of salt. And that perfectly functioning plastic watch your brother wears. Is that it?"

I shake my head impotently.

Nick grabs my forearm, just above the wrist, and we both stop walking. He swings my arm back and forth lightly, then strokes my forearm, his fingers feeling for the bone just beneath my skin. I've taken to stiffening whenever he touches me like this, brazenly, on purpose. It's not danger I feel, not exactly, but something close enough to it, something like danger stripped of threat. A vigilance that's instinctual and animal. Nick moves in front of me so he's positioned like a large, contorted reflection. His head bends down, his face growing grotesque as it gets closer, all bridge of nose, eyes like an insect, his lips too large, as though inflamed. My ears ring as his mouth meets mine. The sun is beating down on my back, the heat driving against me angrily, and I feel a weak dissolving sensation, the stiffening thawed to sickly slush, a fever. Nick's tongue is in my mouth, tunneling like a muscular worm. His body presses into my chest, my stomach, my hips, shifting like it wants to be everywhere at once but can't make itself comfortable anywhere. He pulls away and steps back. His hand is still wrapped around my forearm, and then he takes that back too. His breathing is loud and strained. It's the only sound I hear for a moment, and then the sounds of the desert explode into the background again, filling the empty space. The thrum of occasional bees and cicadas; the sad, flat cooing of mourning doves; the rustle of a small mammal absconding into its shadowy burrow.

If Nick meant this to be a prelude to asking me more questions, he seems to have forgotten his intent. Dirt and rock crunch under our feet as we start walking again. Sometimes it seems like Nick has no idea what he's doing, and sometimes it seems like it's just me who has no idea what he's doing, no idea what I'm doing, no idea of anything.

"Look at us," says Nick. "Spending all our time playing in the dirt. Soon, it's going to get too hot for this. What do you do when it gets too hot to go outside during the day?"

"We go outside at night," I say.

"Like little nocturnal animals," Nick says.

"Yeah, cactus mice and kangaroo rats."

Nick laughs, an agitated sound that seems to burst convulsively out of him. I watch him, trying to figure out what's funny about what I said. Maybe the sun is making him delirious, or maybe he's releasing pent-up energy from another emotion, like fear or pain. Once, when Wulf crushed one of his fingers under a cinder block he was moving when we were patching a wall, instead of crying he laughed mirthlessly for a long time, howling until he had used up all his breath and then some, rocking back and forth, clutching his hand. Dad and I didn't touch him until he got all that crazed laughter out of him, and then Dad made a splint out of wood and a strip of cloth torn from a shirt in case any minor bones were broken.

"We probably shouldn't tell anyone about the container," I say when Nick stops laughing.

Nick inclines his head and draws a long breath. "Because you're worried what Isaac would say, or because you still think it's toxic waste?"

"I just don't think my dad would like it. We can say we're doing something else."

"Something else," Nick repeats, a note—I think—of humor in his voice.

"Like looking for something else. Fossils, maybe."

"Sure, fossils." Nick grins. "We can say that."

When we arrive at the settlement, Dad is kneeling on the ground, scooping dirt into a glass jar. He lifts his head when Nick and I come upon him, his neck extended long like a tortoise's. He screws the lid on to the jar, then pushes himself up off the ground. The sun glints against something on the ground, and my eyes are drawn down to four more jars at Dad's feet, all partially filled with dirt. He gazes down at them as well. "Just taking care of a little housekeeping," he says nonsensically. "Everything in order?"

"Everything in order," Nick says, glancing at the jars as well.

Dad tilts his head down with finality, dismissing us. But either Nick doesn't understand that Dad's ended the conversation, or chooses not to, because he just stands there and grins widely at Dad, who clears his throat, looking ill at ease.

"How's Vanessa doing?" Nick asks.

"I believe she's in her building, if you're looking for her," Dad says.

"Nope," says Nick. "I'm not looking for her."

"Well, then," Dad says. He bends down to pick up his jars and struggles for a moment to figure out a way to hold them all. He ends up with the five jars grasped against his chest, his fingers splayed over them. He walks stiffly to his building. Nick watches with a satisfied expression, almost amused.

"What was that about?" I ask.

Nick turns to me. He has a trickster's glint in his eye, a half smile playing over his mouth. He says: "I think Isaac's developed a little crush on Vanessa. No big deal, these things happen." He stretches his arms out and rolls his neck. It cracks unpleasantly, the sound stepping on little bones makes. "Whew, are you as tired as I am? That sun is brutal today, isn't it? I don't know how much more sweat and grime my skin can handle before I start getting a rash. You want to show me how to take a bath around here? If I'm allowed one, that is."

"You're allowed," I say distractedly, watching Dad stoop down the stairs to his building. Nick's words about Dad and Vanessa are prickles of heat rash on my skin, abrupt and irritating. What does he know? I try to tell myself. But the uncomfortable truth itches at me—he knows a lot more than I do about these kinds of things.

I lead Nick to the glass house, where we keep the water for bathing in one of the cisterns, and bring him a bucket, soap, and cloth rags from the basement. I tell him we usually wash under the ramada, where there's shade, and where the ground slopes slightly, so any water runoff will eventually make its way to the garden and give extra water to the plants.

"Just out there in the open?" Nick asks.

"There's no one here to see you," I say.

Nick raises his eyebrows at me. "Not unless someone looks."

"Why would they look?"

"Wow, okay. Brutal. But I can take it."

"I didn't—" I try to say. I can feel pink warmth coloring my ears.

"No, no, don't try to explain yourself."

He's trying to be funny, I can tell, but the humor isn't connecting. The attempt just makes me feel vaguely distressed, like I've taken a wrong turn in the conversation, picked up on the wrong thread. This isn't what I want to talk about, I imagine myself snapping. How did we get here? Some of these thoughts must show up on my face, because Nick's own expression changes. He observes me for a moment, the corners of his mouth downturned.

"You okay?" he asks.

"I'm fine," I say, the words hard, defensive.

And then Nick's expression sours again, like he's suddenly grown tired of talking to me. "Yeah, yeah," he says. "All right. You're fine. I'm fine. Everyone's fine." Then he shakes his head. "Sorry. The sun makes us testy, doesn't it? Or maybe just me." He reaches his hand out to touch my cheek, his hand chapped and clammy with sweat. "You're a pretty little thing, you know that? Even with your face all flushed and red."

A pretty little thing, a pretty little thing. The words scuttle around in my head like beetles. I leave Nick to himself and make my way to the library, thinking that I'll wander around and pick out some books at random. I've been spending too much time with Nick, too much time with myself, too much time with Nick and me together, and the library arrives suddenly in my mind as an antidote. I'll fill my head with facts about thermodynamics, Roman columns, maize production, and censuses, even circuit boards or radio waves, why not, and the scraps of knowledge will shove everything else out of the way. The plan alone is soothing. I can feel a softening in my limbs, a looseness slipping into my blood, at just the thought of it.

I open the door to the library, and—with a jolt, and then a sinking feeling, an *of course* arriving unprompted to my mind, as though it's somehow inevitable—there's Vanessa in the far corner, sitting at the small table. She's leaning over it, her neck bent deeply, writing in a notebook with a plastic pen. She doesn't glance up immediately, though she must have heard the door open. I watch her continue writing, finish a thought or a sentence. Finally, she looks up at me and our eyes meet, and she smiles warmly, effusively, like she's welcoming me into her home. Maybe this has become the home she's made for herself—it occurs to me, with a disorienting lurch, that I haven't been paying attention. What do I know about what she's been doing? Maybe she's been spending hours here every day without me even noticing. What do I know about what she's been doing when she spends time with Dad?

"Have you ever thought of painting the walls in this place?" Vanessa asks, like we're picking up an old conversation. "The adobe in here is great—a nice change from all the cement—but I was just imagining what it would look like in a dusty pink or a yellow."

After a confused pause, I shake my head.

"I know it's probably not high on the list of projects around here," Vanessa says, smiling mildly. "It's just something that popped into my head. I've always painted the walls in every apartment I lived in, even if it wasn't allowed in the lease."

"Are you working on your essay?" I ask, my gaze drifting to her notebook.

"Just bits and pieces," Vanessa says, closing her notebook. She picks up her pen and twirls it, moving it from one finger to the next.

I'm still standing by the door, so I take a few steps forward, just to the nearest shelf, and run my hand along the flat surface. It has a deep layer of dust on it, and some dried, tight bundles of long grass stacked at the far end, an abandoned attempt to make a broom.

"Were you talking to my dad about painting the walls?" I ask.

Vanessa shakes her head. "No, no, it was just a passing thought. Isaac would hate the idea, wouldn't he? All those solvents and heavy metals in paint." She sweeps a few strands of hair from her face and then reaches her arms back to undo and retie her ponytail.

Not the right question, I think, disappointed—not the right question to pick at what Nick said earlier. As though there's a right one I just have to stumble onto and then I'll have my answer, some answer, anything at all. Even if there were, trying to find it is a pointless venture—a fairy-tale task like searching for a single grain of sand—or just impossible, like trying to resee a particular shape in the clouds when it's windy and the clouds are forming and unforming constantly, creating a new cloudscape by the second.

Vanessa is looking at me closely, her gaze steady. "Can I ask you something?" she asks.

"Sure," I say, suddenly aware of my heartbeat, as though it was just switched on.

"Do you remember when Isaac brought up the Domes when we were weeding? When he brought up the power failure? Has he talked to you any more about that? I'm asking because he mentioned it to me again today. He told me it turns out there were a couple of deaths from damage to the water filtration system."

"Deaths?" I repeat, confused. "No. There were deaths?"

"From chlorine poisoning," Vanessa says, watching me. "Pretty gruesome, apparently. Isaac seemed pretty upset about it. He asked me what my thoughts were and, to be honest, I wasn't really sure why he was telling me and what he wanted me to say. I was wondering if you might know."

"He didn't say anything about it to me."

"It's never happened before, from what I know," Vanessa says. "They've had a lot of issues at the Domes, but never deaths."

I shake my head. "I don't know why he told you," I say. "Or what he wanted you to say."

"Hmm," says Vanessa. "Well, anyway." She smiles at me again, her smile placid, blandly friendly. "Were you looking for something to read?"

"No, I was just—no," I say, illogically.

"It's too bad you don't have any novels here," says Vanessa, looking around at the bookshelves. "I get the feeling we could have gotten into some good conversations about them, you and me. But I can understand why Isaac doesn't want them around."

"You do? Why?"

"Well, it's like what Plato said. Have you read Plato?"

I shake my head no.

"He said that art is so removed from reality that it's basically a lie. It seems like Isaac thinks the outside world is full of those. Everyone going around believing in and telling each other their different versions of reality. He's lost patience for that, hasn't he? He's found the truth, and meanwhile, the world is running out of time. There's no point in wasting it tolerating alternatives to his reality." Vanessa smiles. "I don't mean to be critical. I just like novels, personally. Sometimes I want to have someone else's voice in my head."

"Is that why you talk to Dad so much? To get someone else's voice in your head?"

"Well, that's different, that's a conversation. It'd be nice if it were more like reading a novel. I've thought sometimes, when talking to people for an article, wouldn't it be nice if they just wrote down all their thoughts on a piece of paper and handed them to me? There wouldn't have to be any badgering, or figuring out a way in, or having to decide what's relevant, or what's true and what isn't, in the moment. It'd be much more efficient and effective."

"You don't like the conversations?"

"It's not my favorite part of my work, to be honest. But it turns out I'm pretty good at it. At getting people to talk to me."

"Nick too," I say without thinking.

Vanessa raises her eyebrows. "You think so?" she says.

"Maybe," I say, my voice quickening, embarrassed. "I mean, you both ask a lot of questions."

She takes a breath, and I'm sure she's about to start in on a troubling line of interrogation that I won't be able to untangle myself from. But she doesn't. She exhales audibly, slowly, closing her eyes as she does it, and then keeps them closed and remains very still, nearly not breathing. Then she flashes her eyes open, and they meet mine for a moment before she drops her gaze down to her notebook. "I should probably get back to this before all my thoughts get away from me," she says. "They tend to do that if I let them."

It takes me a few moments to realize that she's waiting for me to leave. When I realize it, I leave hastily, without even taking a book with me, bizarrely struck with the feeling that I'm intruding, a guest who's slow to take a hint, who's overstayed her welcome.

For the rest of the afternoon, I stay inside my building, keeping my curtains drawn. I tidy my bedroom a little, rearranging my objects and fossils, dusting them with a rag. Time seems to move forward and rewind, spool on, and then stop, but it's just a trick of the light outside, the sun dimming as it goes down, brightening my room for a brief, triumphant moment, darkening again. I sit cross-legged on the edge of my bed and reach underneath for the books between the mattress and the slats of the wooden frame.

The book I pull out is *Moby-Dick*, a short, fat paperback that would make a noticeable lump in my mattress if the mattress weren't so lumpy already. The pages are fragile, a crumbling and pungent brown-yellow. The print is small and crowded together, hard to read in the now poorly lit room, but I thumb through the pages, stopping when I reach the cetology chapter, at which point I raise the book close to my eyes and reread the chapter carefully. Not facts, exactly, but close enough to what I wanted. Valuable oil and baleen, humps and mystery, spouting fishes with horizontal tails. A classification system left unfinished. My mind wanders to the steel drum, still stuck in the dirt. Should we leave it where someone purposefully left it? It's an idea, a thought threatening to spoil the sterility of the facts I'm filling my head with, but I stubbornly continue reading, not letting myself dwell on it.

I leaf through the book until I come across a word that strikes me, read a few pages or chapters until I get drowsy, and work my way through the book like that until it's time for supper. Vanessa's taken the reins on cooking almost entirely by now. Tonight, she's made nopals cut up in little pieces and quick pickled, which we eat with mesquite bread.

The meal doesn't last long. Supper isn't usually rife with conversation, but today the atmosphere feels especially strained, every sound magnified: plates clinking on the table, chewing noises, small coughs, chairs scraped back and scraped back in again. Dad is staring at his plate intently as he eats, eyebrows tipped down. I think back to what Vanessa said in the library—accident at the Domes, two dead. Is that what Dad is thinking about now? Nick keeps knocking his fork against his plate, the clinks getting louder, sounding his irritation as the small, slimy pieces of nopal keep slipping off his fork. Vanessa's eyes dart around like she's waiting for something to happen. Wulf keeps glancing over at Dad. A memory of the saguaro graveyard drifts lightly, soft as pollen, to my mind. Wulf asking: What did I think would happen? Did I think we'd live happily ever after all together? I try to catch his eye, but he ignores me or doesn't notice. What did you know? I ask with my stare, boring the question into his stubborn refusal to look at me. What did you know would happen, and is it? Is it happening? What is it?

Because something is happening. I can feel the shift, the season-ending change. A sudden chill or an ominous heat wave, cacti rotting overnight, ground turning into quicksand. That's what it feels like, the discomfort growing between all of us, the contractions and expansions, the stretching separations. Long, unfathomable distances, and at the same time, spaces closing in, inscrutable as two birds chittering to each other. An inexplicable wrongness, strange dread.

When we finish eating, and Nick trudges off with the dishes to clean, it's a relief to leave the table. I scrape back my chair with a haste that makes even Dad glance in my direction. But once I'm outside, the restlessness doesn't go away. I talk myself into walking around the settlement, and then out of it a little way, my steps focused and disciplined, so it looks like I have a purpose. It's fully dark out now, the moon gauzing the cacti into prickly ghosts rising menacingly into the sky. The shrubs hunch into their spindly branches, the cholla are dark masses I have to step around. There isn't a cloud in the sky, and the unfiltered darkness is crisp and bright, the stars twinkling, razor edged. In the distance, a coyote yips and barks, the sound desperate, almost frantic. I stand still for a moment, breathing the uncertain air.

Eventually, I turn around and head back to the settlement. I walk all the way back to my building before I stop and retrace my steps and walk to the glass house instead. I open the door soundlessly, just enough to slip through, and walk across the building to the side that's fully glass. The wall is smooth and dark, polished like black stone, all the streaks of dirt invisible at night. The light of the moon hits in a way that lets me see both the desert and myself, a ghostly, incomplete reflection.

My face smallish, my hair reaching to my shoulders. It's coarse though I comb it regularly, wash it once a month with vinegar. I tuck it behind my ears, then untuck it. The memory of Nick's mouth on mine rises up in my thoughts, and a squirming heat spills into my body, a lolling wave. I try to look at myself objectively, to see myself as someone else would, but it's difficult to step outside of myself. It's like trying to decide if the mountains on the horizon are beautiful or aren't. They're just the mountains, always there.

I adjust my shoulders so I'm standing up straighter, tilt my head a little to the side so I can see my profile. My face looks better this way, I think, my nose straighter, the rounded end coming to a point instead of sticking out like a bulb. Is that what people think about when they consider faces? My face is pale in the glass, an unsettling see-through color. When I focus my eyes differently, my reflection is cut across by spindly shrubs and mesquite tree branches.

"We can say we're doing something else," I say quietly to the glass, watching my reflection. I wince at the uncertain waver in my voice, the consternation on my face. I try again, repeating the words louder, lifting my chin, smoothing out my expression.

"I should probably announce myself," says a voice behind me, and I freeze.

It's Vanessa, pushing herself up off the ground a few yards away, from where she must have been sitting by the drums of water. She stretches like she's been sitting for a while and her limbs are cramped, then rights herself and walks over to me. Rigidly, I turn back to the glass. When she's standing next to me, I force myself to look at her reflection. Her eyes are narrowed in unfocused concentration, like she's trying to peer outside, to look past the reflected interior at what's out in the desert.

"Funny how we keep running into each other today," she says. "I heard you come in, but I was too far gone in my thoughts to say anything right then. Sorry if I startled you."

"That's fine," I force myself to say.

"Have you ever looked at yourself in a real mirror?" asks Vanessa, nodding at the glass. "I haven't seen any around the settlement. Glass works okay, but it's not really the same. I have one if you ever want to use it. It's just the little round mirror that comes with my concealer." She laughs a little, then says: "I know it sounds stupid to bring concealer with me, but it's sunscreen too. SPF 50. You can never have too much SPF protection."

I only have a dim idea of what she's talking about, but I nod.

Vanessa gazes steadily at the glass, her body still as stone, her face motionless. "I wanted to ask you—" Her words spill out in a rush, like she's decided suddenly to open the floodgates. "Is Nick bothering you?"

"No," I say, my mouth dry.

"Is something going on between the two of you?"

"He's just helping me look for fossils."

Out of the corner of my eye, I see Vanessa smile tightly. She says: "I don't know if it does anyone any good to pretend a situation doesn't exist. It's obvious that he's taken an interest in you. I shouldn't be surprised. You're just his type." She pauses like she's waiting for me to say something, deny it maybe, but I can't bring myself to. It feels almost like sleep paralysis, like I'm caught in a dream and cognizant, unable to wake. Vanessa's voice is calm, but there's a sharpness behind it, a sting I think she's trying hard to tame. "I should warn you that it's a pattern," she says. "Did he tell you about why we moved out here? Why I decided this would be a good time to drop everything at home and work on my book project?"

I nod shortly.

"He told you about the intern?"

"Yes," I say after a pause.

"Did he tell you it was a habit of his to court pretty young women, to find excuses to exchange numbers with them and then patiently put in the time to make them feel admired and understood, to remember their birthdays and buy little gifts for them, before bringing them to our house, where he'd fuck them on our sofa while I was at work or out running errands?"

The intimacy of these details crashes into me like cold water. They settle leadenly, like rocks thrown into a lake, millions of years away from weathering into anything resembling sand.

"Nick can't handle feeling guilty," Vanessa says, her voice tired. She closes her eyes. "Of course he would tell you. Though he probably spun it in some way that makes him seem like a better person. It's selfish, isn't it? Spilling out all your wrongdoing like it absolves you of anything. Confessing, crying a little, and then moving on, feeling righteous and smug. Meanwhile, the situation you've created still exists, and the only difference is that now other people share the burden. I'm sorry," she says, opening her eyes. "I shouldn't be talking about all this to you. I really just wanted to make sure you're doing okay. I think it's safe to assume you don't have a lot of experience with sex."

I try to swallow, my breath caught in my throat. "That's not—"

"I wasn't sure if I should bring this up," Vanessa continues. "Honestly, I have no idea what he thinks he's doing. Maybe trying to remind me that he exists, acting out to get back at me for bringing us here. He just ignores me when I bring it up. I can understand why he doesn't want to talk to me right now, but this is over-the-top ridiculous. Obviously, this is not the time nor the place. What would your father think if he found out? What would he do? Banish us? Make us walk to our deaths into the desert deadlands? It's not—the worst of it isn't even that you're so young, it's that you're so—unformed," she says, a helplessness in her voice, sounding more pitying than angry.

"It's not like that," I make myself say. "And I don't need you to look out for me."

The words come out flat but leave me feeling spent and light headed. What I'm trying to communicate is that I'm fine, that I'm completely fine, and also that I'm sorry. That I'm toggling between wanting to stay away from Nick and wanting to spend more time with him, that sometimes I think he's repulsive and sometimes I'm like a moth, hungry for what I learn from him, lured in by the attention. There's a distant, dim part of me that feels wretched about what I'm watching myself walk into, what I can't help walking alongside, gaping like an onlooker watching a wildfire, but wildfires aren't always a bad thing, sometimes the destruction wrought by them is not only inevitable, but necessary.

Vanessa's face hardens almost imperceptibly. "I'm trying my best here, Georgia," she says. "Despite everything, I'm trying my best to be a good person. I really am. I'm trying to be aware of the particulars of the situation we've found ourselves in and the particulars of the lives of everyone involved and to not point fingers at anyone, because that isn't the point. I'm trying to say that I don't blame you, and that I'm here if you want to talk to me about anything. As uncomfortable as that would be for me and you both."

"It's not like that," I say again, the words strained. "There's nothing to talk about."

"Well, what I said still stands," says Vanessa.

A vague unease lingers between us as we observe each other in the glass.

"I'm going to bed," Vanessa says finally. "Good night, then."

Her quiet footsteps patter across the floor, the door opens and shuts. I stare at myself in the dark glass for a few more minutes. My body looks small, pitifully dwarfed by the tall, empty building, and I feel exhausted. All I want to do is crawl back to my building and sleep, but walking all the way there feels like it would take an energy that I've been drained of. It's easier to just keep standing here, unmoving as the moon beaming through the glass.

Finally, I dredge up the energy I need to make it back to my building. I walk slowly and carefully, making almost no noise, every determined step moving deliberately into the next. It's only when I get to the stairs leading down to my door that I stop short, my eye catching on a small flat rock lying on the ground just before the stairs that I haven't noticed before, that looks—perhaps, just possibly—like it was placed there purposefully. I bend down to pick it up and examine it by the moonlight. There's a faint hint of a spiral on it that could be taken to look like a shell, something an untrained eye could see as a fossil.

A dull, fluttering unease rises up in me. The light in Nick's house is off, but I wonder briefly if he's placed it here. Whether it's a message and, if it is, what it's supposed to communicate. Maybe I'm meant to steal into his building and ask him one of these questions. After wavering for a moment, I accept that I can't bring myself to do it, so there's no use in trying to decide whether I should or shouldn't. I squeeze my fingers around the rock and press it painfully into the center of my palm. I tell myself he's probably sleeping already anyway.

10

By some unspoken agreement, Nick and I take a break from visiting the buried steel drum. Nick hides out in his building, blaming the temperature, which has shot up recently. I hardly see him until Dad calls a meeting after morning calisthenics and sends Vanessa to fetch Nick, who never partakes in exercise. When the two of them come trudging back, Dad leads all of us out of the bounds of the settlement. He's holding two plastic buckets in his hand, bright red. They swing and bump against his knee as he strides forward in his lunging, headfirst gait. When we've walked to where we can barely see the settlement behind us, Dad stops. He sets down the buckets and turns around to face us. He points to a patch of ground.

"You see that?" he says.

There's something lying there, a small, brown shape with an irregular silhouette. For some reason, my first thought is that it's a piece of clothing one of us dropped, a shirt clumped into a dense, dried-up heap. Carelessly forgotten, and that's what Dad's mad about. Then my brain reshapes the image, imbues it with clarity and meaning, and I see that it's a dead bird lying beak-down in the dirt.

Dad crouches down and turns it over with a stick. One wing splays out beside its body. "Georgia? Wulf? Can either of you identify this specimen?"

"European starling," I say, the name popping into my head swiftly.

"Correct," Dad says. "A common enough bird. Not a tragedy in and of itself. But this is the sixteenth dead bird I've found this month.

That I've found," he repeats, looking at each of us in turn, as though to make sure his words are sinking in. "Who knows how many more there's been?" His eyes are small and narrow, eyelids puffy from allergies or lack of sleep, and the skin of his face looks waxy, losing structure somehow, like dirt rendered into mud by rain.

"What happened to it?" asks Vanessa, stepping forward to crouch down beside him. She peers at the bird cautiously, keeping a safe distance.

"Hard to say with certainty," says Dad. "Hard to make a judgment like this, with my limited capabilities. Biology isn't my specialty. I don't have the tools one needs. That being said, I do have my theories. There's nothing stopping a layman from developing theories, so long as suppositions are taken one by one and no great leaps are made prematurely. If one observes carefully, expands the reach of one's vision and awareness, there's a surprising amount of knowledge that can be attained that way. And what I've come to conclude—what I've come to theorize—is that I shouldn't be surprised at what I'm seeing. After all, what's happening the world over? Would anyone among us call our planet a safe place? It would be foolish to think that my physical distance, my opting out by living where nobody else wants to live, means that I can completely evade all the consequences and ill effects of humanity's mistakes."

I glance at Wulf, who's standing with his hands shoved into his pockets. He looks up to meet my gaze instinctually, sensing my movement. Then he ducks his head back down, a scowl forming on his face.

"Not catching your drift," Nick says.

Dad stands up slowly, using his hands to push himself off the ground. "When I moved my family here, I knew it would only be a matter of time before the outside world caught up to us. Before it encroached upon us, no matter how hard I tried to keep it at bay. It likely comes as no surprise to anyone here that I've been keeping an eye on the nearby Domes project, and what I've seen, lately especially, troubles me. It looks like, after all these years, the world is knocking on my doorstep, bringing its ills along with it."

"To be honest, some dead birds doesn't sound all that bad," says Nick after a pause.

"It's not just the birds," says Dad. "It's what they mean."

"Dabbling in augury, huh?"

"No, Nick," says Vanessa, standing up as well. "An indicator, not an omen."

"Exactly," says Dad, nodding his thanks to Vanessa.

"I guess I'm just not following," says Nick. He snaps a spindly branch off the bush he's standing next to, snaps it in half, then in half again.

"What killed these birds?" asks Dad, his voice pedantic.

"Could have been anything, right?" says Nick. "Coyotes, or some bird disease. Maybe it just died of old age. Why is this a big deal?"

"There are no bite marks," says Dad. "This wasn't the work of a predator."

"Okay, so not a coyote," Nick says.

Dad shakes his head, a slow sweep back and forth. "I've lived in this desert for a long time now. I know how it feels when everything is functioning properly, and I know when something isn't right. I can feel it in my body. Soon enough, even my forsaken share of desert in the deadlands won't be safe for habitation."

"You're forgetting that Vanessa and I actually live out there," says Nick. "It's—well, I won't say it's *fine*, but it's livable. Definitely habitable. A hell of a lot more habitable than your little settlement here. At least we've got some creature comforts like plumbing and air-conditioning and normal medicine. You're acting like we're on some toxic planet like Saturn or Jupiter and you're the only one who lives in a compound that protects you from the air."

"Saturn and Jupiter are gas planets," says Vanessa.

Nick looks at her blankly. "So?" he says after a pause.

"You wouldn't be able to build a compound," she explains. "There's no ground."

"Nobody is speaking about the air," Dad says impatiently. "I'm not quite sure what it is yet, but it's unlikely that it's airborne. I'm not discounting it, it certainly remains as a possibility to keep on the radar, but we'd be seeing more effects in ourselves if that were the case. My guess is that this contamination comes from the ground—in the groundwater, maybe. Spillage of—who's to say?—pollution, mismanaged sewage, pesticide chemicals, radiation. Any of it may have gotten into the water table."

"Radiation?" Nick says incredulously.

"From the nuclear reactor," says Dad, looking at Nick levelly through his glasses. "Nuclear energy is slated to be a core component of the Domes, though I wouldn't be surprised if that particular element of the endeavor is downplayed in certain circles. A project like that, poorly planned, developed quickly, a vacuous idea from the start that never would have passed muster if regulatory bodies cared anymore about what goes on in the deadlands. Let's just say it wouldn't shock me if the proper precautions weren't taken."

"Does, ah—" Nick frowns. "Radiation in the groundwater? I mean, I'm not an expert, but I don't know if it works that way."

"What are we going to do about it?" Wulf cuts in, and all of us turn to look at him, which makes him jut his head down, his posture stiffening.

Dad prods the bird's wing back against its body with his stick. "I don't quite know yet, Wulf," he says. "I don't quite know, but I'm considering our options. If this contamination does originate from the Domes, from the nuclear reactor, then it won't be long before the problem is taken care of. But we'd still have the damage already done to contend with, and regardless, my theory could very well be proved false. This world is full of hazards—dangers we couldn't even imagine, problems stewing that we aren't aware of before it's too late. For now, I think it's best if we get our bearings. Do a small survey to figure out how bad the situation is. A little reconnaissance and removal." He looks over at us, eyes piercing. "Birds, rodents, small mammals, any death you find, bring it here. It's always animals that feel a disaster first. Plants we can look at on a case-by-case basis. If it looks severely, unnaturally, harmed, make a note of it. We're not going to strip the ground, we just want to get a better sense of things. Use sticks and the buckets, not your hands. Don't touch anything that you don't need to, and don't touch your face with your hands. Wulf and

Georgia, you two go together. Vanessa and Nick, you'll come with me, and we'll handle the search closer to the settlement."

Nick and Vanessa exchange a look, which jerks something in my chest, a rough pull. What do they have to say to each other? I think, incredulous. Their unspoken communication complicates itself like skin zoomed in to skin cells, unfurls like a cactus flower that sprouts and blooms and shuts again, mute to the world around it.

"Let's go, Wulf," I say firmly, and pick up one of the red buckets. I start walking and don't check to see if he's coming, but I hear his footsteps a few seconds later, and then he's next to me. We walk slower than usual, our heads bent to scan the ground. Soon, we've left the others behind, their voices faint and dim and then gone, and the only sounds we hear now are the hot wind, our feet crunching against rocky dirt, and distant, melancholic birdcalls.

"What do you think?" I ask Wulf.

He pauses to frown at a pile of stones. "Dad will figure it out," he says.

"What was Dad talking about with the Domes? About the nuclear reactor being taken care of? Is that what you're planning?"

"No," Wulf says.

"The Hermit or Eduardo, then?"

"Shut up," Wulf says, glancing at the retreating figures of Nick and Vanessa. "Dad hasn't told them anything about Herm or Eduardo. They'll hear you."

"You're avoiding the question. Is Herm or Eduardo supposed to do something to the reactor?"

Wulf vacillates. "I don't know," he says without meeting my eye.

A strained silence passes between us.

"All right, fine, we won't talk about it. But do you think something's really wrong, or that this is just in Dad's head?"

Wulf's forehead creases. "Why would Dad make it up?"

"I'm not saying he's doing it on purpose."

Wulf shakes his head vigorously, his body tensing in a way I know means he's getting angry. "You're spending too much time with them," he says.

"What's that supposed to mean?"

"They're just talking to you so they can get information out of you. Why would you believe anything they say? Why wouldn't you trust Dad?"

"Who said anything about not trusting Dad?"

"You spend too much time with them," he repeats, his face set, obstinate.

"Is that what Dad's been saying?" I ask.

Wulf bends down to pick up a long, sturdy stick and then stabs it into the ground. It barely penetrates the hard ground and bounces back a bit, making Wulf fumble to catch it. "No," he replies petulantly. "He doesn't have time to talk about stupid stuff like what you're doing."

"He seems like he has plenty of time to talk with Vanessa."

Wulf ignores me. He's walking ahead of me so I can't see his face. "Look," he says brusquely, using his stick to point at the ground. "Is that something?" He's pointing at a lump of dirt-colored fur, torn up and soft looking from decomposition and scavengers picking at the flesh and bones.

"Jackrabbit," I say.

Wulf spears the stick through the decomposing body, and some of the fur and skin fall away. The part that stays on the stick looks even less like a rabbit than it did on the ground. Wulf raises the skewered animal in front of him like a torch. We continue milling around the desert silently, keeping our eyes trained on the ground.

In the end, Wulf and I return with just the rabbit, our bucket empty. Dad, Nick, and Vanessa come back with all kinds of things Dad found troubling: two dead rodents; a snakeskin that was too flaky; a clump of red yucca that looked too stringy; a small piece of unidentifiable cactus with a black hole of rot; clay Dad says is siltier than it should be, which he says may be a sign of quickening geologic change. We stand around the bucket in a circle as Dad elucidates the meaning of its contents one by one. "What does this tell us?" Dad asks, looking around at each of us, waiting for one of us to produce the right answer.

"Things die," Nick volunteers tartly.

"Is it really that much more than usual?" Vanessa asks Dad. Two wrinkles form between her eyebrows, like she's considering whether to be worried. "I mean, it might look concerning if you put it all together, but is that just because we're paying attention? We don't go around collecting dead animals on the regular, so I don't know if we have anything to compare it to. I just don't know if we should jump to any conclusions yet."

"Trust me, there's enough to merit our attention," Dad says.

"Oh, sure," says Nick. "Trust the guy who's keeping us hostage. No problem." But his animosity sounds routine, an obligation even he's grown tired of, and nobody reacts, not even Vanessa to quiet him with a glance.

"We've had trace levels of toxicants in our groundwater for decades here," Dad goes on. "My filtration systems have made me well aware of that. It's not the contamination itself that's rare. But this is something different. It isn't as easy to understand, and therefore it's currently impossible for me to address. We may have reached a point that's serious enough to merit action, not just attention."

"What does that mean?" asks Vanessa. "What kind of action?"

"We'll watch and wait for a while longer," says Dad. "We might need to take a small trip in the future to find out more. I'm assessing our options and determining the best path forward, but I wanted to give everyone here the courtesy of forewarning should the need transpire."

"A trip? Oh goody," Nick says. His voice is sarcastic, but he's watching Dad alertly.

Vanessa looks thrown by the idea. "A trip where?" she asks.

"I'll let you know when you need to know," Dad says.

"Would we walk?" she presses.

"That's right. Walk at night and sleep during the day. Three nights walking, two days of rest. The first night will be the hardest because you'll be wanting sleep, but you'll adjust by the second night. It'll be easier from then. But we're getting ahead of ourselves. We may not go at all. I'm still thinking through these plans."

I look over at Wulf, and he meets my eye again. We know exactly where Dad's thinking of going now—the Hermit's. There's no destination we know that's placed precisely three days away but this one, and nowhere else we ever go, regardless.

"But let's return to the present," Dad is saying. "It's time to move on to the removal part of our reconnaissance mission. After I take some samples, I believe the best way to deal with whatever we have on our hands is to burn it. We'll take these buckets to the firepit, and from that point forward, I'll take care of it. Nobody is to go near the fire while it burns. We don't know what toxins are lingering and their possible effects if we make them airborne. I'd advise everyone to stay inside or stay away from the settlement."

"What about you?" says Vanessa.

"This is my settlement," Dad says. "I'm prepared to take on the risks involved."

"Sounds fair to me," Nick says. He raises his arms above his head in a stretch and groans in an ostentatiously satisfied way. "I think I'll go with the staying-away option."

Vanessa gives him an inscrutable look, disappointed or reprimanding.

Dad picks up the two buckets, signaling that it's time to go, and we wordlessly trudge behind him back to the settlement. When we get there, Vanessa and Wulf break away to their buildings, and Dad heads to the firepit. Instead of going to his building, Nick lingers at the edge of the ramada. He watches Dad bend to add kindling to the firepit, crouch down, and strike a match. I linger, too, keeping my eye on Nick, moving my gaze between him and Dad.

"So what's this trip he's talking about?" Nick asks.

"Probably more reconnaissance," I say curtly, evasively.

"Seems like he has a destination in mind."

I shrug and turn my attention to Dad, who's standing back up, stepping away to wait for the flames to catch. He looks small from where we're standing, a wiry, fragile person. It's a strange way to see him. I have the urge to look away but can't.

"Has he always been like this?" Nick asks.

"Like what?" I say.

"You know." Nick waves his hand vaguely. "This martyr act he's putting on. Like he's making some big statement, protecting his territory, this dumb thing with the Domes as a threat to him—attacking them, shielding himself—now telling us it's the cause of some *contamination*," Nick says, making air quotes with his fingers. "Like he's living some big cosmic drama, good against evil, dark against light, little guy against the big bad monster. He's acting like any of this is a big deal—but you know what? It isn't. Nobody cares. Barely anybody lives in the Domes. It's some stupid government project that's going to fail by itself anyway, without Isaac's help. Just like this settlement-commune-whatever-it-was did a century or something ago. That's what everybody thinks. Everyone outside is just rolling their eyes at it and complaining about how much it costs, because it's a stupid idea. Earth's going to continue to become a wasteland, every continent's going to be a deadland, and most of us will die, and then there'll be fewer people around to create problems and pollution, and then eventually things will start regrowing and get better, and then we'll repopulate the world and create the same problems all over again. That's the circle of life with humans on Earth. What any of us do really isn't that important. It—doesn't—matter," Nick says, pausing to accentuate each word.

Nick's words slip off me like water slips off drought-stricken land, pooling heavily without absorbing. A part of me thinks there may be truth to what he's saying. That Dad is picking up the feathered carcasses of facts and exploding them into a theory about contamination and conspiracy that doesn't quite fit. But another part, a deeper part—the child memory, the me who's been taught everything I know by Dad, who grew up trusting, the way Wulf still trusts, that Dad had the answer to everything—can't let my brain believe this fully.

What does Nick know? this part of me insists. Nick may very well know about the outside world, but here, in the world of our settlement, Dad is still the highest, the most reliable, authority. Who but him knows what minute of the day the sun burns brightest? Or how many

109

uses can be extracted from a cactus, or the number of steps separating the mountains from the flatlands? Who but him has built up this home we have, here on this stretch of dirt that's been forsaken by the rest of the world as dead? And doesn't that prove that he knows something we don't know? That he has information and insight we don't have?

Dad has the fire going now, orange flames leaping up through a smoky haze. It occurs to me again how vulnerable he looks against the fire, how human. He coughs into his elbow, ducking his head. Then he leans down to pick up a bucket and thrusts his upper body forward to dump the bucket's contents into the blaze. He steps back quickly when a swarm of sparks flies up, turning his face away.

"There's nothing wrong with those animals," Nick says, following my gaze. "If there was, burning them would be the stupidest thing he could do. There's no way he doesn't know that. Releasing toxins into the air? Making toxic ash so it can spread everywhere? Give me a break."

It's a surprisingly lucid point, a part of me admits. The other part of me says: What does Nick know about toxins, about the dangers of the desert? Who does it make more sense to believe? Nick, who's careless enough to get stung by a scorpion? Or Dad, who can recite the venomous properties of every snake that slithers or rattles around the settlement?

"He's a showman, your dad," Nick says, nodding at Dad fanning the flames. "Fooling only himself." He shakes his head, like he's ridding himself of the train of thought. "The important thing is, How are we going to occupy ourselves while we're supposed to be making ourselves scarce?"

"We don't have to make ourselves scarce," I say. "We can just stay inside."

"Where's the fun in that?" Nick shades his eyes with his hand. "Sun's not too bad yet. Shall we go visit our fossil?"

11

"Don't be mad," Nick says once we've walked out of sight of the settlement. "Here, let me take that backpack. I'll carry it."

"I'm not mad," I say. But I grip the backpack straps tighter and quicken my pace so I'm out of reach and he can't take it.

"I shouldn't have said anything about your dad," says Nick. "Forgive me? My opinions of him aside, I do realize that he's your family. Loyalties run strong. We can't help that. You should ignore me, really. I have a bad habit of talking without thinking about what I'm saying. Word vomit just comes out, you know? I don't mean anything by it."

"I'm not mad," I say again. And although there's irritation in my voice, it's true, what I'm saying. There's too much clutter in my mind for me to really be angry, too many competing thoughts bouncing against each other to focus in on any one of them, and anger requires a single-minded focus, an all-consuming concentration. I breathe deeply and still smell fire, so I hold my breath for a moment, but that only forces me to breathe more deeply when I let myself inhale again. Nick's words about toxins in the air clang around in my head alongside Wulf's about Dad knowing what he's doing. Dad knows what he's doing, I repeat in my head, and then force myself to continue thinking it as I walk, one word accompanying every separate step.

"Let's talk about something else," says Nick. "Something palate cleansing. I've been thinking, we need a better cover story for this so-called fossil of ours. What if someone asks us what it looks like? We've got to be on the same page. What kind of paleontology enthusiasts would we be if we didn't have a guess about what it is, hmm? What are we digging up here? What new species have we unearthed?"

"I don't think anyone's going to ask us about it," I say.

"Humor me. Let's pretend. What ancient beast have we got on our hands?"

"I guess we could say it's a whale."

"A whale?" Nick exclaims. "All right, sure. Go big or go home, right? Why not?"

"They found whale fossils in a desert in Chile."

"Well, there you go. A prehistoric species of whale. What are we going to name it?"

I tell him it would be in the genus *Balaenoptera* and briefly summarize what I know about the rules of naming: If the species name is an adjective, it has to agree with the genus name in gender. If it's a noun in the genitive case, it would end in *i* or *ii* if masculine, or *ae* if feminine. If it's a noun in the nominative case, the two parts don't have to agree in gender. Species names can be reused in multiple genera, so repeats are okay. Traditionally, a person naming a species wouldn't name it after themselves.

"So you couldn't name it *Balaenoptera georgiae*, but I can," says Nick.

"I don't want it to be named after me," I say.

"We could name it after me instead. *Balaenoptera nickii*. With two *i*'s. Actually, no, that sounds stupid. *Balaenoptera nicholasii?* Nope, still sounds dumb."

"It's usually last names."

"*Balaenoptera wrightii?* My name is just not cut out for this, is it? What about *Balaenoptera renoae?* That one sounds pretty good."

"I already told you I don't want it named after me."

"We're not naming it after you, we're naming it after your family."

"It's not even our real last name."

Nick raises his eyebrows at me. "No?"

"Dad picked it when we moved here."

"What's the real last name?"

"I don't know. I just know this one isn't the one we had before we came here."

"What, was Isaac running afoul of the law even back then?"

"Dad doesn't talk much about life before we came here," I say cautiously.

"And you never asked?"

"When I was a kid, I did. I just didn't get a lot of answers."

"You're smart, though. You probably picked up and put together some pieces."

I continue walking without answering, squinting through the sun that's getting close to directly overhead. My shoe brushes against a plant with dry, dark-brown burrs, and I pause to pick them off my sock while Nick watches.

"Not going to clue me in?" he asks.

"About Dad before we came here? I know he was always involved in—things like what he's trying to do to the Domes now. He met my mother when they were both protesting a lithium mine. And he studied computer science because he thought it was the most effective way to try to hurt corporations who were making the planet less livable. Hacking into them and slowing down drilling projects, or messing up deals to buy up and cut down forests. Things like that."

"Was anyone actually paying attention to him, though? Enough for him to change his name and become a fugitive from civilization? Or is he just your run-of-the-mill paranoiac?"

I frown. "What do you mean?"

"I mean, he's on the extreme side, but he's not exactly a unique breed. Idealistic nuts are always trying to sabotage corporations for their so-called noble reasons, even in the Center States. Actually, just before

Vanessa and I left Ohio, some college kids tried to plant bombs in my father's law offices, apparently because he defended a big corporation's right to drain an aquifer. You know what happened? Security guards caught them and essentially just gave them a slap on the wrist. Shooed them away like flies to make trouble somewhere else. That's how it works—we just move those making trouble along. It's not like the little law enforcement we have left cares. And out here, in the deadlands? Forget about it. I'm just saying, it's not like anyone's hunting down Isaac. Whatever trouble he's trying to make for the big and powerful, he's nothing but a mosquito to them."

"I don't know how you can know that," I say testily.

"All right, all right, I'll lay off," Nick says, raising his hands in mock surrender. "I'm not doing a good job of keeping my promise of not saying anything about your dad, am I?"

"You never promised that," I say.

Nick grins, and we start walking again. "You're right, I didn't. I didn't even really apologize, did I? Bad habit of mine. Anyway. To get back to the important conversation. It doesn't really matter what your real last name is. I mean, *real*, what does that even mean, right? All names were just made up by someone at some point, anyway. Speaking of which—how'd your brother get his name? I thought your dad wasn't literature's biggest fan. Does he make an exception for the Geats?"

"The Geats?" I ask.

"Right, the Viking dudes. Like in *Beowulf*."

I shake my head.

"What, you don't know it? The Old English epic?"

"We don't have it here," I say. After a pause, I add: "You know a lot of books."

Nick laughs. "Just their names, really. I have the fancy private schools I grew up in to thank for that. My folks would have been very happy to hear that someone thinks I'm more learned than I am, though. I unfortunately did not turn into the upstanding citizen they thought they were grooming me into becoming and following in the footsteps of a long line of corporate lawyers and bribable statesmen. Sorry—states-people. We're equal-opportunity despicable in my family. But, hey, at least we can all pepper our conversations with intelligent references to great literature."

I wave a hornet away from my face.

"What about your name?" Nick asks. "Do you know? Maybe you're named after Georgia O'Keeffe. Or maybe your parents liked the name George, but you ended up being a girl. Or, if we want to go more obvious, you could be named after the state. *Or*, now that I'm spit-balling here, maybe your name hails from the homeland of the noblest of cheese breads."

"The what?"

"Don't tell me you've never had khachapuri." Nick shakes his head in mock pity. "Ah, Georgia, how much of the world is unknown to you. I'm joking," he says, throwing a glance at me as if checking to see if he actually made me feel bad. "I've never had khachapuri either. It's a cheesy bread from Georgia, the country."

"I've never had any kind of cheese," I say.

Nick puts his face in his hands. "You're killing me. All right, it's settled. That's the first thing we're doing when we find ourselves back in civilization. We're getting you some good old American cheese."

I keep my face blank and don't look at Nick. I don't dare to ask: We? You and me both? When we find ourselves back in civilization? I don't want to know whether he means anything by it, whether he actually imagines leaving the settlement and me leaving along with him, or whether he's just talking mindlessly—word vomit, like he said earlier. I hold the strange future of the sentence at a distance, a dust storm blurring the horizon, its path uncertain.

"On second thought, maybe some good old French cheese," Nick says. "That is, if we can find—"

Suddenly, he stops talking. His face contorts, and his body lurches forward, so he's slightly hunched over, his hands on his knees. His body spasms again, and his mouth opens with a violent retching sound, but nothing comes out. He stares at the ground, his expression troubled. Then, with a final lurch, he vomits onto the ground, a thin pinkish stream. He hacks to clear his throat, spits, and stands up. He stares at the pinkish puddle, then squeezes his eyes shut and rubs his face hard, moving his skin around like clay.

"Are you okay?" I ask, alarmed.

"Don't know what happened there," he says.

"How do you feel?"

"Fine now. My stomach just felt like it needed to get something out all of a sudden." He picks up his foot and shakes it, as though to get off the splash of vomit that's landed on the fabric. "Didn't get much on me, thankfully. Do you have that water?"

I pull the bottle out of my backpack and hand it to him. He unscrews the top and pours a trickle into his mouth, sloshes it around and spits, then lifts the bottle higher above his mouth and swallows the stream greedily, stopping just before finishing off the bottle. I indicate at him to go ahead, and he doesn't need convincing, his throat working frenetically to gulp down swallow after swallow. The fetid smell of vomit wafts up from the ground. Nick's skin looks grayish and clammy, but color is slowly returning to it. He wipes beads of sweat off his forehead with the back of his hand and returns the empty bottle to my backpack.

"I've been having some digestive issues lately," he says, his expression pinched like he's eaten something unpleasant. "Nothing to worry about. It was like this in Phoenix too. Just not used to the bacteria in this part of the country yet."

"You think it's something you ate?" I ask, watching as the puddle of vomit soaks into the earth, becoming dark-brown mud.

"Maybe those javelina leftovers. I'm too used to refrigeration."

"Should we go back?"

"Nah, let's keep going, I'm fine now. Really," he says to my skeptical expression.

When we get to the part of the desert where the steel drum is buried, we settle into our jobs easily. We've been leaving our trowels behind so we can start back up the next time quicker, and we're almost finished now, the drum only barely attached to the earth in a few places where the dirt's hardened so much, it's almost like chipping away at stone. Nick and I are on our knees, leaning heavily into the ditch we've dug around the drum, straightening up and stretching when our backs start to hurt.

We work quickly and silently, metal tinging against rock the only sound between us. It's almost melodic, the repetitive tings, and I drift into a memory of music as we worked years and years ago, the work blurred in my memory—building a fence? molding clay for adobe bricks?—and the music a clash of recollection, singing and a plucked stringed instrument, my memory trotting out possibilities, none of them quite right.

I adjust my grip so I'm holding my trowel more steadily, then strike it into the dirt again and again, clanging against the metal of the drum sometimes, the sound reverberating. Dirt mixes with my sweat and collects in rivulets in the creases of my palms, turning my palms chalky textured. And then, a few more tings and clangs, and Nick pushes the drum to one side and then the other, rocking it back and forth to snap off its remaining ties to the earth, and suddenly I know it'll be freed, and then it is. Nick exclaims victory, and after some adjusting of our grips and maneuvering, we drag the drum out of the ditch, turn it right side up—its contents rattling, a brief, discordant sound of shifting—and place it on the ground. We step back to get a good look at it.

"There she blows," Nick says. "Shall we open it?"

For some reason, my throat feels constricted, and all I can do is nod.

Nick leans over the lid to pull on it, digging his feet into the dirt for traction, tugging. The lid comes off with a rusty creaking and a pop, the suddenness making Nick stumble back, which makes him laugh once he regains his footing. We step forward and look inside.

It's hard to make out the contents at first, hard to put the parts together and give the whole contents meaning, like the bird Dad showed us. Except it's not a bird inside, but bones. Dusty and grayish, a jumble of them. Skulls and ribs and blocks of vertebrae; femurs and ulnas; and cracked, curved pieces, maybe parts of a pelvis, piled to the top of the drum, a tight, packed arrangement. I have the urge to dip my hand in and comb through them, and then immediately after, a strong revulsion. I want to slam the lid back down and rebury the drum deep in the dirt. A panicked feeling seeps into me like water bloating a dead body, a sense that we've disinterred something terrible, worse than something toxic.

Nick is standing as still as I am. "What the fuck?" he says. He looks over at me, his expression searching.

I shake my head.

"These are human, right?" he asks.

"I think so," I say. "They look like it. Yes."

"What are they doing here? What is this?"

And I shake my head again, and we both fall silent, staring at the bones, like we're expecting something to happen, a genie to swim out of the container, an answer to reveal itself.

"Pretty weird thing to find," Nick says finally, breaking the spell. "You think we should—"

"Tell someone?" I offer when he doesn't finish.

"Yeah, I mean, shouldn't we? What do you think?"

"No."

"No?"

"He wouldn't want to hear about it."

"Your dad? Why? How do you know?"

How do I know? I ask myself, and I can't answer—I just do, as well as I know the bones are human and not animal.

"We should put it back," I say out loud. "We should bury it again."

"It feels like we dug up a grave," says Nick, his voice jumpy, unsettled. "I mean, that's what we did do, but we didn't do it on purpose. It's not like there's a marker or anything. Who puts bones in a steel drum and not just in the ground, in a normal grave? I guess it's kind of like putting ashes in an urn. Bones in a drum. But all of them together like that—why? Why keep them all together? Why not separately?"

"Maybe they died at the same time and they didn't know whose bones were whose."

"Yeah, okay. That makes sense. Maybe. What do you think happened, then? Mass murder? A natural disaster? Mass heatstroke?"

"Maybe," I say dubiously.

"You think it was those people Vanessa's supposed to be researching? The ones who built this place? Or someone else who camped out here between you and them?"

"I don't know," I say, my tone clipped, suddenly irritated with Nick's questioning. "I don't know any more than you do."

"These aren't people you've all killed who've stumbled on this place like me and Vanessa have, are they? Just, you know, checking."

"That's not funny," I say.

Nick shrugs distractedly. "Eerie, though, isn't it?" he says. "Gives me the creeps."

I take a step closer to the drum to peer down into it. The bones are so close together, it looks like a spider's nest inside, a web of ashy white. Almost without thinking about it—the thought, if it's a thought, floating independently of all other thinking, barely skimming the surface of my awareness—I reach down and close my fingers around a piece of bone, long as my hand and slightly curved, like a blade. It slips out easily. I move it out of my shadow and into the full sun. The edge that's been broken off is porous like a sponge and jagged, but the rest is smooth when I rub my thumb against it. A fine dust comes off on my skin.

"What is it?" Nick asks.

"A piece of rib."

"You going to take it as a souvenir?"

I shake my head no, but I don't return it to the container. Instead, I place it on the ground carefully, a few paces away from where we're standing. Nick doesn't say anything as he watches me. I walk back and pick up the lid to the container.

"Ready?" I ask. "To bury it again?"

"Right," Nick says. "You're probably right. Let's get it over with, then."

The sun is glaring overhead uncomfortably, and I think both of us feel overwhelmed at the task ahead of us. The container is easy enough to lift back into the hole, and the dirt we unearthed is piled in a mound that only reaches my knee, but it's past noon now, nearing the hottest part of the day, and we don't have any more water. Still, there's no discussion. We've agreed without saying it that if we're going to rebury the drum, we have to do it now, to close the chapter firmly and forget about it.

We replace the drum into the hole, move the dirt with our hands and feet and trowels. We cough when we breathe in too much dust from working so quickly, spit when sand gets in our mouths, making our tongues gritty, our saliva dark like mud. We don't talk, to preserve our energy. The sun is painfully hot against the top of my head and my forearms, scorching whatever exposed skin it can reach. We didn't think to bring hats when we left. Nick's face is red and shiny, the sweat making it look wet, making me think of water. I swallow dryly, shove more dirt into the hole, pause to stretch my arms, and then continue pushing in the dirt. Small rocks cling to my knees as I kneel, to my palms as I press them against the ground. Dirt crams itself so deeply under my fingernails that the tips of my fingers hurt.

When we finish, Nick smooths the dirt and rocks down with his foot, and then the spot looks nearly the same as the ground around it, a loose collection of rocks and clods of dirt. It would be difficult to find tomorrow if we were to return, but I know we won't. From the grim look on Nick's face as he surveys the spot, I know we'll stay away. Quietly, I pick up the piece of bone I set aside and hold it inconspicuously at my side. Whether from exhaustion or disinterest or distaste, Nick doesn't remark on it.

The walk back feels like it takes barely any time at all. Suddenly, the settlement is right in front of us, as though it's a mirage that's popped up because we were wishing for it. But it's real enough, the mesquite trees and creosote clinging to the edges of the falling-apart fence; the squat, low buildings; the smell of a fire recently put out, smoke and wood sap. I know everyone must be inside, spending the hottest part of the day ensconced in the cool concrete of their buildings, but there's a deserted quality to the place, a feeling of abandonment, like everyone's left and Nick and I are the only people left on the planet. The thought that everyone else is gone dawns on and fastens to me—not that they've been taken violently or that they're gone because of any tragedy, but that they've been quietly swept away like sand, erased without a trace. It's like when Wulf and I were kids and would climb on top of one of the buildings and lie on the roof flat-backed so that all we could see was the turquoise sky and puffy clouds above us, and after a while, if we tried hard enough, we'd manage to convince ourselves there was no ground beneath us, that it was just turquoise sky all around and we were floating in it, as though we were resting on a flying carpet or gliding the wind currents like hawks.

At the glass house, Nick and I drink cup after cup of water. The world feels a little sturdier as the water rehydrates my body. It's only at the edges of my vision that the world lingers, wavering. Nick sloshes some water onto his chin and nose from drinking too quickly, and coughs. The sweat drying on my skin leaves a salty itch. It's hard to breathe in here, the glass magnifying the heat intolerably, white-hot in our eyes. When Nick and I step outside, I still feel dazed, and the settlement, stripped of glass, settles itself around me unevenly. There's a shuffling in a creosote bush nearby—a javelina? a cottontail? a crow?—and when I blink to try to see better, the rustling is gone, mocking me for ever thinking it was there. The bush sways languidly in the hot, slow wind, and then the wind hits my face, and I flinch.

Nick motions for me to follow him to his building. The silence of the desert roars in my ears. Our human bodies are loud and jarring in it, every step and breath amplified. The rasp and grind of the door opening and shutting behind us. Nick sighing at the coolness and the dim light inside, rust colored from the curtains.

Is it inevitable, what happens next? It's easy to think that way, to shed cause and effect like a snakeskin. The concrete floor is chilly and hard against our legs when we ease ourselves down to it. We're too hot to imagine sitting on the sofa, too tired to contemplate dragging ourselves onto the stiff chairs. I curl on my side, cheek pressed against the floor. The bone scrapes against the ground under me, and I twist to pull it out of my pocket and push it away. Nick lies supine next to me, eyes closed. "I'm drenched in sweat," he mutters.

"Sweat helps you cool off," I hear myself say from somewhere far away.

"What?" Nick asks.

I twist so I'm lying on my back, cool cement on my neck, and repeat the sentence.

"Mmm," Nick says, his voice blurred. He stretches out, arms overhead, feet arching, a joint cracking somewhere, another elsewhere, and when he pulls his limbs back, his arm wedges itself against mine, sticky skin, prickly hair. Don't move, the cogent part of myself instructs me sternly. My mind swims feverishly, my thoughts a swampy mess. I can feel the pulse at Nick's wrist, rapid thumps, straining. The room blurs and my eyes close. I feel goose bumps emerge on my skin, a landscape of tiny, firm projections. Mountains rise up, tectonic plates crash into the ground. Time passes endlessly. Go on, the cogent part of me instructs. Where are we going? I think blearily, the question desperate and pointless, like trying to walk or speak in a dream where the rules say you can't. At some point, I'm aware of Nick's hand on my knee. He lifts off his palm and taps it back down, off and on again, like he's testing the handle of a saucepan to see if it'll burn him. Does that happen or do I dream it? When I turn my head to look, Nick is asleep, his shirt in a heap under his head. He's breathing audibly through his mouth, pink lips parched and scaly. I strip my clothes off methodically, as though I'm about to bathe. The water is so cool against my skin, a leaden pressure. I drift on its surface, let myself be carried. Where are we going? I ask again, and the cogent part of me frowns in rebuke at my insincerity, says I know very well that where I'm going to is the somewhere I won't be able to return from. A loop in the river cut off, its course changed. A sea dried to a seafloor turned into a desert.

Nick is sitting up now, watching me. I shift under the intensity of his gaze, lift up my torso, lean back on my elbows. Dirt from the floor sticks to my skin, dust and tiny pebbles. How much time has passed? My thoughts skip and sink, fleeting, heavy. When Nick leans over me, I'm alarmed at first that he's falling, losing consciousness, but then his teeth are biting my lip, and I realize, no. His mouth tastes sour—the vomit, I remember. His hand reaches over to squeeze my breast, like it's a rag he's squeezing clean of water. He runs his hand from my chest to my stomach, then lower, his hand curling. I shift uncomfortably. He swings his leg over and lowers himself down, a heavy shadow. His heartbeat is rapid, his breath fast, heat from his skin emanating. He reaches his hands around to pull me tighter against his pelvis, scratching my bare skin against the fabric of his jeans. "You feel that?" he asks close to my ear, his voice strange, almost strangled. Hot air on the side of my face, the sour rotting smell, and the smell of sweat between us, wood-like and mineral. He kneels to peel off his pants, taking a long time with the button. His penis sticks out from a mess of hair, and I stare at it, blinking, as though I'm only now waking up fully. It's shiny and bulbous, an absurd pink. Nick spits into his hand, and then his hand is rubbing me roughly, shoving his fingers inside like he's reaching for something. "No? Not like that?" he says, and I realize I must have made some kind of sound. His hand stops, and he pulls himself on top of me again, reaches down, and prods me clumsily until he finds what he's looking for and heaves himself forward. I bite the inside of my cheek against the shock of pain, taste blood in my mouth as the pain softens, confusedly, briefly, into a siphoning of thought, a dull, engulfing pulse, before returning. Nick's body knocks against mine repeatedly, crushing my hip bones into the concrete. I turn my head to the side and stare at the piece of bone. Nick's eyes are open, but they're glazed and staring at the floor just beside my head. His forehead is beaded with drops of sweat. My spine presses against the ground painfully. The rubbing begins to burn, and a rush of hate rises up inside me, a swelling crash of anger. My instinct is to bite or claw, to lash out like an animal, but I brace myself. So much time has passed—eons, ages. I want to see it through to its end. Who wouldn't want to see what's on the other side? I dig my nails into my palm and count the seconds. "Almost there," Nick says.

The sudden absence is so relieving, I nearly cry out. Nick hunches over himself, moving his hand back and forth, and then he grunts as his body collapses inward. A cloudy liquid pools on my stomach like glue. Nick rubs until more drops dribble out. I watch as he turns softer in his hand, the shiny, taut skin wrinkling up. He lets himself fall heavily down beside me. "Shit," he says. He turns to me. "How was—how do you feel?"

"Fine," I say. "Good."

"You sure?"

I nod sharply, the movement sending a stab of pain down my neck.

"That was good," he says, moving his head back so he's staring at the ceiling. "I wanted to come inside you so bad." He runs his hand down his face. "Maybe that wasn't the smartest thing to do," he says, closing his eyes. "God, I'm tired. I need to sleep." His breathing evens out almost instantly, his chest rising and falling deeply. I watch the sweat on his shoulders dry to a sheen.

My body pulses dully with discomfort, and suddenly I realize I'm exhausted, too, that all my energy has siphoned out of me. My mind drifts into a half dream, and I give in to it, letting myself drift. There aren't any bones here, no desert or bodies. Not a word but a rustling, formless sound, what language is before it means or says. It could be anything: sand at the bottom of the sea or dirt covering a desert before people and animals ever stepped on it, before plants were seeds or seedlings caught in sandstone. There's nothing around me but space, nothing inside me but my body lapping mutely like a wave of silty water.

12

I worry, at first, that Nick will try to talk to me about what happened and that this conversation will go similarly to the one we had after he kissed me in the desert. Short and uncomfortable, casting the situation as something different from the tenuous thing it is in my head, relegating it to a crude, simplistic *don't tell anyone*. But, instead, the opposite happens. Nick conspicuously keeps his distance, walking past me or ducking into a building when he sees me, his smile vacant. A question of space grows between us, wide and gaping.

Or maybe it's just an extension of the space stretching apart all of us. An oppressive tension, taut as a spider's web, has settled over the settlement. Ever since Dad mentioned the contamination, he's sequestered himself in his office. When he does show up to meals, he's reticent about his plans. I take to keeping the bone fragment in my pocket and fidgeting with it, my fingers nervous. Wulf takes to heading off to hunt nearly every day, but it seems like he's not even trying. Day after day, he comes back empty handed.

When Dad finally announces one morning that we'll be taking the trip he'd alluded to earlier, there's a visceral loosening in the room, the relief of knowing what we're doing next. With crisp efficiency, Dad informs us that we'll be leaving today, at dusk. He tells us how many bottles of water to bring, which jars of food to pull out of storage or prepare, the shoes we should wear for the walk. And even though he warns us that we'll have to be wary of signs of contamination, even while he reminds us that the trip isn't without its dangers, he speaks animatedly, almost with a hint of elation.

It's midday by the time we finish packing the provisions and organizing ourselves. Dad calls us to lunch and has us all eat several helpings of rabbit stew he's cooked, to give us fuel for the walk, he says, but also to make us drowsy, so we can get some sleep before we set out. He keeps urging us to eat more, repeating the instruction with mechanic regularity, and we keep murmuring our agreement and accepting another ladle, already lethargic from having had several servings. All of us sit around the table in a tired stupor. Finally, Nick works up the energy to stand. He gathers up the dishes, taking his turn to clean them. On my way back to my building, I pass him scrubbing bowls with juniper branches and sand. I hesitate, unsure of whether to approach him or not. He starts when my shadow falls over his hands, but he doesn't look up at me. "Do you think you'll be able to sleep?" I ask.

"I'm going to try," he says.

I crouch down next to him and hug my knees to my chest. Nick sets down the bowl he's finished scrubbing and picks up the next one.

"So, any word about where we're going yet?" he asks, a false brightness in his voice.

"Dad hasn't said anything," I say, watching him.

"Not to me or Vanessa. Maybe not to you, either, sure, I can buy that. But does that mean you really don't know? It's funny—the more I think about it, the more unlikely it seems to me that you really have no idea. I'm starting to get the feeling that everyone here knows more than they're telling. But that's just me. Just me thinking out loud, idly speculating."

"Hey there, you two," a voice says.

Vanessa is striding toward us with a pile of plates, which she deposits in front of Nick. "Isaac gathered up some more from the last few days," she says. She picks up a bowl from the finished pile and examines it. "Hmm."

"What? Not up to standard?"

"Probably as good as it's going to get without water."

"Thank you for your benevolent understanding," Nick says, bowing his head. He looks up at her, squinting against the sun. Vanessa readjusts a few pieces of his hair, and I try not to stare, bewildered at them suddenly so familiar with each other. Vanessa says: "I still have those sleeping pills with me. Do you want one?" She combs Nick's hair down and glances at me. "I'd offer you one, too, Georgia, but I can imagine Isaac wouldn't approve."

"I'll take one," I say.

Vanessa doesn't reply immediately, as though waiting for me to say I'm joking. When I don't, she says: "Are you sure? You might have weird dreams, and it'll make you groggy if you have to wake up before it wears off."

"I'm sure," I say.

She studies me, and I stare back. Finally, she shrugs and takes a hard plastic tube the length of a finger out of her pocket. She shakes out a small blue pill and hands it to me. "There you go," she says. "But if Isaac finds out and wants to know how you got it, I'll have to tell him that you must have gone through my things and taken it."

"What if I tell him that you gave it to me?" I ask, eyeballing the small pill in my hand. It's the color of mold, of a toxic insect's egg—the color of nature warning you to stay away.

"Well, then it'll be your word against mine, won't it?"

When I look back up, she's smiling at me, and I feel thrown, like I've misstepped.

"Sure," Nick says.

"What?" Vanessa turns to him.

"You asked me if I wanted a pill, and I'm saying sure, yes." Nick holds out his hand, and Vanessa shakes a pill into it with a flick of her wrist. "Cheers," Nick says, and pops it into his mouth. "Well, don't leave me hanging. It's no fun if it's just me."

"Finish the dishes and let's get you to bed," says Vanessa. She crouches next to Nick and then looks up at me, as though suddenly remembering I'm there. "You might want to lie down before you take it, Georgia. It might make you dizzy."

Reluctantly, cradling a vague grievance, I walk to my building, the sleeping pill tight in my fist. When I'm inside, I unclench my fist. The pill has leached a light-blue stain on my palm. I pluck off the pill and lick my palm experimentally. The blue reminds me of sugar from candy Herm brought me and Wulf years ago, but with a strange, bitter aftertaste. I examine the pill for a few more seconds, then place it on my tongue and swallow.

I don't feel anything at first, but by the time I've stuffed two shirts and a pair of pants into my backpack, my thoughts start to feel dense and slow, as physically substantial as they are unfinishable. It's a different feeling than being tired: a heaviness encroaching, a wave that I can see coming to subsume me. It would be frightening if my brain weren't as heavy as the rest of me. Hazily, I decide that I've packed well enough and put my backpack aside. I curl up on my bed and watch as the world turns darker and duller, my consciousness seeping out of me as quick as water running through loose sand.

Soon, I'm on a raft of branches in the ocean, a storm rocking me violently. With a start, I realize that there's a blue whale just beside me, whacking its tail frantically against the water, making the raft plunge into and out of the water at wild angles. I make a feeble attempt to talk to it, to convince it to stop moving, as though a whale could hear or understand me, but no sound comes out of my mouth. It's only a matter of time before I'm flung into the water. I try to grasp the edges of the raft, but my fingers are made of stone, thick rods, inflexible. They knock against the sides of the raft uselessly as I try to grab ahold. My entire body is made of stone, I realize with dawning horror. I'm only moving because the waves are knocking me around. "Come on," an angry voice says. "We're all waiting for you." I open my eyes to Wulf's face looming over me. He shakes my shoulder again. "Get up," he says.

Something in my body shifts, and I'm free to move my limbs again. I take a couple of long breaths, and then pull myself up to sit. Wulf takes a step back, as though I'm some dangerous animal. He has his backpack on and a wide-brimmed hat that's big for his head.

"What time is it?" I ask, blinking.

"Nine," Wulf says. "Nine at night. I've been calling at the door."

"Okay," I say, trying to clear the grogginess from my throat. "Sorry, I didn't hear you. Give me a few minutes. Tell Dad I'll be right there."

Wulf rocks on his heels, not leaving.

"I'm just going to change my clothes and finish packing," I say.

"What's wrong with you?" he blurts.

"Nothing's wrong. I just woke up."

Wulf kicks one of the legs of my bed lightly. "Everyone's acting weird," he says. "Dad and this trip—he isn't talking to me about it. We never visit Herm in the spring. It doesn't make sense. And Nick and Vanessa, they're like zombies. What's wrong with them?"

"It's just the medicine they took to help them sleep."

"Is that why you were sleeping?"

"I was sleeping because we're going to be walking all night, Wulf."

"But you took their medicine, didn't you?"

I wave my hand, annoyed. "It doesn't matter," I say.

"It does," says Wulf, and he sounds so grave, like he's mourning the death of something, that I feel a pang of strange guilt in my chest.

It doesn't take me long to get ready after Wulf leaves, but every movement takes extra effort, like the air has turned to viscous mud I have to wade through. My backpack is mostly packed, filled with my share of the food and water, clothes and spare socks, a book. I scan my room hurriedly and add a few more items. A pocketknife, a whistle, a few small cloth bags for foraging food. After a moment of wavering, I pick up the bone fragment and nestle it deep inside the backpack. It feels wrong not to take it. I swing my backpack, adjust the straps and stretch my arms, and hurriedly climb out of my building.

"Nice of you to join us, Georgia," Dad says, his tone reprimanding. "I believe we're finally ready to leave. Does everybody have their water and allotted provisions?"

"Yep," Nick says, but Vanessa is distracted, her eyes directed at Dad's hip. My gaze follows hers to a glint of metal—the gun Dad takes whenever we make the trek to Herm's, smaller and somehow more lethal looking than the rifle he uses to hunt at the settlement. Dad realizes what she's looking at the same moment that I do. "For the coyotes," he explains. "They smell our food. Not a danger so much as a menace."

We follow Dad toward the mountains in a loose cluster. He walks slowly, making sure we're pacing ourselves. Twilight clings to the air around us, coloring the dirt and shrubs with blue that turns darker imperceptibly. Birds coo and hoot softly. Rodents and small mammals are just starting to leave their burrows, scampering invisibly through the desert. By the time we've walked to where our surroundings are unfamiliar to everyone except Dad, it's dark out, the half-moon our only light, our eyes adjusted already.

No doubt because of the medicine I took, my brain still feels swaddled in a gauzy-thin sheet of sleep, and at moments I wonder whether I'm really awake or if I'm still in a dream, sleepwalking. After a while, I decide I'm awake, but by that point, I'm barely cognizant of anything except irritations. My shoes pressing against my toes, the rocks under the shoes' thin soles. The moonlight too white, the shadows that every cactus and rock casts too dark and oddly angled. My skin is unbearably itchy from dried sweat, and whenever someone coughs or says something, I feel an unaccountable burst of rage, as though they're shaking me out of a deep hypnosis with every syllable, preventing me from getting even a few moments of rest.

Wulf begins updating us on the hour. Ten, he calls out, followed by eleven, then midnight. By one in the morning, we're still walking at a steady pace, but by three, everyone seems to have reached the point where their energy is depleting exponentially. Nick lags behind, dragging his feet slightly, tripping every now and then. He veers off to relieve himself with an odd frequency, waving at us to go on ahead.

Whenever Vanessa notices herself slowing down, she speeds up again, but only momentarily. Dad pauses every now and then to stretch and take a carefully rationed sip of water. Wulf's voice falters when he tells us the hour, and the updates become more sporadic. Three thirteen, four oh two, four thirty. I bite back my irritation, walk with my head bent down. We take more water breaks, stretching out a single sip by rolling it around our mouths, letting it sink into our gums instead of swallowing. Slowly, the black sky starts showing signs of blue again. A little farther, Dad says.

We press on into the coming day, the blue-black turning to dark blue, then fading lighter, then lifting away from around us. There are more shrubs than cacti here, and occasionally the shrubs stretch tall enough to be called small trees. The terrain we've been walking across has been jagged with boulders, the elevation rising steadily, more chaparral than desert. We walk and walk, and a little farther ends up being hours.

Dad leads us up a path that only he seems to see. It rises toward a jutting cliff, our elevation increasing slowly. When we're closer, we see how the rock shelves jut out of the bulging reddish-brown sandstone, creating shadow. There's a dried-up ravine at the base, plants crowding against its sides, poised for a flow of water that comes rarely.

This is where Dad stops. He shrugs out of his backpack, sets it heavily on the ground, and rolls his shoulders, flinching. The rest of us follow his lead and then wordlessly stake out places to sleep. Mine is a bed of dusty sand in between two creosote bushes. I pull out a tarp from my backpack and prop it up with a stick, then crawl under. Inside, I curl up on my side and, despite the rocks digging into my hip and shoulder, fall asleep within minutes.

It's an uneasy sleep, the air hot and stuffy beneath the tarp. I wake up what feels like every half hour, the light more glaring and saturated as the day goes on. My dreams are scattered, tense and fleeting. Repeating scenes of the desert at dusk, of waking up and starting another night of walking. The dreams play out so logically that every time I really wake up, I'm disoriented for a full few minutes, unable to figure out why I'm suddenly lying on the ground, staring up at a sky of blue plastic instead of walking, why everything is so jarringly illuminated instead of dark. My sleep is flimsy, a transparent curtain. It's only in the afternoon, when the light begins to dim, that I sleep for a few deep, uninterrupted hours.

When I wake up at dusk—my eyelids sticky, my pupils dilating in the absence of sun—I'm relieved that it's finally time to get up. My body is stiff, and my hair is matted with sweat. I pull my tarp off as I sit up, blinking at the clouds illuminated with the last of sunset, drawing in a breath of warm, creosote-scented air.

Wulf is standing a few feet away and stretching his right arm across his body. Nick and Vanessa are rummaging around in the packs, pulling out jars. Dad is standing apart, his gaze moving from Nick and Vanessa to Wulf and me and then around the desert, assessing everyone and everything at once, like a bird surveying the landscape.

"How'd you sleep?" I ask Wulf, pushing myself up to stand.

He flinches in surprise and drops his arm. "Fine," he says.

"Herm's going to be surprised to see us this time of year," I say.

A moment of silence, and then Wulf shrugs.

"He'll think something's wrong," I say.

"Something is wrong," Wulf says.

"Right," I say, and pause. "It'll be nice to see him again."

"Dad doesn't want us talking about him."

"About Herm? Even now?"

Wulf glances at Dad, who's still absorbed in surveying the landscape.

"Did Dad tell you that?"

"I told you, he isn't talking about it to me," Wulf says, his voice low. "He didn't say that we're going to Herm's, that's just what we're guessing. We shouldn't talk about it where they can hear us. If Dad wanted us to talk about it—if he wanted them to know—he'd say."

"You mean Nick and Vanessa? You think he doesn't want them to know? Why does it matter? They're going to see him in a couple of days anyway."

"Shut up," Wulf says, looking away from me, his expression fierce. "Just shut up. You're making everything worse."

"What are you talking about? What am I making worse?"

"Just stop, or I'll tell Dad."

"What'll you tell him? That I'm talking about Herm? All right, go ahead."

"I'll tell him what I know," Wulf says. He's staring at the ground by his feet, and his face is flushed. Inexplicably, he looks like he's about to cry.

"What are you talking about?"

"I'll tell him what you did."

"What I—?" I repeat. My mind reels frantically. "The sleeping pill?" I ask, hitting upon the memory. "Is that what this is about? Wulf, that wasn't—it didn't matter. I just thought I'd try it to make the walk easier. It doesn't mean—I don't know if this is what you think—that I'm turning into one of them."

"You are turning into one of them. And it's not that."

"What, then?"

"I saw you. You and him. Nick."

My legs feel like all the strength has gone out of them. The desert around us contracts and expands dizzily, the movement nauseating. My ears ring loud as cicadas, a shrill barrier. What could Wulf have seen? He couldn't have seen inside Nick's building, the delirious sea inside, what happened in it. So what did he see? Us out in the desert? At some level, isn't that what I wanted? To cross a line? To swim past the point of no return? A part of me, yes. But only a part of me. The shore behind me suddenly looks a terrible distance away. My body feels like it's about to seize up, unable to swim any farther. Like I'll sink and drown right here, a heavy stone, my body calcified, all mineral. "Saw what?" I hear myself say.

"I won't tell. Not unless I have to. But I know. I saw you."

"Unless you have to? What's that supposed to mean?"

Wulf twitches his shoulders. He's trying to look calm, like he's talking about supper or the weather, but there's a buzzing tremor to his body, his limbs wound up and tense.

"What's that supposed to mean, Wulf?" I force myself to ask again.

"Everything was fine before they came," Wulf spits. He scuffs the ground with his shoe, kicking at a rock stuck in the dirt, loosening it from the sand.

"Maybe for you," I say.

"Stop," Wulf says, his voice inexplicably verging on hysteria. It comes out louder than he means it to, I can tell, because even he looks startled by the volume. I have a fleeting, irrational urge to embrace him, and then the urge dissipates just as quick, leaving only formless fear, a prickling anger. Nick and Vanessa look over at us from a distance, and Vanessa smiles tentatively. Out of the corner of my eye, I see Dad make his way toward the pile of backpacks, toward Nick and Vanessa. "Everybody ready to eat?" Dad calls. Vanessa answers, but she's turned away from us, and I can't make out the words. "Wulf, Georgia," Dad calls. Without another word to me, Wulf stalks toward the others.

Our supper is canned tepary beans, warm from the heat of the day. Vanessa finishes eating faster than the rest of us, licking her spoon. Nick seems to have a harder time, swallowing large gulps like it's medicine, or else scraping his spoon against the crust formed on top, placing a speck on his tongue. Wulf watches him, disgusted, and I have a feeling Nick notices and is exaggerating his ambivalence toward the beans just to get on Wulf's nerves. Nick takes a final bite, chews painfully slowly, places his spoon neatly back in the jar, and sets it on the ground.

"So, how many of us know where we're going and why?" he asks pleasantly.

I can feel Wulf's eyes burning into me, accusatory. It's clear—it's probable—that Nick heard fragments of our conversation. But, contrary to Wulf's worries, Dad doesn't look alarmed or angry. Instead, he just looks distracted, blinking like he's surprised to be addressed.

"We're paying a visit to a friend of the family," Dad says. "We call him the Hermit—Herm—although his given name is Daniel. You're free to call him as such if you prefer. He'll answer to either name."

"Well, that tells me a lot," Nick says.

"I don't know if sarcasm is necessary," Vanessa says.

"What sarcasm? I'm acknowledging that our names say a lot about us."

"Did you meet Herm out here?" Vanessa asks Dad, pointedly turning away from Nick.

"No, no. Herm and I go way back. We went to university together. When I first met Herm, he was already well on his way to finding revolutionary evidence for controversial theories about Earth's development during the Late Cretaceous, as well as independently researching super photons. You can imagine the kind of mind he has. Unfortunately, the possession of a mind so dedicated to study and learning has made it difficult for him to sustain many human relationships. The solitary existence agrees with him in that respect. Although, in other respects, it's a nuisance."

"What do you mean?" asks Vanessa.

"As difficult as it is for Herm to live with others, it's perhaps even more difficult for him to live without others' help. He forgets about basic necessities like food and water. It's impractical to expect him to provide for his own subsistence."

"So, what? Does he live alone or doesn't he?" Nick says.

"He does," Dad answers. "I believe this should suffice as an introduction to Herm. It may be wiser to simply wait until we arrive at our destination to meet him rather than asking me more questions. We'll be there soon enough."

"Soon enough," Nick says ruefully. "How long did you say that would be again?"

"Three days," answers Vanessa. "Well, three nights and two days."

"Good memory, Vanessa," says Dad. He stands up, and, unexpectedly, he turns to me. "Georgia, I'd like you to take a walk with me," he says. Then he begins strolling into the desert, hands clasped behind his back, and I scramble up to follow.

We walk slowly as our eyes adjust to the coming darkness. We walk until we can barely hear the clatter of the others cleaning up the camp behind us, and then Dad stops. He's turned away from me, his eyes directed at the desert, as though he's addressing the darkening patches of cacti and sagebrush.

"I've noticed that you've been spending time with Nick, Georgia," Dad says without preamble. "Taking him along on walks, shepherding him around the daily work of our settlement—quite a lot of time, if I'm not mistaken."

My body stiffens, bracing instinctually.

"I wanted to ask whether you've had a chance to speak much, or if the time is largely spent in mutual silence," Dad continues.

"We speak, I guess," I say stiltedly.

"Don't guess, Georgia," says Dad. "Consider and come to a thoughtful conclusion. I know you're a thoughtful girl. Woman, I should say. Did you know your mother and I were only a couple of years older than you are now when we met? Your mother and I had a partnership that should have lasted through the ages. As you know, I'm not a religious man, but the fact that we seemed to know each other intimately from the first time we met is the only thing that's ever made me wonder if there's something supernatural in the world. I'm sorry you didn't get to know her better." Dad clears his throat. "However, at other times people simply have relations because it's what their bodies crave, the way we crave food and drink. Or two people come together because it serves a mutually beneficial purpose. My parents, for example, stayed married during my own childhood because it was a sound financial idea and it provided me with the most stable upbringing they could offer, which was a value they espoused. I bring all this up because it may be that Vanessa's role here changes. The two of us have arrived, I believe, at a certain closeness over the course of our extensive conversations. My hesitation, however, is the effect this would have on Nick. We have a fragile ecosystem here when it comes to social relations. I bring up Nick and the time you've spent together because I wonder whether he's mentioned anything to you about Vanessa."

"About Vanessa?" I say, my mind reeling. I open my mouth and close it, waves of confusion washing over me, ebbing and receding. A certain closeness, Dad is saying. My thoughts flash to Vanessa's interactions with Dad: how, from my vantage point, they've always been, and still are, dominated by Vanessa's scrutiny—her endless stream of too-genial questions; the studious, almost hungry, way she listens to the answers. I think back to Nick's words about Dad—*Isaac's little crush*. They sound insulting—one-sided and silly, a juvenile characterization. It embarrasses me to connect them with Dad. But I realize I can't dismiss them outright. It's unnerving to consider that maybe, just maybe, Dad is capable of deluding himself.

"Well, Georgia?" Dad says, still waiting. "Has Nick mentioned anything?"

"Sorry. I was thinking. No. Not much."

"Vanessa rarely talks about Nick as well," Dad says, nodding. "It's what leads me to believe that they may not engage in conjugal relations. As well as the fact that they've opted not to share a building in our settlement. Regardless, people who have partnered have a certain loyalty to each other. They may not know it exists until the moment it comes under threat. It's a territory on which to tread carefully." Dad half turns to me. "That isn't to say that both of them don't remain objects of suspicion. I believe it's unlikely they brought this contamination we're seeing with them, but we shouldn't discount the possibility yet. It could have been something on their clothing, something they carried in unknowingly. We've seen plenty of cases of similar situations happening in history when people who live in vastly different environments come into first contact. I should have been more wary of it when we first met, if I'm honest with myself and with you. That was a failing on my part as a father. It's lucky nothing has happened up to now. Perhaps you've already mulled over this possibility. You're a critical thinker, Georgia. That's why I've kept you at arm's length these past few years. Why I haven't tried harder to rein you back in after you distanced yourself. Women's brains develop faster than men's, and yours is at a junction of adolescence and the completion of its growth. You're not so blindingly loyal to parental figures anymore as Wulf remains, and you're intelligent, but not quite wise enough yet to come to the correct conclusions at all times. It's important I share my work with people who come to the correct conclusions right now. I hope that, in the future, this situation can change."

I nod after a moment, the only answer I can manage.

But Dad doesn't seem to be looking for an answer. His eyes are sweeping over the rocky ground, his mind already moving to other matters. He pulls a small cloth bag from his pocket and crouches down to fill it with a handful of dirt, then pockets it. He says: "Herm will be able to look at the samples to give us a clearer idea of what's happening. That's my hope, in any case." He glances up at me as though to check if I'm giving him my full attention, then stands up clumsily. "I want to prepare you for an unpleasant possibility," he says. "Not to frighten you, but to warn you. It's possible that, when we arrive at the Hermit's house, we'll find him dead."

A chill runs through my body, even with the day's heat still hanging in the air.

"The hazards of solitary living," says Dad. "He's more susceptible. It's not necessarily what I'm expecting, but I wanted to give you the courtesy of forewarning, in the event you hadn't considered the possibility yourself. Of course, I don't know if the contaminants have spread to his area or what we're looking at here in terms of toxicity. Physiologically, he may have fought it off if something did get to him. Considering his quality of life, the fact that he's lived this long should be an indicator to us that his body has its natural defense system intact. But this is only one of the countless possible outcomes that could stem from the situation. This is just a warning of what may happen, not what will."

"Thanks for thinking of me," I say after a moment. "I mean, for thinking to warn me."

"I'm always thinking of you, Georgia," says Dad. "Everything I do, I do it with you and Wulf in mind, as well as the coming generations you represent." He glances in the direction of the camp. "Let's rejoin the others, shall we?"

Everyone looks more awake when we return. Wulf is sitting on the ground, stretching, and Nick and Vanessa are speaking together quietly by a neat pile of backpacks. They stop when they see Dad and me, and Vanessa smiles brightly. We all pull on our backpacks, and Dad leads us out of camp.

We're becoming acclimated to walking at night, to our new waking and sleeping schedule, and our pace is faster than it was yesterday, our arrangement less regimented, as though we're getting more comfortable walking as a group. Depending on the terrain, we fan out or wander closer together, forming loose, small clusters and then disbanding. I keep an eye on Vanessa and Dad, who walk together at the front and occasionally exchange a few words. Wulf keeps his head down and walks to the side of everyone. I try not to look too much at Nick. I tell myself not to, but I can't help stealing glances. After we've been walking long enough to watch the moon arc across the sky, when everybody has been walking fairly far apart from everyone else for a while, Nick sidles up next to me. He murmurs something that I don't catch.

"What?" I say, keeping my voice down.

"Did he say anything about you and me? Isaac?"

I shake my head no.

Nick takes a deep breath, lifting his shoulders, and exhales. I watch Vanessa laugh at something Dad says. Her mouth moves as she answers, and she gesticulates with her hands. Wulf is walking to the right of us, his neck bent and his upper body lurched forward, stumbling over rocks and regaining his balance with a scowl.

"You lied, you know," Nick says, his tone pleasant. "The day I wandered off, when I got bit by a scorpion. You said nothing was around."

"Herm isn't around. He lives a long walk away."

"Well, 'around' is relative. I'd argue that a walkable distance qualifies. But don't worry, I don't blame you. I'd say the same thing if the roles were reversed. If we'd taken you three hostage instead of you three us." Nick laughs at the thought, a caustic sound.

The word *hostage* pings around my head unpleasantly. I watch Nick out of the corner of my eye. He's deliberately creating a barrier. Dividing everyone back into their proper places—him and Vanessa on one side, and me, Dad, and Wulf on the other. But it's more complicated than that now. Nick has to see that, regardless of what he says.

"If we were your hostages, I'd convince you to let us go," I say.

"Oh, really? How would you do that?"

"I'd use my wily charms," I try to joke, the words halfhearted.

"I wouldn't count on that. Doesn't seem to be working for me." Nick quickens his pace, and soon we're not walking beside each other anymore, and I'm left to think about his words. I tilt my head up as we trudge on, watching the moon complete its arc across the sky and clouds drift over spatters of stars. By the time the night is halfway through, everyone's energy has worn off, and we all float along in our separate worlds, concentrating on putting one foot in front of the other.

We make camp at dawn again, this time amid pinyon pines and stunted junipers, half their branches bare, the others twisted like wrung-out rags. The earth is reddish brown, powdery with dry grasses holding it together, speckled with barrel cacti and ocotillo and sprawling manzanita clinging close to the earth. We spread out far from each other so we each have the cover of our own bush or tree to sleep under, extra shade on top of our tarps.

I use my backpack as a pillow this time, and maybe that, maybe the bone inside, is what makes the dreams come on so quickly. Shimmering at the edges, glinting like flecks of sand, they race to reach me almost before I fully fall asleep. I'm on a ship on a sea of rocks and bones that rattle when the ship moves, scraping against each other horribly. I shiver and turn, wake up and sit up, and pull off my tarp. The sky is a brilliant turquoise, painful to look at. I hear a coyote yipping, a hysterical, wretched sound. Dad is up, standing motionless by a bush, his head tilted up to the cloudless blue sky. I slip back beneath my tarp and sink into a cluster of dreams that dart away the moment I open my eyes again, hours later. This time when I take off my tarp for fresh air, I notice Nick sitting up, leaning heavily against the juniper he's been sleeping under. I lie back down, adjust my backpack under my head. When I wake up next, the sun is wobbling over the horizon, perched to set. Nick and Vanessa are sitting close together on the ground, and I'm about to look away when I notice that Nick's body is hunched unnaturally and Vanessa's hand is on his back, steadying him. I rub my face, stuff the tarp in my backpack, and make my way over to them.

"It's nothing," Nick says when he sees me approaching.

Vanessa frowns at him. "He woke up shaking," she says.

I study Nick more closely. His mouth is set, but his teeth are chattering lightly. He readjusts often, moving his legs and arms so it's hard to tell, but I can see his hands and shoulders shaking as though racked by a deep cold, a temperature foreign to our desert. Before long, Dad and Wulf have joined us, too, everyone huddling in a circle around Nick and Vanessa. Nick wipes his forehead with his palm, rubs his neck. His eyes are glassy. He blinks a lot, like he's trying to see better.

"I can't say I'm surprised," Dad says. "It makes sense to me that one of you would be the first to feel it. Your immune system is already degraded from living where you do. The air you people breathe is toxic, not to mention the food you eat. This does, of course, lessen the likelihood you brought it with you. And it comports with my theory, the fact that it's starting to attack us the closer we get to the Domes. We'll have to be on guard. Our understanding of it is growing, regardless."

"Of what?" asks Vanessa. "What do you mean?"

"The contamination," Wulf says.

"You think that's what this is?" Vanessa asks, frowning up at Dad.

"That's not what it is," says Nick, his tone irritated.

"Have you been feverish?" Dad asks Nick. "Have you noticed any other symptoms?"

Nick waves his hand. "It's just stomach issues. Just give me half an hour. I'll be fine then."

Dad doles out the rabbit jerky and water. Nick chews slowly at first but comes into himself the more he eats, and by the time he's finished his bottle of water, he says he feels ready to walk if we start out slowly. Dad takes his customary lead, and Wulf, as usual, keeps to the side of our group, about five feet distant. Vanessa stays by Nick's side and leans in to speak to him quietly. Whatever she's saying seems to annoy Nick because he pulls away each time. After an hour, she seems to reach the limit of her patience and drifts to walking at her own pace, a little faster, catching up to Dad. I linger where I am, keeping my eye on Nick. I quicken my step determinedly, then change my mind and slow down again. Finally, I match my stride with Nick's.

"Don't ask me how I'm doing," he says.

"I wasn't going to."

"Liar."

"I've got more interesting things to think about."

"I don't doubt it. What's a sick old man like me to you?"

"You're not old."

"No," Nick says. "A little sick, though. Damn it—hold on." He stops to pick a rock out of his shoe, hops a bit when he loses his balance. "There," he says, flinging the rock away. "The last time I went on a miserably long trek like this was when I was a kid on a Scouts trip. And, miserable as that was, it wasn't even this bad."

"Why didn't you like it?"

"It was too much of a pain to get to any nature. More trouble than it was worth."

"You lived that far away?"

"Most people do. That's how it is everywhere—everywhere people live, at least. Where we lived in Ohio, there was what we called a forest a couple hours' drive away, but it was really only a buffer of trees growing around the city's landfill and sewage dumping ground. Some city initiative had a trail built around it, but you can imagine what it smelled like, walking next to millions of people's trash and shit."

"But people still walk there?" I ask.

"Some crazies convinced they need the *fresh air*," Nick says with air quotes.

"What about if you drove out farther?"

"Yeah, you'd get to some wilderness eventually. But you'd have to take roads nobody uses anymore. It's a stretch to even call them roads. Like the ones around here. At least here, you've got the hot, dry weather to preserve them. We've got freak blizzards all year, flooding, tornadoes. It's not pretty. It's only the highways the government keeps usable, the ones that get you from one metropolis to the next. Nobody lives anywhere else, except people like you."

"I don't know if there's anyone else out there like us."

"Well, there's a lot you don't know, Georgia," Nick says, and there's an edge to his voice, almost reproachment.

We walk and stop, walk and stop. I'm glad we're making progress at a pace that's less punishing, but all the stopping makes the walk harder, every pause reminding me of my draining energy. My body seems to sense that we're close. It craves desperately to give in to exhaustion, and I have to force it to keep moving. It's still dark out, only a couple of hours past midnight, when Dad gestures at something up ahead.

"See that hill?" he calls to everyone. He's gesturing at a short mountain, still a few miles up ahead. Trees, even some ponderosa pines among them, cluster at the bottom of the slope and climb up sparsely to the top. It doesn't look drastically different from the landscape we've been walking through, but I recognize it the moment Dad points it out. The trees poke into the dark sky familiarly, thicker at the base of the hill, then thinning out. "That's where we're going," Dad says.

The air is slightly cooler here. We've trekked to a higher elevation, slowly climbing up a barely perceptible slope. Rocks jag out of the soil, like we're walking on a bed of rocks that's only thinly disguised with a carpet of dirt and the leggy plants that manage to straggle out.

"Have you ever thought about moving up here?" Vanessa asks Dad.

Dad raises his arms above his head, stretching, and takes a deep breath. "I'll admit, the air is refreshing. Unfortunately, this location is too close to an artery of the transportation system. A highway passes some miles north of here. Even if the trucks are few and rarely stop, it doesn't bode well for my peace of mind. No, my purposes are better met in a place the world has judged uninhabitable."

"Herm doesn't feel the same way?"

"The life Herm chooses to live is more worldly."

Vanessa glances at the wilderness around us.

"It's a matter of degree," says Dad.

13

The sun is just beginning to rise when we come upon the cabin. The shadows are long and quiet, the air a deep blue that's slowly disappearing. Herm's cabin is hand built out of adobe bricks and logs hacked into halves and fourths and nailed haphazardly together. The roof is covered by a tattered, bright-blue tarp that's pegged to the ground on three sides. There's a smaller structure next to the cabin that's storage for the Hermit's riches: shelves and shelves of food in dented tin cans, crates of useful and useless metal, a jumble of plastic objects from the outside world that he rescued to repurpose. A bulky mechanical device that Herm uses to take core samples sits stationed in front of the cabin. Parked to the side is Herm's truck, and I watch as Vanessa's and Nick's eyes are drawn to it.

"Herm, it's Isaac," Dad calls, his voice dwarfed by the trees.

There's no answer. No sound comes from the Hermit's hut.

"Herm," Dad calls again, louder. "It's Isaac here."

Suddenly, we hear the sound of twigs and dead pine needles crunching coming from behind the house. A moment later, a four-legged black-and-white blur comes bounding around the corner, and I recognize Moonpie just as she jumps on Wulf, paws pedaling his thighs. Wulf kneels down to pet her, and Moonpie can't contain her excitement. She does a series of small jumps, pressing her thin front legs on Wulf's shoulder and licking his face, his neck, his ears. Wulf lets himself laugh brusquely and rubs his hands up and down her back as she licks his cheek. When he stands up, she bounds over to Dad, who gives her head a couple of pats, and then she gallops over to me, drumming her paws on my legs, turning her small snout up to me and whining desperately. I bend down to take her into my arms and scratch behind her ears.

"Is that—your dog?" asks Vanessa.

"Moonpie," I say.

Vanessa frowns down at Moonpie, as though she can't fathom that she's really seeing the dog she'd been searching for with Dad. Moonpie barks happily and nuzzles my hand.

"Animals always sense danger before people do," Dad says vaguely.

A series of noises comes from the hut, a knocking-about inside. Moonpie barks and runs to the door, then back to us, then repeats the circuit as the noise continues. Finally, the door crashes open, and there's a man standing in the doorframe, corpulent and barefoot, holding a hunting rifle pointed in our direction. When his eyes fall on us, he leans forward and blinks rapidly. His grip loosens on the rifle, and the barrel droops and rises, pointing precariously at our feet, then at our chests. "Is that you, Isaac?" Herm says, squinting.

"Indeed it is," says Dad.

"Couldn't find my glasses," mutters Herm. "You caught me when I was still sleeping. Do I have—no, I don't have my dates off. It's not even summer yet. What're you doing here?" He looks around at the rest of us. "Who's all this?" His mouth twists into an open-mouthed grimace, revealing his incisors, as he stares. "There's Georgia and Wulf. What about the rest of you? That isn't Eduardo, is it? No, it isn't. You're shorter. Skinnier."

"Why don't you invite us in, Herm," says Dad.

"There's an idea. Come on in, come in." He waves us through with his rifle. "Not loaded," he explains. "Just a prop to ward off intruders."

The inside of the hut is just like I remember. Dusty and grimy, crowded with variously colored and shaped rocks piled on any surface—on the ground, on each other, on furniture in various states of disrepair. There's a small bed in the corner with blankets piled on top of it, and a desk in the corner with one computer and three monitors, tangles of wires running along the walls. The door has a table next to it with a hot plate and a stack of dirty plates and a few empty tin cans. In the middle of the room sits an armchair and a peeling leather couch. Herm pulls up a couple of rickety wooden chairs from the wall, moves off the rocks piled on them, and arranges them by the couch. "Make yourselves at home," he says, waving at the seats.

Dad takes a small object off the desk and slips it into his pocket with a metal jangle. "I see you found my dog," he says mildly, opting for a wooden chair.

"She just showed up here one day and wouldn't leave," says Herm. "Even when I tried to shoo her. But that's my fault. I fed her some cat food I got on my last supply run, and then she'd keep whining so pitifully that I'd have to feed her some more the next day and the next. Kept meaning to cut her off, but she doesn't make it easy."

"You have a cat?" Nick asks, glancing around the cabin.

"I do not," says Herm. He groans as he lowers himself into an armchair and taps his hand down on the crate next to it absentmindedly, as though by habit. His fingers grasp something, and he holds it up triumphantly—a pair of wire-rimmed glasses. "There we go," he says, hooking them over his ears with some difficulty. "Now, let me get a good look at you all."

"Herm, this is Nick and Vanessa," says Dad. "They've been staying with us."

"Visitors?" Herm asks, frowning. "On purpose?"

"I wanted to write an essay," says Vanessa.

"Ah," says Herm, scratching his cheek. "Well, I've thought of doing that myself."

"No, I mean I'm a writer. I was writing a long essay about the people who built the settlement where Isaac lives now. That's how Nick and I got there."

"How'd she find you?" Herm pans his amazed expression from Vanessa to Dad.

"Trial and error," says Vanessa.

"Huh," says Herm. "Does she know about the—what we're—" He trails off.

"Yes," Dad says.

Herm waves his hand to Nick. "Both of them? Or—"

Dad shakes his head.

"Mmm," says Herm.

"Vanessa and I have been getting along quite well," says Dad. "After some initial misgivings, I've taken to enjoying explaining my way of life to her and why I've taken it upon myself to take certain actions against certain entities. Thanks to her probing mind, we've had a series of illuminating conversations that I believe have strengthened my convictions more than ever. Her husband, Nick, has been acclimating less easily, but he's been making progress. But that's neither here nor there. It's not what I came here to discuss with you."

"I was going to ask," says Herm. "That's why I had the gun, see. Wouldn't have even thought to expect you, unless something went wrong with the—well, I'll shut my mouth about that. We know how it went. Go on, keep talking, don't mind me."

"I'm concerned about a possible contamination event," Dad says with the air of someone who's been waiting patiently to continue. "Originating from the Domes, potentially. That's why we've been working to stop them, isn't it? The damage we always knew they could cause, the adverse effects. This isn't far from what we've discussed about them. Well, are we surprised now that something's gone wrong over there? It's a working theory, but it's the best explanation I've been able to come up with. We came to you, Herm, because I thought you might be able to help shed some light on what we're seeing."

Herm frowns deeply. "What've you been seeing, exactly?"

"Plant rot, animal mortality. I've been watching birds dying off for months now. No obvious reason why. You know how closely I live with the earth, Herm. There's a sickness I can feel. A malaise. I thought it might be an environmental contaminant. Something to do with nuclear or chemical waste, by-products of the build. But that's only one theory. Maybe it's directed energy attacks they're testing. Microwave pulse weapons, or a new technology. It wouldn't be the first time the government's tested their covert weapons out here in the desert. Whatever it is, I can't study it the way I'd like to. I have my theories, but I don't have the right tools or expertise. That's why I came to you. Have you noticed anything around these parts? Anything strange?"

"Well, let's see," Herm says slowly. "Can't say I've noticed anything I've been worried about. Only thing I can think of is Eduardo going AWOL. Could be that his signal's down. Did you have rain in your parts in the past few days? I had a freak storm here, ten minutes and then gone, like a monsoon, but it's too early for that. I had to climb on my roof and do some rewiring to get everything back to working. Your dog near went crazy barking, watching me up there. Could be that Eduardo had something similar over at his place."

Dad's body has stiffened. "Eduardo didn't go through with it?" he asks sharply.

"Nope. You didn't know? Well, I guess you wouldn't, walking here and all. Nah, no news about anything happening to the reactor." Herm glances over at Vanessa and Nick, his forehead creasing abruptly. "You want us to have this conversation later, or—"

Dad shakes his head impatiently. "It doesn't matter anymore," he says.

"Up to you," Herm says, but there's surprise in his voice. "Well, the news sites, like I said, they sure reported about the things you and I made happen. The power failure, the water system going down, the—you heard about the deaths?"

"I heard," says Dad, his face inscrutable.

"Yeah, unfortunate, those. No problems with news coverage about that. Anyway, with Eduardo, either something didn't work right or he decided not to go through with taking down the reactor. I sent out a communication but didn't get anything back. Not that that really tells us anything. My bet is that something's gone wonky with his internet. We probably just have to give it a few days, and—"

Herm stops because Nick has stood up suddenly.

"Excuse me," Nick says, and rushes out the door.

All of us stare after him. From where I'm sitting, I can see a part of him hunching over and then hear a retching sound. He rights himself, stands uncertainly like he's afraid he's going to topple, and then comes back inside. He stands in the doorframe, blinking, almost like he doesn't know where he is. "Could I get some water?" he asks in a weak, shaky voice.

"Course," says Herm, springing out of his armchair. "Course you can. What happened there? You feeling okay? Sick with something?"

Nick nods, walking unsteadily to the water pitcher.

"Sit down, I'll get that for you," Herm says. "Sit down, go on."

Nick takes the chair next to Vanessa, and Vanessa leans over to examine his suddenly pale and sweaty face. "Nick? What's going on?" she says.

Herm brings Nick a tin cup of water, and Nick gulps it down.

"Another sign," Dad says.

"Sign of—what, the contamination you were talking about?" Herm asks.

Dad inclines his head.

"Huh," says Herm, studying Nick. "Well, if it's some kind of environmental contaminant, something from the Domes, it'd be mighty strange if it was only affecting our friend Nick here and no one else. Everyone else has been feeling fine, haven't they?"

"There may very well be invisible effects," Dad says. "We don't know what's going on inside our bodies. As for why Nick is visibly sickening and the rest of us are not, it's likely that his immune system is especially weak. In that case, it's not surprising that he's experiencing the effects before the rest of us."

Herm squints at Nick, his eyes thin crescents. "You been getting diarrhea?"

"On and off," says Nick, his mouth a thin line.

"What about sulfur burps?" Herm presses.

"Sulfur—what?"

"Sulfur burps. A burp that tastes like sulfur. Like rotten eggs."

"I don't know," Nick says, his brows knitting. "I don't think so. Maybe."

"Sometimes that symptom takes a while to develop." Herm nods knowingly. "You might have a touch of giardia. A parasite. Giardiasis can develop slowly, so it's hard to diagnose early. Some people just have diarrhea for weeks. You been feeling tired a lot?"

"We don't know the extent or the severity of the threat," says Dad, his voice ringing out, as though to drown out Herm and Nick's conversation. "But we do know one exists. Nick's symptoms reinforce it. What you've told me about Eduardo, Herm, only solidifies my conviction. Something is gravely wrong. Something that, if it hasn't reached us yet, is coming. Eduardo wouldn't have reneged on his part of the plan. His intelligence is such that he would be able to fix whatever problem he may have encountered. So why haven't you heard from him? Where does that leave us? In a world with Eduardo dead. He lives closer to the Domes than any of us. Now we have a clear indicator of the contamination's source and direction. If we can take anything from Eduardo's death, it's a warning. Heeding it would do honor to his memory."

"Whoa now," says the Hermit. "Whoa. Let's slow down. Nobody said anything about Eduardo being dead. That's a pretty big leap there."

"I believe there's sufficient reason to make the leap," says Dad.

The Hermit rubs his face with his hand. "I don't know, Isaac. You're a smart guy, but I don't know, I think maybe you've got this one wrong. I don't see any reason to jump to that kind of conclusion about Eduardo. And seeing some dead animals and plants—well, it's nearing summer. It's hot. Lots of things die off every year just because of the heat. I don't mean any—don't take this the wrong way, but maybe you're just getting the heebie-jeebies."

"Pardon?" says Dad.

"You're spooked. Starting to see patterns where there aren't any from your nervous energy. Those deaths at the Domes—I know that must be hitting you pretty hard. Don't know how much you read about it, but I read that they were young people, a guy and a gal in their twenties, two of the engineers. The gal was on temporary assignment, had a husband and a little one back home. The other one, the man, supposedly he used to be a volunteer firefighter. Well, they always write nice things about dead people. Who knew what they were really like? Maybe the world's better off without them. No way of knowing, I guess. Anyway, I'm rambling. I was just thinking that's probably hard for you, thinking about them. I know you didn't want something like that to happen."

"We always knew there might be sacrifices," Dad says stiffly.

"Well, sure, maybe. I mean, maybe you did. Not something we ever talked about directly. But even if you thought about it, it's different seeing it actually happen. Different when it's real instead of abstract."

"That may be you projecting, Herm," Dad says.

"Yeah, maybe, maybe," says the Hermit. "Anyway, the way I see it, we wait and see. How about you hang around here for a few days and we keep an eye on it? We'll wait and see—maybe Eduardo's just late. If nothing shows up in the news after a while, we go from there. Regroup and decide how to figure out what's going on with him. And in the meantime, we'll do some poking around about this contamination business."

"I've been collecting soil samples," says Dad.

"Sure, we can take a look at those," says Herm. "We can run some tests. We can start that right away—well, maybe first you'd like to rest. Are you all tired? You'll probably want to stay up to reset your sleep schedules. I'll boil us up some tea. Got a good stash of nice tea bags of Irish breakfast on my last supply run. Water's running a little low, but we can figure that out. You want to start setting up camp? A couple of you can fit in the cabin here with me. For the rest of you, there's tents in the storage shed. Should be a place to sleep for everyone one way or another. I'll call you in when I've got the tea ready."

"We're appreciative," says Dad.

"Well, then," says the Hermit, pushing his hands against his knees to stand. "I'll leave you to it. Georgia, you want to stick around for a minute? Got some new fossils for you I've been collecting. May as well give them to you now instead of waiting around until I was supposed to see you all next. Nick, you can stick around, too, if you want. I might have some antibiotics somewhere in here. Might help, might not, but hey."

We all stand, and Dad leads the small delegation of Wulf and Vanessa out the door. Moonpie cheerfully trots after them. Herm pours the rest of the water in the pitcher into a saucepan and turns on the hot plate. He studies the shelf nailed to the wall above it, pushing aside a couple of jars and tins, muttering to himself. "Here we are," he says, extracting a cardboard box from behind a stack of small tins. The box is red, white, and blue and decorated with a picture of a tall clock tower. I know Herm will save the box for me so I can add it to my collection.

Herm fishes out a square tea bag from the box and drops it into the saucepan, where it floats desultorily, hardly coloring the tepid water. He picks up a dirty fork and pokes the tea bag around. "That'll do," he says. Then he walks over to a stack of plastic crates, crouches down, and moves one crate aside, then rummages through another until he finds a small plastic box. He pulls out several pairs of scissors, a pair of tweezers, and a pincushion stabbed with needles. Then he digs through a collection of pill bottles, plastic baggies of lozenges and foil-backed packets of pills, rolls of gauze. He brings a few bottles and foil packets up to his eyes, baring his teeth as he squints to read the tiny lettering. Finally, with a grunt, he motions for Nick to hold out his palm. "No antibiotics," he says. "But we've got a multivitamin, a motion sickness pill, and this big yellow one that's supposed to do something good for the stomach. Forgot what, exactly. They're expired, but one of them might still do something. Worth a try, anyway."

"Cheers," Nick says with a small shrug. He pops the yellow pill into his mouth and swallows, flinching as it moves down his throat.

"So, what do you think about all this, Georgia?" Herm asks. "Are you worried about what your dad's been saying?" He moves to a shelf made of wooden crates. It's crammed with tools, rock samples, buckets of dirt, and heaps of miscellany shoved into every spare nook left over. He seems to deliberate where to look. He moves aside a pick to look behind it, appears not to find what he's looking for, then lowers himself onto his knees to search a lower shelf.

"It's like Dad said," I say uncertainly. "There's a lot we still don't know."

"You think Eduardo's dead?"

"No. But I don't think he isn't dead either. I don't think anything yet."

"Spoken like a scientist," Herm pronounces, still crouched on the ground. He pushes aside a metal box that makes a screeching noise. "That's good, that's good. Keeping an open mind. Innocent until proven guilty. All that good stuff."

"He didn't tell me about the deaths," I say. "I knew about them, but only because Vanessa told me. I guess he mentioned them to her."

"He did, did he? Well, that's interesting. Why, do you figure?"

"I don't know, but maybe—when Vanessa told me Dad had talked to her about it, I thought maybe he wanted to gauge her reaction—to get an outsider's perspective. To see if she'd be horrified, or if she wouldn't act like it was a big deal. Like maybe he was trying to figure out how bad it was, really, that he caused some deaths. I don't know. It was just a thought."

"Could be," says Herm. "Like I said, it makes sense he'd be shaken. Sabotage is one thing, but something like that—well, in all the times he's tried to stick it to the big powers he says are ruining the world and whatnot, he's been careful not to actually hurt anyone."

"Are you—" Nick says, pointing between Herm and me. "Are you talking about the hacking and sabotage stuff? The stuff Isaac's doing to the Domes?"

Herm turns around to glance at Nick, his expression sour. He walks back over to us and deposits two small light-gray rocks in my palm. They're nearly identical, the surface of each covered in a ladder of close ridges.

"Bivalves?" I ask, turning one over.

"From the limestone south of here," says Herm.

"Thanks, Herm. Thanks a lot. They're great."

"Well, they're nothing special," says Herm.

"So, are you just going to ignore me, then?" says Nick.

"Nick, is that right?" Herm asks, turning slowly to look Nick over. "That's your name, is it? And the other one of you is Vanessa? How much do the two of you know? What's Isaac told you?"

"Ha," Nick says. "We haven't really had a chance to sit down and chat, Isaac and I. I've had to get my intel via other means."

"I told him some of what Dad's doing," I explain.

"I see," Herm says, raising an eyebrow at me.

"I didn't tell him about you or Eduardo."

Herm shrugs. "I don't mind. I just don't know if you should be telling him anything Isaac doesn't want him hearing."

"Dad's been telling a lot to Vanessa," I say.

"Hmm," says Herm. "Well, speaking of which." He glances out the window, hazy with grime. "Do you want to tell them to come in and get some tea? I'll try to dig up some food for breakfast."

Herm shuffles back over to his crate shelf, and Nick and I go outside.

"So, who's Eduardo?" Nick asks me once we close the door behind us.

I consider not answering, or lying, but I don't have the energy. The air has a thin quality, like there's less oxygen in it. Does it matter what Nick and Vanessa know now? It seems pointless to hide anything now, everything fraying, threatening to unravel. My brain can't grasp the situation enough to assess anything. Has Dad given up on hiding everything? Suddenly, I can't remember why we kept anything secret in the first place.

"Eduardo's a friend of theirs," I tell Nick.

"They just keep coming out of the woodwork, these friends, don't they? First the Hermit, now Eduardo. Your dad's a pretty social guy, it seems. How many more people does he have caught up in all this?"

"That's it. There's no one else."

"So, this Eduardo guy was supposed to do something to the nuclear reactor up at the Domes, but he didn't? What happened there?"

"I know as much as you do about that."

"And now Isaac thinks this Eduardo guy bit the dust because whatever he was supposed to do didn't get done, huh? How likely is that, do you think? That he's really keeled over? Can't they just go and check up on him? Or does he live even deeper in the middle of butt-fuck nowhere and it'd take months to walk to him? Looks like Herm's got a car, though, so maybe not. What do you think? Are we finally going to take that road trip?"

"Certainly not," says Dad's voice.

Nick starts, his face almost comically guilty as Dad comes around the corner of the cabin. Vanessa, Wulf, and Moonpie follow in tow. "God, you scared me," Nick says, composing himself.

"Nobody will be taking the car anywhere," Dad says coolly. "I took the liberty of confiscating Herm's car keys when we arrived, and I've just finished removing the car's starter relay, rendering the car unusable. Admittedly, these precautions are a little extreme. The car only has enough charge for Herm's very precise purposes. As none of you know Herm's precise route, the car would strand you in the desert if you tried to drive it. Regardless, as I've already explained to Vanessa and Wulf, I thought it best to prevent an unpleasant situation like that from occurring in the first place. Herm uses the car exclusively to resupply, and none of us, not even I nor Herm, will utilize it for any other means."

"Why?" says Nick, staring. "Why not use it to check up on your friend? Or are you not going to tell me?"

Dad returns Nick's gaze levelly. "You may have noticed that I've decided it no longer especially benefits me to remain discreet," he says. "We have more pressing matters to attend to. Eduardo lives too far for us to check on him, and too close to the Domes and other people. The risk isn't worth it. We have our protocols. Herm and I communicate with Eduardo exclusively electronically, just as Eduardo and I communicate with Herm exclusively by trekking up here to see him. Neither of them communicates with me unless I reach out to them first. We keep ourselves safe that way. Besides that, if the contamination has reached Eduardo already, what do we have to gain by chasing it? If it's killed him, nothing but likely death awaits us there too."

"So how exactly do you imagine this Eduardo's supposed death happened?" Nick asks. "Like, do you think he just keeled over and died one day, while drinking his morning coffee? Radioactive poisoning or some biochemical weapon floating through the air suddenly attacking him with no warning? Or is he writhing on the ground in your mental image, in dramatic death throes? Because, if you don't mind me saying, both those options sound a little—how do I say this—deluded? Unrealistic? Let's go with deluded and unrealistic."

"I'm not going to speculate on the specifics," Dad says tersely.

"You've got to have an image in your head if you've been leaping to all these conclusions."

"I'm not sure why you believe you know what's going on in my head, but I'll warn you right now that it's a fool's errand," Dad says.

A tense silence settles between them, each eyeing the other with distaste. Vanessa catches my eye, then looks back at Dad. Moonpie whines. She stands on her hind legs and pedals her paws against Wulf's leg. Wulf scratches her head and murmurs something to her.

"Herm says the tea is ready," I say.

"The tea?" Dad frowns at me like I've said something nonsensical.

"Herm made tea," I say.

"I see," says Dad. "That's right. In that case, let's go drink some tea."

Although we're all exhausted from walking all night, Dad agrees with Herm that it's better if we force ourselves to stay awake until evening. We drink cups of hot black tea in Herm's cabin, and then Dad announces that he and Herm will begin their investigations immediately, starting with the soil samples.

He sends the rest of us outside to find the tents in the shed beside the cabin, which is packed floor to ceiling with objects Herm has scavenged on his supply runs. Broken plastic containers and watering cans with holes in them, a termite-eaten door, wooden crates full of dusty knickknacks that have all turned the same faded color of dust. Cardboard cartons full of anything and everything, mostly broken, and steel drums stacked precariously to the ceiling. There's so much clutter that we need to rearrange the objects every time we want to move, making a new space to stand.

"Look at these," Nick says, holding out a handful of what look like lumps of dirt twisted in tiny bags of thin paper. He squeezes himself into the narrow space of open floor by the door and flings one of the lumps at the ground. It explodes with a cracking sound and a tiny flash of light. I flinch, and Wulf startles. Vanessa sharply catches her breath.

"Poppers," Nick grins. "There's a box of Fourth of July supplies back there in the corner."

Vanessa peers cursorily at the box. "We're supposed to be looking for tents," she says.

"Just trying to lighten the mood," says Nick, shrugging.

It doesn't make sense for all four of us to be inside the shed together, but nobody offers to step outside, maybe because nobody's in the mood to talk, or maybe because everyone wants to be doing something instead of counting down the minutes until we can go to sleep. We just continue navigating around each other in the small space, crouching down on the ground or flattening ourselves against another wobbly pile of objects to let each other pass. The caffeine in the tea has put me on edge.

I flinch whenever someone sets down an object too loudly, jolt away when anyone accidentally brushes against me.

It's Nick who finally finds the tents, five of them folded up, lying beneath a pile of muddy clothes that have dried into a solid lump. We unfold them to pick out the four with the fewest holes, then take them outside to pitch them on the other side of the cabin. Vanessa and Nick work together to pitch the two red ones, and Wulf and I take the other two, one gray and one blue. I hold the poles in place as Wulf nails the stakes into the hard ground. When we start on the second tent, we realize it's missing all its stakes, so Wulf withdraws into the storage shed to find something we can use in their stead. He returns with a handful of bent silverware. With the help of some digging and angling, three forks and a butter knife manage to keep the tent up.

When Dad emerges from the cabin to check on our progress, he's enthusiastic, fizzing with energy. He walks around the tents several times, crouching down to peer at the stakes, shaking the poles to make sure they're stable.

"Excellent," he says. "Excellent work, everyone. I believe Herm has a collection of tinned food in the shed. I'd like you to collect the tins of fruit and stack them outside. There's enough liquid in them to help stretch our water supply. When you finish, you can start building a fire-pit. Just a circle of stones with a grate. There'll be one in the shed. You see where I'm pointing? Keep it equidistant between the cabin and the edge of the clearing. Go ahead and begin collecting firewood as well."

14

My sleep that night, when Dad finally lets us retreat into our tents, is fathomlessly deep and dreamless. I don't wake up until long after the sun has risen. It's the heat that wakes me, the sun beaming persistently at my tent until the air inside is too stuffy to breathe. I sit up in my sleeping bag and rub the sleep out of my eyes. For a confused moment, I think we're still on our way to the Hermit's, that I need to lie back down and fall asleep again, to sleep through the day until dusk. Then I think, no, we haven't even left yet. Finally, slowly, yesterday's events filter back to my memory. I stretch my arms to my toes, then crawl forward to unzip my tent.

I'm not the only one who slept late. From the drowsy way they're milling around, Nick and Vanessa look like they've only recently woken up as well. Vanessa yawns as she places a saucepan over the firepit, on the rusty grate I dimly remember finding in the shed yesterday. She notices me and gives me a small wave. I lift my hand in response. Nick steps out of the shed, holding two very dented cans. I scoot out of my tent and make my way over to them.

"Where's everyone else?" I ask.

Vanessa points with her chin to the cabin.

"Dad hasn't been out yet?"

"Nope," says Nick, sawing the lid off a can with a flimsy knife. "They've been holed up in there since we've been up." He grips the lid with two fingers, pries the rest of it open, and dumps the black mush of beans into the saucepan. Vanessa stokes the coals with a stick, making them glow red.

"How long has that been?" I ask.

"Fifteen minutes? Twenty?" Nick says. "I woke up when I heard Vanessa making a ruckus."

"I was not making a ruckus," Vanessa says. "I was just having a hard time with the zipper on my tent." She presses her left wrist against one eye, then the other. "I could use some more of that black tea," she says, opening her eyes wide as she takes her hand away. "It's going to take a few days to get readjusted to being—whatever the opposite of nocturnal is."

"Look at you, starting up a caffeine addiction again on day two," says Nick. "Tsk, tsk. After giving me such a hard time about complaining about it at the settlement." He prods at the beans with his knife. "I hope these aren't expired. Do they smell weird to you?"

"Diurnal," I say. "That's what the opposite of nocturnal is."

"Oh, is that it?" says Vanessa. She leans down to sniff the saucepan. "The beans are fine."

Nick flinches and rubs his abdomen.

"What?" says Vanessa.

"Hmm? What?"

"Why are you touching your stomach? Are you in pain?"

"Not pain, exactly," says Nick, grimacing.

"Then what?"

"I'm just going to—" Nick motions indistinctly into the distance. "Come find me if I don't come back in ten minutes. Just in case I'm being mauled by a wolf or something."

Vanessa raises her eyebrows. "Any wolves here we should be aware of, Georgia?"

"We may have had a Mexican wolf ranging around the settlement five or six years ago, but they're very rare. Maybe extinct, actually. Dad thinks it was just a coyote, but the tracks were different. I don't think he took a good look at them."

"Okay," says Vanessa. "I was joking, but good to know."

Nick salutes us stiffly and trudges off into the trees.

By the time he returns, Vanessa and I have finished the beans and put the saucepan away, and Wulf has just shown up, lugging a sack of cut nopals over his shoulder. Moonpie trots alongside him, her tail wagging. Dad and Herm must have been keeping an eye on us through the window, because they, too, emerge from the cabin. Dad nods a greeting at everyone, rigid and formal. "Good morning," he says. "I hope everybody has had sufficient rest. Georgia, if you would be so kind as to clean the nopals Wulf has foraged, we would be grateful. Has everyone eaten already, or have you been waiting?"

"I could eat more," Vanessa offers after nobody answers.

Moonpie barks cheerfully, and Wulf crouches down to pet her.

"I'll get her some cat food," Herm says.

After I finish cleaning the nopals, Vanessa volunteers to grill them over the fire. Herm brings out a plastic pitcher of water and dumps a can of syrupy pears into it. He mashes them up with a fork, so the water turns sweet and pulpy. The sugar is welcome, though it makes my teeth hurt. The nopals taste tough and sooty, but everyone eats everything on their plate. The sun is high in the sky now, making our meal closer to lunch than it is to breakfast. The fire's embers are glowing red and white, flakes of ash floating up and away when the wind stirs them. We eat in silence, forks clanging quietly against tin plates. Moonpie, having finished her bowl of grayish cat food, is dozing beside Dad's chair.

"So, any word from Eduardo?" Vanessa finally asks.

Dad finishes chewing. "No word," he says, swallowing. "Unsurprisingly, seeing as all indicators point to him being deceased. As I have already said."

"What about the—have you found out anything about the, you know, the contamination?"

"We're progressing with our research. We might be here longer than expected."

"Oh, really?" says Vanessa after a pause. "Because of—what you're trying to find out?"

"It may be in our best interests," says Dad.

"You can't monitor the situation back at the settlement?"

"It isn't only monitoring that we're dealing with, Vanessa. It may be that regrouping will be involved. We may have to analyze and reassess, to decide on the best path forward, given the circumstances. Which, at the present time, aren't readily apparent. In the interim, I appreciate everybody's flexibility and patience."

"The quarters are kind of cramped," Herm says apologetically. "I'm not used to having so many guests. We might have to do something about food. I think the water situation will be okay, but I've been due for another supply run for food. Stash is running low. Don't know if you all want to keep eating cactus every day. Good and healthy as it is and all."

"We'll make do," says Dad.

"It's just that I didn't bring my notebooks with me," Vanessa says. "Not even a pen. I'm not sure what I'll do with myself in my spare time without them."

"We'll keep you busy," says Dad. "There's a lot to be done around Herm's."

As though eager to keep his promise, Dad sets Vanessa, Nick, Wulf, and me to work on a series of tasks as soon as we finish eating. We uproot our tents and pitch them between the cabin and the shed, where Dad now says they're at decreased risk of trees falling on them in case of a dust storm or an early monsoon. We gather firewood and divide it into three piles: small twigs, thin branches, and thick pieces of wood. We further clear the clearing, picking out any stray wood or pine needles or dried grasses around the firepit, the cabin, the shed. Dad even has us pick out the larger stones from the dirt, explaining, when Vanessa gives him a questioning look, that we can use them for a building project later, and that it makes the terrain more amenable to planting.

Dad flits in and out of the cabin, checking on our progress before hurrying back inside, like he's minutes away from making an important discovery, like he's in the middle of research that can't be left unattended. In the late afternoon, he asks us to search through the shed for parts to rig up a Geiger counter to detect possible radiation, but when none of us, not even Wulf, can figure out what this device is supposed to look like from Dad's description, he gives up on trying to explain it. He says it would likely be useless, anyway. His energy has deflated a little, his previous vigor waning.

"We're all tired," he says, perhaps to justify our failure. "It's understandable. Your bodies, like mine, are still readjusting to this schedule. We'll eat dinner soon. In the meantime, I'd like you to survey the area for edible plants."

"I think I'll just hang around here," Nick says, stretching his arms out widely.

"Suit yourself," Dad says, and strides back into the cabin.

"Why?" Vanessa turns to Nick. "Are you still feeling sick?"

"Just don't want to overexert myself," Nick says. "Though now that you mention it, maybe I'll ask Herm for another pill sampler."

"Pills won't help," says Wulf. He flinches when we all look at him, but then he thrusts his chin forward the slightest bit, committed to finishing whatever he wants to say. "Medicine can't get rid of the contamination."

"That's what your dad says, huh?" says Nick.

"Yes," says Wulf.

Nick arches an eyebrow significantly.

"If medicine could help, Eduardo wouldn't be dead," Wulf goes on doggedly. "He can get medicine whenever he wants. He would have tried it if he felt sick. And he's smart. He would have known what to take. But he's dead, so obviously medicine doesn't help."

"Eduardo isn't dead," Vanessa says impatiently.

"How would you know?" Wulf says.

Vanessa opens her mouth, then closes it firmly. "Well, that's what we're here for, isn't it?" she says. "We're sticking around here to wait and see. Isaac and Herm are looking at the situation, and as far as I know, they haven't reached any conclusions yet. So neither should we."

"You don't know what you're talking about," Wulf mutters.

Nick glances at Vanessa, who shrugs her shoulders. I watch irritably as a silent exchange passes between them, unreadable to anyone else.

"Come on, Wulf," I say, my tone clipped. "Let's see if we can find some food."

Wulf and I head off by ourselves. Moonpie trots just ahead of us and glances back regularly like an attentive guide. We walk through the scrubby trees for a while, scanning the ground for cholla buds or juniper, but it's mostly just dry red pine needles and sticks with the occasional stubby cactus poking out of the dirt. Sometimes Moonpie barks at something we can't see and goes bounding off into the trees, then gallops back when we whistle to her. For the first time today, I start to notice how tired I am, feeling it a little at first, then all at once. Suddenly, it's difficult to keep walking when all I want to do is lie down on the hard ground and sleep. I feel like I'm walking through a storm, as though I'm fighting against the elements to keep walking forward. I try to take deep breaths, hoping an influx of oxygen will help me stay awake. The trees take on a bleary, blurred quality. I drift into a daydream of olive green, dusty brown, and red. When Moonpie barks, my heart leaps, and I'm suddenly wildly confused about where I am. Then I'm alert again, and I stay that way until I start nodding off again while walking, and the cycle continues.

Wulf bends down to pick up a gnawed pine cone. He tries to pry it open with his hands, flinching at the splintering scales, then shakes it beside his ear.

"Anything inside?" I ask.

Wulf shakes his head. He tosses the pine cone into the air. Out of nowhere, Moonpie comes galloping toward us and leaps into the air magnificently to catch it. She shakes her head back and forth, growling, then drops the pine cone to the ground and bites it again, growling even louder, wood scales splintering between her teeth. Wulf and I make eye contact and start laughing almost simultaneously. It's a strange sound to hear, Wulf's laughter. It's an unstable echo of mine, slightly deeper, occasionally leaping up an octave. I laugh more than I need to, just to hear the sound of his longer. Moonpie drops the pine cone to bark happily at us. She bites it again and brings it to Wulf's feet like it's a toy she wants to play with. Wulf obliges. He picks up the pine cone and throws it forcefully, and Moonpie darts to retrieve it.

"How long do you think we'll be here?" I ask, watching Moonpie.

"As long as Dad says."

"Come on, Wulf. What do you think?"

Wulf chews his chapped lower lip. "Probably longer than usual," he says.

Moonpie comes bounding back, panting. The pine cone is nowhere in sight—maybe she couldn't find it, or maybe she lost interest in looking—but Wulf scratches her ears anyway, murmuring that she's a good girl. She runs off again, and we start walking. The silence between us sinks into something surprisingly companionable. The trees are scraggly but tall, their brown-red pine needles dry and so high that we can't reach them. A warm wind blows strands of hair into my face. Wulf and I don't find much that's edible, but we gather dry twigs for tinder. We stop to examine a manzanita bush, the reddish branches thin and smooth.

"Dad thinks it's safer here," Wulf says, picking a tiny leaf off one of the branches.

"What?" I ask.

"He told me before we left that he thinks it's safer here, at Herm's."

"Why? Aren't we closer to the Domes here?"

"I think it's because of the trees. Trees clean up the air, so there's no contamination. Or less contamination, anyway."

"Maybe," I say.

Wulf studies me. He seems to decide that this response is acceptable.

There's a crackling and a rustling to our right, and we turn to see Moonpie's small body weaving in between the trees and brush. There's something white in her mouth, the bright color flashing every time she comes into view, and my heart nearly stops. The bone, I think. She's gone into my tent and found the human bone in my backpack, and now she's bringing it here to chew on it or play. But no, I realize a second later. It isn't. She hasn't, I reassure myself. Whatever she's found is larger, the shape different.

"What've you got, Moonpie?" Wulf says.

Moonpie drops the object at our feet, mouth open, lightly panting.

Wulf picks it up. Square teeth, a boomerang shape.

"Deer jaw," I say.

Wulf turns the jaw over, brushes off some dirt. "Do you think it's old?" he asks.

"It has to be. There aren't any deer here."

Moonpie sticks her nose into Wulf's hand and licks the deer jaw. Then she lightly tugs it from Wulf's grip. She looks so pleased with herself that Wulf laughs again.

"It'd be fun to see a deer," he says.

"So you can kill it and eat it?" I ask.

"No," Wulf says, and when he looks at me, his expression is odd, almost hurt.

"I was only joking," I say. The words hang uncomfortably in the air, and I cast around for a peace offering. "Maybe we'll see one when everyone finally leaves the deadlands for good, and it's just us here. When the Domes are gone too. You never know. The deer could still be out there somewhere. They could come back someday."

"No," Wulf says, "they're gone." But his expression has softened, no longer mad. It's a nice change to see. Despite my exhaustion, my mood lifts.

We end up returning to the nopals patch Wulf found in the morning, and we gather up some of the cactus pads in a small cloth bag. On the walk back, we come across juniper bushes that we missed the first time around and fill our pockets with the hard, dusty berries.

Herm makes supper at sunset, heating giant tins of pinto beans. The sky is sweeps of orange and pink, clouds ablaze against a background of purple blue. Moonpie sniffs at the spoonful of beans Herm offers her and licks it experimentally, then decides to stalk into the trees, perhaps to try hunting something better. The rest of us take our seats around the firepit and eat our bowls of beans without complaint.

The day feels distended, strange and endless. It feels like we've been here for days, for years, like we've always been here, living at Herm's. We clean up our dishes, and everyone begins a slow, tired filtering into the cabin or a tent. Wulf hangs back beside the fire, poking at the coals with a stick. After putting away the dishes, I wander back to the fire, too, drawn thoughtlessly to it like an insect. I've reached that state of being tired where it no longer feels like a desire to sleep but like a thin, breathless energy that's egging me on to stay awake. The heat of the day is still hanging in the air, but I hold my hands out to the coals to feel the warmth from the fire.

"Want to play cards?" Wulf says without looking at me.

"Cards?" I frown at him, not understanding.

Wulf pulls a deck of playing cards out of his back pocket. "I found them in the shed. There's two missing. Four of diamonds and jack of hearts. Herm taught us to play some games one time we were here. Don't know if you remember. It was really long ago."

"I remember," I say. "Okay, we can play. What game?"

"I don't know. War? If you remember it."

"Sure," I say, pulling up a chair and sitting across from him.

We arrange a third chair between us, and Wulf deals out the deck. We lay down card after card in tandem. Out of the corner of my eye, I watch Vanessa and Nick zip up their tents. For a while, there's a dim glow coming from the cabin, a bluish electronic light, but it shuts off by the time Wulf and I are on our second game. Moonpie succumbs to sleep at my feet, curled into a ball, her belly lifting and falling with her breathing, deep and slightly wheezing. Dusk makes our bodies and chairs cast bulky shadows. Wulf puts down a king, trumping my four of hearts, and adds both cards to his deck.

"It's not so bad," he says. "Being here."

We both put down sixes, so we each turn up one card facedown and one card faceup. Wulf's card is a jack, and mine is another six, so he scoops up the cards again and adds them to his deck with a satisfied expression.

"Yeah," I say belatedly. I glance at the tents. "I don't know why, but it feels better than it was at the settlement."

"It's kind of like old times," Wulf says. "Being here at Herm's."

"It is," I agree. Something about Herm's presence, or maybe the change in location, has shifted the dynamic, reminding us all that Vanessa and Nick are the outsiders here, separate from the rest of us. Alliances are being redrawn, people pulled back into their proper orbits. I can almost imagine that everything is as it should be between me and Wulf and Dad.

"But it isn't," Wulf says, his tone suddenly stern, like he's remembering himself.

I slip a card from my deck and turn it right side up. Wulf does the same, but we both just stare at the two cards on the chair without doing anything. All of a sudden, real exhaustion hits me, more forcefully this time than last. My eyes start closing all on their own. I don't know if my ears have just started ringing, or if I'm just now becoming aware of it, but the sound drowns out all other thought. Wulf seems to be feeling it too; his motions are slower, his reactions delayed. Finally, he takes the two cards up, and we go on playing. Neither one of us seems to want to suggest giving up. It feels like it would be a capitulation, reversing the fragile peace we've strung between us. It's been years since Wulf and I played cards together. The night deepens, our cards dimming into fans of dark rectangles. Every time we put more cards down, I wonder how much longer we can sustain it.

15

By the time a week has passed, we've finished organizing the shed, dug out clay to repair the adobe parts of Herm's cabin, and planted a small nopal plot in the clearing. Though we've tried to get the Hermit to grow some of his own food before, he's always forgotten to tend it. We help Herm set up new rabbit traps and consolidate the water from multiple smaller tanks into one large one. Wulf starts tinkering with Herm's water machine, which has only been eking out a small trickle of water, but soon abandons it.

In the mornings, Wulf and I fall into a routine of foraging for food. We check the rabbit traps and set new ones, pick the season's last cholla buds and sagebrush. Moonpie plays the part of our faithful companion, staying close and getting underfoot, whining when we don't give her enough attention. We don't talk much, except to point out something edible or to briefly deliberate which way to walk next, but when there's silence, it's comfortable, like a worn blanket that we've lost and found again. Every day, we venture farther and farther in a slightly different direction, familiarizing ourselves more than we ever have with this landscape.

Sometimes Vanessa accompanies us, and other times she busies herself with chores around the cabin. Only Nick doesn't do much to help. He complains of being tired all the time and spends more and more time lying around in his tent. He eats little, saying all food makes him queasy. Herm digs up some other medicines for him to try—pills rattling around in a small orange bottle, chalky tablets that pop out of foil wrappers, a bottle with an inch of viscous red syrup—but they don't do much, or whatever they do, they don't do it for long. Once, Nick's back breaks out in small red welts, which disappear just as mysteriously a couple of hours later.

"Does he have a history of being a malingerer?" Herm asks Vanessa in a low tone once, after Nick excuses himself yet again after hardly eating anything at supper.

Vanessa shakes her head lightly, watching Nick walk away.

"Could be psychosomatic," Herm murmurs. "You know, stress."

"Occam's razor, Herm," Dad says, his tone sharp, edging toward irritation. "The simplest solution is usually the correct one. We can connect Nick's illness to the contamination, even if we don't fully understand how yet."

As the rest of us fill our days with the tasks Dad assigns us, Herm and Dad go on reconnaissance missions, trekking into the desert beyond the ponderosa pines, sometimes staying away for an entire day. They analyze samples of dirt and rock they bring back, pore over indecipherably small pages of data on Herm's computer, spend hours conferring quietly.

Vanessa asks for updates during meals, but Dad is cagey, refusing to offer details. The only direct answer he'll give is that there's still no news of Eduardo, further bolstering his theory that Eduardo is dead. Herm clams up completely, shifting his full attention to whatever canned food is lumped on his plate. It's hard to guess what, if anything, their research is telling them.

On the morning of our ninth day, Dad decides to fix the water machine himself. Before anyone else has woken up, he's pulled it apart carefully and scraped all the brown scum off the metal pieces, even the hard-to-reach places in the filtration mechanism.

Now, the rest of us stand around listening as Dad narrates the process of correctly putting the pieces back together again, so everyone knows how to clean the machine if asked to. Herm's forehead is furrowed in concentration, as though he's trying to memorize the steps. Dad runs the water machine: a low suctioning sound and a gurgle. We watch until the collection container fills with an inch of water, then pass around a jar so everyone can take a tiny sip. When Vanessa wets her lips, her eyebrows raise.

"What do you think?" asks Dad.

"Wow," says Vanessa, holding the jar up to her eyes. Her voice sounds falsely polite, almost placating. "It actually tastes like water. What have we been drinking up to now?"

"Several varieties of mold," says Dad. "Anybody care to guess which?" Wulf opens his mouth as though to answer but then closes it. When nobody else says anything, Dad takes off his glasses and polishes them clean with his shirt. His face looks bald without them, the skin around his eyes pink and mole-like. When he puts them back on, he's back to his serious, authoritative self. "Regardless, nothing dangerous," he says briskly. "Not in the small quantities we've been drinking. Our stomach acids are strong enough to kill the pathogens. But it does make a difference, doesn't it? I think the effort justifies the quality-of-life improvement. More importantly, now we'll have an increase in supply. What do you think, Herm?"

"Doesn't taste all that different to me," Herm says gruffly after Vanessa hands the jar back to him to have a taste. He passes the jar to Wulf, shrugging.

Dad squints up at the sky, where the sun is straining toward its highest point. "Even with the increase, we'll have to start rationing more carefully. Soon, we'll have to come up with a more permanent solution. Herm and I will be looking into drilling a well."

"A well?" asks Vanessa, looking between Dad and Herm. "Wouldn't that take a while?"

"We'll look into an interim solution to get us through," Dad says.

"But what about going back to the settlement?" Vanessa asks, her forehead creasing.

"No," says Dad. His face is still tilted upward, his eyes thin crescents.

"No? What do you mean?"

"We won't be returning to the settlement. It's become clear to me that we're safer here. Herm and I haven't figured out the exact nature of the contamination yet, nor have we verified its source. Regardless, there are some facts we do know. The elevation, the geologic features, the terrain up here—it ensures that certain risks we may have to contend with at the settlement are less likely to be present. Additionally, there's safety in numbers. Six people are stronger than five. The rational course of action is to stay where we are permanently. I've decided that we'll rebuild here. We'll begin a new settlement."

"You can't be serious," says Vanessa.

"I assure you, I am," Dad says, his voice maddeningly calm.

I look between Wulf and Herm, to see whether they already knew about Dad's decision. Wulf's gaze is fixed firmly on the water machine, and Herm is rocking on his heels, gazing off into the distance. Neither of them looks surprised. They must have already heard the change of plans, then, or they'd look as stunned as the rest of us. It's an extreme course of action, even for Dad. I think of all the things we left behind at the settlement—drums of water, months' worth of mesquite flour and pickled fruit, stashes of bullets for hunting. Our clothes and blankets and beds. The cactus gardens we've painstakingly cultivated.

"We're not going back at all?" I venture. "Not even to collect supplies?"

"An unfortunate loss," Dad says without looking at me. "But I've come to accept that the risk is too high. To return would be a fool's errand." He raises his gaze to the sky, blinking. "It's getting close to midmorning, and we haven't even eaten yet. I think we're due for a break, if nobody objects."

"Wait," says Vanessa, her voice rising precipitously in pitch. "What about"—she seems to cast around for something—"what about all your computers back at the settlement? Don't you have important data on them?"

"There are ways to remotely reacquire any data I'll need. I'm not in any hurry, regardless. It'll be in our best interests to lay low for a period of time. We'll put our projects on pause."

"You're just going to give up on attacking the Domes?"

Dad studies her impassively. "I didn't know you'd become so dedicated to my project, Vanessa."

Vanessa shakes her head jerkily. "It's just that it doesn't make sense to me," she says.

"It doesn't have to," Dad says, a hint of warning beneath his pleasant tone. "Now, as I said, if nobody objects, let's rest and break our fast."

We retreat inside to eat, where Dad serves us tinned green beans and cups of freshly filtered water. Uncharacteristically, Herm is the only one who makes any attempts at conversation. He's met with only brief responses, the sound of chewing and swallowing, metal spoons tapping against tin bowls. Vanessa takes tiny bites, barely nibbling at a limp green bean speared on her fork. She keeps putting down her fork and then picking it back up, like she's forgetting and then remembering that she's supposed to be eating.

"What about Nick?" she says suddenly, fixing her gaze on Dad. "He's still sick. The medicines Herm's been giving him haven't been doing anything."

"Don't worry about me," Nick says heartily. "In no time, I'll be right as rain."

Vanessa turns her infuriated gaze at him, but Nick only smiles back at her.

"If I remember correctly," Dad says, "Nick's symptoms began at the settlement. Is that not an indication that we'd be returning closer to the source of the contamination if we returned?"

"But we have drugs in our first aid kit that could help him," Vanessa insists.

"There's no need to panic," Dad says, dabbing his mouth with a square of cloth. "Though Nick's symptoms are cycling through various manifestations, they don't appear to be increasing in severity. The body is an amazing machine, astonishingly capable of healing itself."

"There's no guarantee of that," Vanessa says.

"There's little guarantee of anything in life, Vanessa," Dad says calmly.

"This is ridiculous," Vanessa says, her voice rising. She scrapes her chair back and stands, and the rest of us stop eating to stare at her. She strides out of the cabin, leaving behind her bowl of barely touched food.

"Perhaps I broke the news too hastily," Dad says after a brief silence. "It's important that we maintain our sense of camaraderie during difficult times. I'll try to talk to her." He stands and follows Vanessa outside, his own steps calm and measured.

"Wouldn't be surprised if she worried herself sick too," Herm mutters to me and Wulf.

"Nick isn't sick because of worrying," Wulf says, his voice obstinate. "He's sick because of contamination."

"That's right," Herm says vaguely. "I was only talking about Vanessa."

Wulf glances at me, like he expects me to say something to back him up, even though Herm isn't exactly arguing with him. When I don't, his expression hardens, a quick snap. He rises stiffly and leaves the cabin, following Dad.

"That's what happens when you think about sickness too much," Herm goes on. "You get sick yourself. Me, I don't give it a second thought, and look at me. Haven't even had a cold in years. Course, that's mostly because I'm not around anyone to give one to me, but still. No other sicknesses either. Healthy as a horse. You all right?" Herm asks, squinting at me. "You look like you're chewing something over."

"Just trying to get used to Dad's announcement," I tell him.

Which is partially true, but there's something else I'm trying to figure out—something that doesn't sit quite right. Vanessa's mind is clearly elsewhere, but I'm not so sure that it's lingering on Nick. There's an expanding quality to her jumpiness, an unwieldiness that's made me start wondering whether her worry about Nick is a front to hide a different concern.

The thought nags at me into the next day. I watch Vanessa ask Nick if he wants some water and then, just a few minutes later, ask the same question again. She scolds him for not eating enough at breakfast, then for eating too much lunch. She tells him he's spending too much time in his tent in the morning, then later, when he emerges, tells him he should get more rest, then instructs him to look through Herm's medicine stash again.

Nick closes his eyes or stares up at the cloudless turquoise skies, opening his eyes wide, as though to douse them with the wide blue expanse. When he decides to take a walk around the clearing, Vanessa snaps at him. "You're making me nervous," she says as he makes loop after loop. "Isn't he making you nervous?" she asks the rest of us, searching our faces for affirmation. Dad's gaze flits inscrutably between Nick and Vanessa. "Idle hands make fretful minds," he says.

He asks Vanessa to accompany him on a reconnaissance mission. Nick retreats to his tent, and Herm and Wulf drift to tasks beyond the clearing's perimeter, leaving me by myself.

The sun arcs into late afternoon as I go about my chores, its heat fierce and determined. It would be too hot to be outside if it weren't for the slight wind that whooshes through the air regularly. I tidy the inside of the shed, gather more nopals, and de-spine them.

I keep glancing at Nick's tent, wondering whether he's sleeping. I try to think about something else—try to picture what our new life will be like here at the Hermit's—but maybe it's because this is so unimaginable, because it still feels so unreal, that Nick is where my mind keeps returning. It drifts to the day we found the bones, to our unclothed bodies in the delirious ocean, to floating in the bottomless cold, unmoored in the current. It drifts to Nick and Vanessa, to the conversations they have without speaking, an unspoken language apart from us, from me and Wulf and Dad. My stomach clenches, humiliation flooding in, then receding like a tide. What did I think I was doing?

I ask myself. The voice in my head is superior, condescending. What a stupid thing to do, it says. Swimming away, untethering myself. Isn't it better to be walking on dry, solid land?

I sit outside the cabin for a while, then get up and look for Moonpie, calling her name and receiving no answer. The heat is dry and dusty, settling and leaving a residue on my skin. The fabric of Nick's tent ripples in the breeze, unstable like a mirage. With quick, short strides, I walk over to it.

"Nick?" I ask. There's a rustling inside, then silence. I call his name again.

"You can unzip it," Nick's muffled voice says.

Even without leaning into the entrance, I can feel the stifling air inside, hot like breath. Nick is lying on his back on top of a thin sleeping bag. His face has an unhealthy flush, his hairline glistening with sweat. His half-open eyes meet mine, and he clears his throat, a wet and phlegmy sound. "Come in here for a bit," he says.

I look around, then lower myself to the ground and crawl in. It's even stuffier inside, the plastic material capturing the heat and stewing it unpleasantly. The blue fabric of the tent casts a blue light on everything. Nick props himself up so he's resting on his elbows. He pats the space next to him—a useless instruction, since it's the only other place to sit in the tent. I arrange myself to sit cross-legged, my legs cramped and slightly raised. Nick places his hand on my knee, where it rests heavily. "The tent's unzipped," I say, jumpy.

Nick doesn't give any indication of having heard. He lies back down and keeps his hand where it is. It's warm and clammy, and I swing between wanting to shove it off and wanting to sit still so he doesn't move it. Nick's fingers find a mole below my kneecap and worry at it lightly, then stop moving.

"How are you doing?" I ask, trying to shift my attention away from his touch.

"Just resting," says Nick. He takes his hand away and moves it beneath his head.

"It'd be less hot if you rested outside the tent."

"No, I like it better in here. It's like how animals crawl into caves or closets when they're about to die. Some instinct tells them to hide, so they won't be eaten by predators. Nobody wants to get eaten when they're down, even if it's a quicker way to go."

"I don't think you're about to die."

"Come on, let me have my melodrama."

I pick some dried dirt off my wrist. "What do you think about us staying here?" I ask.

"You know, it's not bothering me so much," Nick says. "I guess you could say I've come to terms with my captivity. What does it matter where I'm being held hostage?"

"Is that supposed to be melodrama too?"

"That's right," Nick says, smiling up at the roof of the tent.

"That doesn't seem to be Vanessa's attitude," I say after a moment's pause.

"Oh, you've noticed, huh?"

"Why is it making her so agitated?"

"What, you don't buy that she's just desperately concerned about my failing health?" Nick grins, baring his teeth. "No, you're right. It's not like a multiday journey back would do wonders for me. Something else is on her mind. But your guess is as good as mine. Maybe she just hasn't reached the level of enlightenment that I have. She hasn't learned to sit back and let the absurd world wash over her, to accept our situation for what it is."

"She seemed a lot more comfortable at the settlement," I say.

"Well, yeah, no kidding. We had actual beds back there."

"I don't mean physically comfortable, I mean—"

Nick waves his hand. "I know what you mean. Who knows. Who cares. We're here now, aren't we? Here we are, in the middle of nowhere again."

I frown down at him. "Are you feeling okay?" I ask.

"Fine, fine. Just a little fatalistic."

"Do you want a book?" I ask. "I brought one with me."

"Nah, it feels like too much effort to read."

"Want me to read to you, then?"

He turns his head to look at me. "I wouldn't say no to that," he says.

Outside, the breeze has picked up, sweeping a sap and pine scent through the clearing. The trees sway dreamily, their rustling dry and faint. There's a tense feeling of expectancy in the air. In my tent, I rummage around for my backpack, then for the bundle of clothes I wrapped my book in. My fingers brush against the bone that's next to it, smooth and cool and human. It feels wrong now, having brought it, a bad luck charm. Quickly, I pull the book out from the backpack.

Nick's eyes are closed when I return. I sit down quietly and leaf through the pages. There's a noise outside, something coming from a distance, dull and echoing. "Well?" Nick says, startling me. I flip to the start of the book. "Call me Ishmael," I read.

"It's as good a name as any," says Nick, settling his hand back on my knee.

"Some years ago—" I continue, and then stop, my ears straining.

It's a dog barking, the sound I heard. Nick must hear it, too, because he opens his eyes. All we can see through the unzipped tent flap is a cutout of trees and brush, a patch of sky. It takes me another moment to realize that the barking is Moonpie's, meaning Wulf has returned. Right when I do, the barking stops. Then it starts up again, unsettlingly close.

"I should go," I say, pressing my hands to the ground.

When I crawl out of the tent, Wulf is taking off a boot and shaking the dirt out of it at the edge of the clearing, where he has a clear view of the tent. He doesn't look at me, but Moonpie barks and bounds toward me. I crouch down to stroke her greasy head, and then she bounds off again. My heart beats hard when I stand up.

"Georgia," Wulf calls, his voice hard and accusatory.

I try pretending I don't hear, but he calls my name again, this time so loudly that there's no avoiding it, and I force myself to walk over to him. Wulf tugs his shoe back on, the movements jerky, almost fitful. I study his face to try to glean what he saw and didn't. Is he angry that I was in Nick's tent? Did he see Nick's hand on my knee? Is that why there's fury brewing on his face? No, not fury—betrayal, which feels even more dangerous. I want to try to explain myself, but I don't even know where to begin.

"Wulf—" I start. But I don't know what I want to say next, so his name just hangs there.

Wulf turns on his heel and walks off. Moonpie whines, looking between Wulf and me, not knowing whether to follow or to stay.

"Go on," I tell her softly, "I know he's your favorite." She runs after Wulf until she catches up and settles into a content trot at his feet, glancing back at me only once.

16

Though Dad has announced that we're rebuilding, he hasn't made any attempt to start. None of us are sure of what we should be doing, so we slowly work on the various projects Dad has already started, stretching out the chores as long as we can. We collect surplus water to store it, hammer tin cans flat so we can mold them into bowls and plates, patch up termite-chewed parts of Herm's cabin. We start cutting down the brush and small trees and cacti at the edge of the clearing, slowly expanding the space.

All the while, Vanessa's agitation grows more pronounced. If she's sitting, she suddenly stands up as though she's decided to go somewhere, and then sits back down again just as fast. She stops midway through a task and wanders to another, leaving the first unfinished.

Often, I notice her glancing around the clearing, as though looking for an escape, and I try to figure out why she looks so trapped. What's different now? She's stuck here, but wasn't she just as stuck at the settlement? I watch her eyes take in Herm's car, the cabin, the shed—a puzzle she's trying to solve, a series of lines she's trying to connect. She peers intently at the horizon, like there's an answer hidden there.

And then, abruptly, it's like a switch flips in her. Not quite like she's calmed down but like she's decided to change tack, to test out a different method. The six of us are in the cabin, hiding from the hottest part of the day, and Dad is staring into the computer screen. He clicks around, frowns, touches a few buttons.

"Code isn't doing what I need it to," he murmurs. "Signal's weak."

"Can I help?" Vanessa says.

Dad frowns at her, his expression probing.

"I could be useful," Vanessa says. "I'm not bad with tech."

"I suppose I don't see why not," Dad says, continuing to study her. He offers a small, conciliatory nod. "I'm glad you're feeling inclined to help the effort, Vanessa. I'm happy with this development. Feel free to pull up a chair."

From then on, she makes a point to smile more, to finish her chores early and ask others if they need help. She pays particular attention to Dad, nodding along as he talks, sitting beside him at meals. They start taking walks together again, the way they did back at the settlement, and Dad seems to grow more at ease. His movements are less stiff, and sometimes he even whistles during the day. Strangely, he seems less suspicious of Vanessa's sudden change of heart than I am. Maybe he sees something I don't. Or maybe he's ignoring the inexplicable in his eagerness to believe Vanessa.

One afternoon, I'm searching for more juniper to use for cleaning dishes when I hear voices and a quiet whimpering coming from deeper in the trees. Alarmed, I follow the sound deeper into the trees, trying to account for everyone's whereabouts to figure out who got hurt and how. Their bodies are only flashes between dry branches at first. As I get closer, I see it's Dad and Vanessa—Dad leaning against a tree, his eyes shut tight and a terrible grimace on his face; Vanessa kneeling. Tending to a wound, I think at first. But as I get closer, new parts of the picture emerge—Dad's pants pooled around his ankles, Vanessa's head positioned at his groin, and Dad thrusting his hips forward, the movement convulsive and unnatural, like his body is being jerked around by puppet strings. Dizzy with nausea, I hurry away. I don't even try to make my footsteps quiet; I know that they won't notice me. When I return to the clearing, Wulf is by the firepit with the pile of dirty dishes.

"What?" he says, glancing up. "Where's the juniper?"

"I didn't—" I shake my head, words trailing off.

He stares at me. "What?"

"Dad—" I say.

Wulf's eyes are fierce, as though daring me to continue. I realize in time that it's pointless. That Wulf wouldn't believe me if I tried to tell him what I saw. His faith in Dad is too strong to allow any hint that Dad isn't in perfect control of the situation. I know that even if I dragged him into the trees, forced him to see what I had, his mind would shut it out or rig up a benign explanation.

"Nothing," I say.

"What?" he says again, angrily, like he's being forced to pick a fight.

"I ran into Dad out there, and he said there wasn't any juniper around," I say.

He eyes me suspiciously a moment longer, then shrugs. We end up cleaning the dishes with pine needles, which isn't as good, but works well enough.

Whatever Vanessa is trying to accomplish, either she hasn't done it yet, or she's doing it so discreetly that Dad hasn't noticed. At night, I hear the zipper of a tent and low voices, and know it's Dad visiting her. I'm not sure if anybody else notices it; if Nick or Herm do, they keep their thoughts to themselves. During the day, Dad drifts around like he's under a spell, alternating between spurts of activity at the computer or in the forest and going about rebuilding slowly. He sporadically assigns us chores, only laying out vague plans for the day each morning.

On a particularly hot day, he doesn't give us any instructions at all, heading into the ponderosa pines by himself and leaving us to our own devices. I find myself clearing brush and trees from behind the cabin with Nick and Vanessa. Nick hacks at a bush halfheartedly with what looks like a toy machete he must have found in the shed.

"At least we have more free time now," he says.

"You've always loved your free time," says Vanessa.

Nick's eyebrows raise, but he seems to decide to ignore this. "What I've been trying to figure out," he says, turning to me, "is whether this will all blow over if we wait long enough. Whether Isaac's gotten paranoid like this before and then forgot about it. Does he regularly decide the world's trying to poison him? Or is this time special?"

"He's still trying to figure out what's going on," I say after a pause.

"No," Vanessa says quietly. "He's made up his mind already."

"I guess you would know best," says Nick.

"I don't know what you mean by that," she says, her face a perfect blank.

"Really? You don't know what I mean by that, Vanessa?" Nick says. "Let's cut the crap."

"I'd assumed you'd understand the importance of being on good terms with Isaac, now more than ever," Vanessa says without looking at Nick. "Would you prefer that I build an antagonistic relationship with the man who's holding us hostage?"

"I would prefer that you didn't build any kind of relationship with him, actually."

Vanessa laughs, an empty sound. "That's perfect, coming from you."

"Coming from *me*?" says Nick. "*You're* the one who got us into this mess. You wanted to come here. You're the one who wanted to go on this insane adventure for your insane *work*, and to bring me along as some kind of insane punishment."

"You keep telling yourself what I wanted," Vanessa says.

"I have to if no one else will."

Vanessa shakes her head vehemently. For a moment, there's a glint in her eyes, like they're wet, but she blinks hard, and then it's gone. She excuses herself to work on Herm's solar panels, which we've been trying to clean of grime. Nick drifts deeper into the trees, making as though to clear more brush, but it looks like he's just seeking the shade.

I focus my attention on a patch of land on the edge of the clearing that looks like it could be made into another garden and start digging out chunks of dirt. I pull up wads of dried grass and wedge out scrubby, thick-rooted weeds. The dirt is hard, mostly rock and clay, and I only manage to turn the soil on a small square patch. I stop when the sun starts beating too harshly on the back of my neck for me to stand it, deciding I've worked long enough to justify a break.

After I return my tools to the shed, I make my way over to Herm, who's settled himself in the shade in the front of the cabin. He has large sheets of papers spread over his knees that he's hunching over to read.

"Geologic maps," he says, peering up at me and then nodding at the paper. "Had them printed out big for my purposes last time I did a supply run—investigations into changes to crust thickness since the Late Cretaceous. Isaac had mentioned wanting to know how vulnerable the groundwater is to surface pollution a while ago, so I pulled them out. They're not the right kinds of maps for that kind of thing, but we make do with what we have, don't we?"

"Do you think the contamination is real?" I ask bluntly, before I can think better of it.

Herm frowns deeply down at his map. He doesn't speak for what feels like a long time. "You know, I've known Isaac for a while," he says finally. "I've stuck by his side since we were in school together, so I've had some time to observe him. Not that I'm saying I'm great at that kind of thing, observing people and understanding them. Might actually be what I'm worst at. But Eduardo and I have talked about this some, too, so I'm not just going off my own thinking here. The way I've come to see it is that your father likes to find a clear-cut cause for things. And usually the cause is that someone is to blame. A corporation, or a person, or a project. Sometimes even himself. He fixates on the cause, and suddenly it's the singular reason for everything bad."

I look over at Herm, but he's still staring down at the map. Thin, flimsy paper, swirls of different shades of gray, like a monochrome oil spill.

"Then again," he says, "there's a lot that Isaac knows that I may not always fully understand. It's not my area of expertise. I know rocks and weather patterns. I know some about computers. That's about the extent of it. So I may miss some things that Isaac sees. I try to keep an open mind, see? I'm not exactly a criminal mastermind, am I? Not saying Isaac is, in quite those words, just saying, personally, my mind's not programmed to fight against those things. But here I am, helping him. I've got my reasons. Maybe no one else would see them or understand them, but those reasons are still there. You know what I mean?"

"You didn't really answer my question," I say.

Herm sighs, tapping his map with his palm, then putting his hands on his knees and standing. "I'm going to finish up inside the cabin. Getting too warm out here. You're welcome to join if the heat gets to be too much for you too."

"I'm okay for now," I say.

Herm nods and takes his leave, and I try to make sense of his speech. The contamination isn't real, I try out saying in my head. It's Dad seeing a series of problems—birds dying, likely of heat; Nick getting sick, likely because of stress, bad luck, and his genetics; humanity failing to solve its growing deadlands crisis, likely because of a whole host of different reasons—and Dad picking out a single cause, the Domes, to blame. I float the idea in my mind like a feather. He's being paranoid, I tell myself, trying out the word. The way he's always been. The way he thinks the outside world is only evil, intent on destroying him specifically and itself in general, a chaotic hornet's nest of dangers. A part of me knows this explanation is the right one. Another part isn't ready to believe it yet.

The day meanders on, the sun refusing to let up. Dry pine needles hum with built-up heat, as though ready to burst into flame. My feet crush them as I walk, releasing the scent of fire and sap. Everyone retreats into a tent or the cabin or the trees at some point, too hot and too tired to work outside for more than an hour at a time.

Even Moonpie struggles. In the afternoon, I find her splayed out on her stomach next to the cabin, her body moving with her panting breath. Nick is crouched on the ground, offering her a bowl of water. He stands when he sees me and rolls his neck, stretching.

"Get some rest?" he asks.

I nod.

"Same," he says. He makes small windmills with his arms. "Not that I really got tired today," he adds, his voice resolute. "I'm feeling healthy as a horse. Just some body aches now. Probably from sleeping on the ground. How much longer do you think we'll be living in tents? No small feat, building up a whole new settlement from scratch. Does Isaac have any construction experience? I know he didn't build those buildings back at the old settlement."

"He can figure out how to build anything," I say.

"Still, that doesn't happen overnight, does it?"

"I don't know how long it'll take. We'll see."

"We'll see," Nick repeats, his voice distant. "We'll see, we'll see." He blinks and turns to me. "Shall we take a walk? For old time's sake?"

I scan the clearing, hesitating. "It's going to get dark soon," I say. "But all right."

We keep our eyes fixed on the ground as we walk, wary of rattlesnakes that might slither out of the stones, of small cacti eager to brush their spines against our ankles. Occasionally, I look over at Nick. His hair is oily, the curls clinging together to reveal parts of his pink scalp. He taps his hand against the thin trunks of ponderosa pines as we pass them, as though to count or mark them.

"You know what's funny?" Nick says abruptly. "Now that Vanessa's calmed down, it's like I've caught her bug. With the way she felt when Isaac first told us we're staying here permanently, I mean. I didn't really care at first, but now I'm starting to see what the big deal is. It's like we've gone deeper into this free fall of lunacy he's created. We're following him down a rabbit hole where he's making up all the rules, totally at his mercy. What insane dictate is he going to make next? I know I said it's all the same to me, but at least at the settlement there was some sense of normalcy." He laughs abruptly. "I guess I'd just gotten used to it."

"Maybe you'll get used to it here," I say, but the words aren't convincing, even to me.

"I know I'm not seriously sick," he plows on, as though he hasn't heard me. "But I have this feeling, like I've never been so close to death in my life. Weird, right? And it really makes me think, what the hell. What the hell am I doing and saying. Who even am I, this person I've never met before who does stupid things that don't—I don't know—fit in with this drive for self-preservation we're all supposed to have. What am I doing, acting the way I am out here? Saying I'm completely fine with staying here, that I've accepted everything? Is that the way I really am? Who knows, maybe I've got a death wish. But probably not. Being trapped makes you do stupid things, you know? You can't think clearly. It's like being stripped naked, down to your core or something. First at the settlement, cut off from civilization, from plumbing, and normal food, and all the things we're used to. Now here, where it's even more bare bones, sleeping in a tent. That's how you brainwash people, isn't it? Take away their regular lives little by little so something like this seems totally normal to them, then reteach them everything they need to know in their new reality. Maybe that's why we're here at the Hermit's. To brainwash me and Vanessa. Maybe that's why Isaac doesn't want to return to the settlement." Nick's gaze is boring into me, and I realize that he isn't just talking to himself anymore, that now he expects an answer.

"Dad doesn't care if you agree with him or not," I say.

"Are you sure about that? Doesn't seem like that much of a leap to think Isaac would be happier if we were all in. If Vanessa and I wanted to destroy the Domes, like you do."

"What do you mean, *you*?"

"I mean a collective you. You all."

"I don't have anything to do with it."

Nick closes his eyes and rubs them with his thumb and forefinger. He presses hard, his fingers making depressions. When he opens his eyes, he's staring at me with a strange intensity. It makes me want to step away slowly, like I would from a coyote, but I don't. "What do you think about all of it, then?" Nick asks. "About what your dad is doing."

"I told you, I stopped being a part of it," I say.

"He's not just abstractly fighting an idea, you know. He's killing real people."

"That was an accident."

"Oh, come on. He knew what he was doing. He knew what could happen."

"Power outages and system failures happen all the time by themselves anyway."

"You're saying someone falling off a cliff is the same thing as someone pushing them off?"

"No," I say tersely. "I'm saying that hurting anyone isn't his intention. I don't know what else you want me to say. I'm not a part of it. I don't know what else I can say about it."

"But you're not trying to stop him, are you?"

"What do you mean?"

"I mean, sure, you might have made a choice not to be involved, but you also made a choice not to stop him. So why didn't you?"

"How could I have stopped him?"

"You're smart. You could have figured something out."

"I didn't think about it," I say, confused.

"Why not?"

"He's my dad."

"Ah, there it is," Nick says.

A towering wave of unreality, a moment of being unhinged from time and space. A vast emptiness seems to open up around me, a dark space I should have filled with thoughts but never have. Why didn't I try to stop him? I ask myself, the question echoing. The truth is, I haven't let myself think about what Dad is doing, not that way. I've thought about it abstractly, intuitively, about how my instinct was that I didn't want to help. I've thought about choosing to distance myself, whether it was a good or bad thing. About being left behind, about being judged unreliable or not ready. But I never thought to or let myself consider much what it means to anyone outside our settlement.

How could I have? Sometimes, I'm not even sure that place exists. I have to tell myself it does, like a fact learned from a book that I have to decide to trust. All I really know is what I've seen, and all I've really seen is the settlement. It's hard to feel anything but abstract thoughts for a place you think about as an abstraction, for an idea that you can't see materialized before you. But Nick's words, like a bad spell, are making the shapes fill out. The gray masses I imagine when I picture the world outside are taking on eyes and mouths, faces contorted with pain. I swallow, trying to wash the image out of my mind, then swallow again and again, my throat dry. But what could I have done? What's the right choice I should have made? The questions are impossible, unmapped landscapes. The outside world suddenly feels both larger and closer. I feel it crowding in on me, pressing against me as it never has, stretching endlessly into a world that our settlement is only a tiny, tiny part of. I can't leave, I realize, panicked. The vastness is real and, for its realness, terrifying. Who did I think I was, thinking I'd be able to leave like it was nothing? It's impossible that I ever thought I could have.

"It was stupid, what we did," says Nick, jolting me out of my thoughts. "That's what I'm saying, about not thinking about things."

"What?" I say.

"Obviously, it's my fault," Nick continues. "I should have known better. Now it's another complication on top of a whole lot of other complications."

It takes me another moment to realize what he's talking about. I shake my head, like I'm trying to shake out the memory. "It was nothing," I say, my voice dismissive. A small, sharp hurt blooms inside of me, and I turn away from it angrily.

"It's not exactly nothing," Nick says. "Do you know what could have happened if anyone realized? I don't think you do. You're not a kid, but you may as well be, for all you know about the world. You don't know about these things, how crazy they make people. We weren't thinking about the risk." He laughs mirthlessly. "You know that's the only thing Vanessa ever said to me about it? Her way of telling me she could guess what was going on. Not that she cared personally, but that Isaac would be furious. I mean, that's no great surprise. She had a point, though. We can't just act on any fleeting want we have, not in a place like this."

"A place like what?" I say, my voice defensive.

"I don't mean it as an insult," Nick says. He opens his mouth and moves his hand as though to touch my arm and say something else, but I jerk away. He raises his eyebrows. "All right," he says. "You don't have to be mad at me."

"I'm not mad," I say.

"I don't know what you were expecting, but—"

"I wasn't expecting anything," I say, though of course this isn't true. I expected—vaguely daydreamed, barely let myself imagine—that Nick would be the way I'd leave the settlement. That he'd let me come along when, somehow, someway, he and Vanessa left. I force myself to face it now, this thought that I'd let lurk inside me, this half-formed, nonsensical idea I'd only let myself look at slantwise.

"—but I do have enough self-awareness to realize that I'm not a great person. I may even be a shitty person. A shitty person who is unironically lecturing you about what it means to be a morally upstanding individual. There you go. It is what it is. But hey, look at the bright side. You get a useful lesson out of all this: people will disappoint you. It's a good lesson to learn early."

"I already knew that," I say.

"Oh, yeah? How, by reading about it?"

"No. It's not like nobody ever disappoints anyone here."

"No, but your sample size is pretty small to figure out a general truth about people."

"It's not some novel concept you introduced to me."

"All right, all right. No bright side then." After a moment, half-smiling, he adds: "You must think that I think very highly of myself."

"I've never really thought much about how you think about yourself," I say.

191

Nick grins fully now. "There I go again, thinking everyone's think-ing about me." He glances up at the trees, then pokes at a desiccated pine cone with his foot. "Should we keep walking or go back?"

"We can go back," I say.

"You know," Nick says after a few minutes of walking silently, "I should qualify what I said about people disappointing you. That's a bit of a misrepresentation. They're not all like that. I mean, not everyone is. Not all the time, at least."

"I don't know why you're telling me," I say.

"Telling you—?"

"About the world out there. As though I'm ever going to be there."

"What, you think you'll be here forever?"

I study his face. "You think you won't be?"

"Doesn't seem likely to me, no."

"What do you mean? How?"

"There's always a wrench thrown into things like this," he says, gesturing vaguely.

"Who's going to throw the wrench?" I ask, watching him.

"If I knew that, we'd be out of here already."

"I don't know if that's always true," I say after a moment. "I don't know if it applies here."

"Yeah, maybe you're right," Nick says, scratching his ear. "I really couldn't tell you."

"I wasn't expecting you to."

"Well, well," Nick says, grinning again. "You know, you'd do fine in the outside world."

"Thanks, I guess," I say stiltedly.

The walk back is a short one, and when we return, the others are in the cabin. Twilight blurs its edges, the structure bleeding into shadow. Nick makes as though to go inside, then pauses, leaning against the door to listen for a moment. From where I'm standing, I can't hear anything except the din of voices, two of them, one higher pitched than the other.

"What is it?" I ask. "What's going on?"

Nick waves his hand to shush me, then listens for a while longer. He turns around to raise an eyebrow at me conspiratorially. "Someone's getting in trouble," he says.

"Who?" I ask. "Vanessa?"

"Sounds like she took the liberty of trying to get on the computer when no one else was around, and it didn't go over too—"

There's a sudden, resounding sound—like a rubber hose snapping or a heavy sack dropped on hard cement—and a startled cry, and Nick's face changes. His body freezes up in shock or indecision, and I realize what we heard. I picture Dad fuming, his breathing heavy, his shoulders high and tense. In my mind's eye, I see Vanessa staring back at him, her expression hardening, a mark on her cheek blooming red. Nick glances at the door, deliberating. It's as though time has stopped, the air charged with danger. Do it, I want to tell Nick. Go inside. Do something, anything. If there's going to be a confrontation, let's get it over with already. A sick feeling creeps into my stomach as he continues just motionlessly standing there.

17

A dark mood settles over all of us—a kind of cabin fever, an undefined, amorphous dread. Nobody talks about what happened between Dad and Vanessa, but everyone seems to feel it's changed things. All of us speak to each other less and less. When someone says something, we nod and make closemouthed noises in response. We smile at each other, our mouths stretched, our eyes darting around nervously like they're disconnected from the lower halves of our faces.

Herm, trying for levity one afternoon, suggests we have a barbecue. "Something tells me those rabbit traps finally caught some meat," he says. "I think some nice fresh rabbit steaks are just what we need right now. What do you all say?"

Nobody responds except for Vanessa, who rouses herself into making a humming noise in some kind of acknowledgment.

"You got any barbecue sauce in there?" says Nick, nodding at the shed.

"Sure do," Herm says. "A nice bottle of A.1. steak sauce, only expired a couple years ago. I've been saving it for a special occasion. I'll leave you all to find it while I check the traps. I can't make heads or tails of anything in there since my system's been—reorganized."

"We can do some digging," says Nick, but he doesn't move.

Herm bows shortly in thanks or parting, the top part of his body pivoting toward the ground like a bird pecking seed. I watch him leave until he's only flashes of his bright-green shirt disappearing into the olives and browns of vegetation.

Nick stretches his arms out. "Should have told him it'll be too hot for a fire," he says.

"It'll cool down in the evening," Dad says without looking up. He's examining a contraption he found in the shed, an ancient radio with tuning dials and a broken antenna. He has the back panel open and is examining the mess of wires, small gears, and plastic parts inside, pulling the tangle apart like it's a tough knot.

Vanessa, who's been tearing labels and scrubbing glue off tin cans as per Dad's instructions, abruptly stands. Her foot knocks into the pile of cans beside her, and some roll away, catching the light in bright-silver flashes. I think: a warning, a signal to prepare for danger. Vanessa retrieves them and rubs her neck when she stands back up, her eyes darting around the clearing and into the trees.

"You planning on joining him?" Nick asks.

Vanessa's eyebrows lower. "What?"

"Herm," Nick says. "You keep looking the way he went."

"Oh. No. I'm just looking. Not at anything. But maybe I'll go on a walk."

"Don't be long," Dad says. He doesn't look up from the mess of wires.

Vanessa sticks close to the perimeter of the clearing, where we can see her through the trees and brush, though it seems like I'm the only one watching. Her steps are slow, directionless—or maybe she's being purposeful, her steps slow because she's being careful. When I finish mending the holes in a plastic rain tarp, I move on to scrubbing the cans Vanessa left unfinished. Later, after Vanessa returns, Dad assigns us all new chores. Wulf is sent inside the cabin, Nick and Vanessa and I outside to dig for clay.

We spend the rest of the afternoon digging but don't end up with much to show for it. Dad nods vacantly when we show him the handful of clay we collect, and tells us we can keep at it tomorrow, that Wulf can join as well. Wulf stiffens at this, eyeing the three of us with disdain, like we all have an illness that's both disgusting and contagious.

It's nearing sunset by the time Herm returns. He appears as a bulky figure, his hands elongated and heavy. When he gets closer, I see it's because his hands are full of rabbit. He's carrying three by the ears, the large bodies dangling down to his calves. His laugh drifts to us from a distance. He raises his arms, triumphant. "Took me a while to find the traps," he says when he reaches us. "But I got them."

"Are those rabbits?" Nick asks, incredulous.

Herm lays them out on the ground for us to admire, arranging them carefully, almost lovingly, in a row. "I just had a feeling," he says.

All of us are roused into activity. Vanessa arranges wood in the firepit, and Wulf gets a fire going with flint. Dad and Herm skin the rabbits, careful to strip the skin neatly so we can use it for shoes or patching up blankets, and then Dad splits them open and pulls out the innards. Nick rummages around the shed for the barbecue sauce he was supposed to look for. I make a serviceable spit from plastic twine and tree branches.

"We'll get more use out of them if we boil them," Dad says, glancing at my work.

"Roasting's more celebratory," protests Herm.

"What are we celebrating?" asks Vanessa.

"Maybe *celebratory* is the wrong word," says Herm. "Festive. It's festive. Feels like we could all use some festivity, some kind of change."

Dad doesn't agree, but he doesn't argue, either, so we continue with our preparations. Once the rabbits are roasting, we take our places around the fire, and Wulf takes it upon himself to tend it with a long stick. There's a slight wind that tosses the small flames around, sometimes nearly extinguishing them, then whooshing them back up. Nick was right—it's too hot for a fire. The wind blows hot air in our faces, the heat violent, a shock every time. Sweat prickles uncomfortably at my hairline and under my armpits. My clothes, and even my skin, feel constricting, a muggy blanket of cells and cloth and fat. Vanessa keeps clearing her throat of the smoke. I close my eyes, wishing she would stop, but cutting off my vision just sharpens my hearing and amplifies the sound. Soon, the smell of roasting rabbit fills the air, but it's somehow unappealing—too rich, mixing unpleasantly with the milder scents of tree sap and smoke. The meat crackles and darkens, drops of fat falling into the fire and sizzling. Dad's eyes are fixed on them. He stares at the wasted nutrients accusatorily, like it's a task he's assigned himself.

When the rabbits are ready, Herm takes the spit off the fire and slides the meat onto plates with a pair of tongs, then hands a plate to everyone. He tosses the innards to Moonpie, who attacks them instantly. I dig my fingers into the side of the rabbit, flinching. The meat is slick with grease, painfully hot. Still, I continue picking at it with my fingers, as does everyone. Every chunk we tear off is larger, and we stuff them into our mouths greedily, as quickly as we can. It's as though we haven't eaten for days. As though all of us are trying hard to create a feeling of festivity and bounty, a celebration though the atmosphere feels tense and off kilter, a sense of a brewing sandstorm, of destruction about to arrive, harsh and inevitable. It's only when the plates are littered with more bone than meat that we slow down. I lick my fingers and pick off a final stringy piece of fat clinging to a bone.

"Georgia and Wulf used to hunt rabbits with bows and arrows around here," Dad says.

The words flit into the night air like insects.

"That's right," says Herm after a silent minute passes, turning to Wulf and me. "I remember. You even tried to make the bows and arrows yourselves. How long ago was that?"

"Years," says Dad. "Long, long years ago. When they were children."

I glance at Wulf, who tosses a bone with meat still on it to Moonpie. The conversation feels incongruous, forcing a nostalgia that's out of place between the darkening twilight and the angry orange coals and the nervous way Vanessa is turning her plate on her lap, adjusting it endlessly, looking into the trees, at us, back down at her plate. The words ricochet and echo uncomfortably in the air.

"Can't remember if you ever caught anything with them," says Herm.

"I don't remember either," I say quickly, hoping to end the conversation.

"We did," says Wulf, his voice cutting through the dark air. "Twice."

I study his face, trying to figure out if he really remembers or if he's just claiming that he does to rebuke me. His expression is impassive as ever.

"You two learned quickly that traps are more efficient," Dad says. "I haven't thought of that memory in years. It's funny how memories return to you in moments of peace." His eyes are half-closed, the lines on his face smoothed by the soft glow of the fire. Strangely, he looks more relaxed than it seems like he's been in weeks—maybe months, or years.

Vanessa laughs abruptly, the sound short and caustic.

"Yes?" Dad says, turning to her.

Vanessa shakes her head. "Nothing," she says. "Nothing, ignore me."

"No, please," says Dad, his voice a cold command.

"It's just, I'm not sure why you'd call this peaceful," Vanessa says finally.

Dad tips his head, then inclines it in acknowledgment. "Yes, I see what you mean. The term *peace* might not be the best one. We're at war with a foreign power, for all intents and purposes. We're watching an invader making incursions into our land and remain ignorant of the severity of the threat. Ignorance like that certainly isn't bliss. Uncertainty often causes more stress than the certainty that suffering is imminent. But even in times of war and uncertainty, one can retreat inwardly and find rest. Stress erodes our health, and our health is something we need to protect, now more than ever."

"Maybe it's easier when you're the one calling all the shots," says Vanessa.

"Calling all the shots?" says Dad, turning his face to her slowly.

"Is that not the right phrase for it? You're the one in control here, right? You decide what we do all day, where we live—everything. I'm— well, I'm just saying that I can imagine it's a lot easier to *find rest* when you've got that prerogative."

"Vanessa," Dad says, studying her, "if that's your idea of what control means, then I'm not sure what I can tell you. What kind of control do I have when everything I do is a defensive strategy? A response to an enemy, a threat? If that's what you consider control, then we have all the more proof that the control we feel we have over our lives is a grand illusion."

Vanessa smiles, thin lipped. "For some less than for others, maybe."

Wulf prods at the fire, and sparks fly out like a startled cloud of gnats.

"I'm just going to be honest right now," Vanessa says. "Look—it really doesn't make sense that we stay here. It's barely habitable for one person, much less six people, to live here permanently. That's just—it's just absurd. There's no reason we can't return to the settlement."

"No?" Dad stretches his face into a semblance of a smile. "You think I'm keeping us for the fun of it? That it's some whim of mine, rather than the safest choice for my family and you, who are now my wards? I'm no stranger to having to make difficult decisions. My decisions may not be easy for you to swallow—and trust me, this isn't my ideal situation—but I assure you, I've made them carefully."

"Sure, carefully," says Vanessa, running an agitated hand through her hair, stopping where it gets too tangled. "Sure, I can accept that. The thing is, though, you can still make a decision that doesn't make sense if you don't have all the information you need to make it."

"I take it that you believe I'm lacking some crucial information, then," Dad says, watching her.

"Look," Vanessa says again. "I may as well just—maybe I'm making a mistake, but maybe it's just better if I lay out all my cards on the table. It's that—let me start by saying—look, I didn't find you because I was searching for the settlement because of some history project. It wasn't an accident that I found you living there. You were exactly who I was looking for. I knew—more or less—exactly where to find you."

A jittery confusion floods the air. I feel something soft touch my ankle, and I start, but it's only Moonpie, drowsy and sedated from her meal, settling herself at my feet. I reach down to graze her fur with my fingers. Dad continues to watch Vanessa attentively, his eyes slightly narrowed, like he's reducing his field of vision so he can hear better.

"I knew all about you," Vanessa continues, holding Dad's gaze. "I knew all about how you got there. How you arrived nearly two decades ago with a group of people, sixteen of them, and you planned to start your own community in the desert, a place that everybody else in the world had abandoned. How you thought it was better than the Californian deadlands, where you came from, because at least there weren't fires every other month and at least the air wasn't so unbreathably bad. I know it worked for a while, living at the settlement, but then something happened, and people started getting sick. And you were all alone out there, and you didn't have the right medicine, you didn't even know what was wrong, and then people started dying. Even your wife died, and you were the leader, but you couldn't save them. I know that only seven of you survived, you, your kids, a couple others, Eduardo, Herm. And I know—I think I know—that that's why you're so upset right now. You're thinking of that terrible time, all that death. You think you're going to see it start happening again. But you're seeing patterns where there aren't any. You're imposing the past on a totally different situation. Nobody is dying here. Nobody is sick from any contamination. Eduardo isn't dead. The reason you can't get in touch with him—the reason he hasn't followed through with his part of the plan—is the same reason I know all this about you. He's the one who told me. He told me that he didn't want to be a part of it anymore, that he'd quietly defected, that he hadn't told you, but that you'd realize it eventually. That was months and months ago, back while I was still living in Phoenix, writing about the Domes, poking around and asking questions, and he was working—posing, I guess—as one of the guys building the nuclear plant. He kept to himself, and I knew how to get people who kept to themselves to start talking, so that's what we did when I'd travel up to the Domes. We got to talking. Eventually he told me about you, and how he'd been a true believer at first, but then, what you were doing, it stopped making sense. He'd met someone, he was thinking about getting married, about trying to move out of the deadlands—there was a lot on his mind, he wanted to talk through it with someone, and I—well, I'm pretty good at listening and asking the right questions. And I thought, sure, good for him for wanting to change his life around, but as for me—well, if the Domes made a good story, here was something ten times better. Someone fighting back, someone sabotaging them—a real drama. I couldn't pass that up. You see what I mean? That's why I'm here. That's why everything is fine, why Eduardo is fine, that's the missing information. That's why there's no reason for us to stay here."

When Vanessa stops, the silence we're plunged into is roaring. My ears ring, snippets of Vanessa's words jangling nonsensically. A group of people? Sixteen of them? I try to jam this story into the history that I know—the one Dad's always told us, the one where Dad drove Wulf and me away from the Californian deadlands after our mother died, where he found the settlement in the desert deadlands and we made a home there, just the three of us together. And then Vanessa's words—*all that death*. They repeat and overlap and shift and skip in my head, rearranging themselves. The two stories don't make sense together.

Herm is staring at the ground, the creases in his forehead deep canyons. Nick is looking around expectantly, like he's waiting for someone to explain everything to him or to start laughing, all of it a big joke. Wulf meets my eye, his open face asking a thousand questions, but I shake my head, distractedly look away, trying to untangle it all myself. Only Dad appears unfazed. His controlled demeanor coalesces everyone's attention.

"I'm not sure what your intention is," Dad says.

"My intention?" asks Vanessa.

"It's quite a story," says Dad.

"I was planning on changing your names, all the personal details, when I wrote your story. I was always going to make sure you stayed anonymous, to—"

"Do you expect me to believe that Eduardo told you all this? It's a good story. Well thought out. I'll credit you that. But what's the motive? What reason would Eduardo supposedly have for telling you this story? Did you have a chance to think that up?"

"I didn't think up anything," Vanessa says emphatically. "I'm telling the truth. From what Eduardo told me, I think he started to see what you were doing in a different light—not as something noble, a fight between a big Goliath and a little David, but as your personal cosmic battle against what had happened all those years ago, when all those people died and nobody quite knew how or why. A kind of retribution. A homing in on a target and channeling all your blame on people that had nothing to do with it. At least, that's what it started sounding like to me. You'd always felt guilty for what happened all those years ago, Eduardo told me. I think maybe you've convinced yourself that this would be your atonement, the punishment you'd dole out to make someone else pay. For a while, Eduardo was convinced that it all made sense, your idealism about how the world should fix its problems and how it shouldn't, your motivations. But then, slowly he started to see it differently. And when he did—well, that's when he decided to cut off contact."

For a brief moment, it seems like some of Dad's composure is threatening to crumble. But perhaps it's a trick of the light, the orange glow in the dark shifting the shadows on his face. A flicker of fire later, his expression is unreadable again.

"Inventive," he says. "I have to give you that, it's a creative telling."

"Okay," says Vanessa. "I realize I might not be accurate in reading your motivations. And maybe some of the story from Eduardo I got isn't true either. I can't vouch for all the details. Maybe there was some misremembering or misinterpretation. Your motives—whatever they were or weren't—aren't the reason I'm bringing all this up. The point is, Eduardo is *fine*. Alive and well. There's no question about that. The reason you haven't heard from him isn't because he's dead from some contamination that's also somehow threatening us. *We're* fine to go back to the settlement."

"Yes, you've made your position on that clear," Dad says icily. He turns to Herm, who's still looking at the ground. "Herm? What do you think?"

"Hmm?" says Herm, lifting his gaze, peering at Dad. "Can't picture Eduardo defecting."

"Do you think it's outside the realm of possibility?"

"No, not exactly. I suppose it would explain things."

Dad turns to Vanessa. "If we're to accept that Eduardo told you the location of our settlement—whatever his reasons were, however you wheedled it out of him—then I take it you're very familiar with the territory. You likely had the map around the settlement all memorized. You could have left any time you liked, if you felt the impulse and were inclined to walk. You were never trapped, were you, Vanessa? Every day, back at the settlement, you were making a conscious choice to stay."

"Well—right—yes," says Vanessa. "I came for a reason. On purpose."

"Whereas here, you don't have the benefit of that territorial aware-ness. Here, you really are trapped. You couldn't find your way home if you wanted to. Certainly not without a great deal of risk. I believe we've hit on the real reason you've been so agitated."

"I guess it's obvious that I've been uneasy," Vanessa says, her gaze fixed on Dad.

"And you'd like us to return to a location you're intimately familiar with? So you have the option of leaving when you'd like? So you can leave and—what?—write about me? Clue the authorities in on my loca-tion? Sell my story and profit at my expense?"

"No," Vanessa says quickly. "I told you, I wasn't going to tell anyone the details they'd need to find you. If I'd wanted to tell the authorities, I'd have told them already. If that was my intent, I wouldn't have come here in the first place. I'm not interested in anything like that. That's got to be obvious to you. And the book—look, I'm not thinking about any of that now. It doesn't matter to me anymore. Trust me. I won't—I don't have to write anything."

"You'd like us to trust you?"

"Please. Yes."

The fire crackles and spits, sending a shower of sparks into the dark air. The hum of cicadas is beginning to drone from the trees, and occasionally we hear the soft, melancholy cooing of a mourning dove, the scuttle of a lizard or rodent, and Moonpie starts up and barks, ears pinned back, before settling at my feet again. Everyone's face is a ghoulish shadow. Dad rubs his eyes, the firelight deepening the wrinkles in his face.

"You've given me a lot to think about, Vanessa," he says.

"Does that mean you're thinking about going back?"

"I haven't come to any conclusions yet."

Vanessa draws a breath. Her pupils are dilated into large orbs in the dark.

"Is she lying?" Wulf says suddenly. "About the people?"

There's a pause, an uncertain moment of silence, and then Dad stands. "It's time we started clearing up," he says. "I think we've all had enough festivity."

We stamp out the fire, and I give the plates to Moonpie to lick clean. Nick excuses himself, lifting his hand and shaking his head when Vanessa opens her mouth to say something to him. Dad and Herm retreat into the cabin, speaking in low tones. It seems like Wulf is about to follow, but then instead he turns to Vanessa, who's crouching on the ground, rubbing Moonpie's belly, her eyes following Nick as he zips up his tent.

"Are you lying?" Wulf asks her. His face is stonily set, his eyes blazing.

"Am I—" Vanessa's hand stills. She squints up at Wulf.

"The people you said who died," Wulf says. "About what happened."

Vanessa glances at the cabin. She stands up and lifts a hand like she's about to touch her face or wave, and then drops it. "All I know is what Eduardo told me," she says. "There were some other people, a few families. Isaac's wife—your mother—you two, and Eduardo, and Herm. And then a lot of them—well, yes, they died. That's what Eduardo told me. He wasn't too clear about the details. It seemed like nobody was really sure what happened. Everyone just started getting really sick and dying. Apparently your Dad took it hard and blamed himself."

Wulf studies her. "You're lying," he says finally. "Dad would have said it was true if it was."

"He never denied it," says Vanessa.

"He will. And he wouldn't have."

"Wouldn't have—?"

"He wouldn't have killed anyone like you said."

"No," Vanessa says, looking startled. "I didn't say he *killed* anyone. Eduardo just told me he blamed himself. That doesn't mean I'm saying it was actually his fault. It's a normal thing, blaming yourself, even when you shouldn't. Of course, a person, even a person in charge, can't really be responsible for the well-being of others, not when an accident happens."

Wulf shakes his head heatedly. "Dad wouldn't make a mistake like that. He studies everything before he does anything. He's careful."

"Accidents happen," Vanessa says. "They happen to everyone."

I'm running through my memories, trying to see if what Vanessa is saying could possibly fit, if I can add and overlay the narrative and still have all I know make sense. A handful of images bobs up in my mind, flashes of movement with people I don't recognize, cooking over a fire, hot and dusty air—and they settle into place now, clicking into Vanessa's story unsettlingly well. And then, suddenly, I think of the bone I brought in my backpack, of the steel drum Nick and I found full of them. A prickly tingling alights on my neck, and then a light-headedness. The pieces connect, and I know it has to be one of theirs, the bone. That the bones we found were those of the people who died in, as Vanessa called it, the early days of Dad's settlement.

"She's lying," Wulf says loudly, his voice verging on hysterical.

"Wulf," I say, distracted by my own thoughts. "Calm down."

"You believe her?"

"I don't know what I—I don't know why she'd make it up."

"To make Dad look bad! To make us side with her and stop listening to Dad. So she can get what she wants from us, whatever she's trying to get."

"I'm not trying to get anything from you," Vanessa says. "Trust me."

"I'm not going to trust you!" Wulf says like it's the most ridiculous thing he's ever heard.

"Wulf, calm down," I say again, my voice firmer.

He looks like a cornered dog between me and Vanessa, his eyes roving between us, growing wider and wilder the further we get into the conversation. "You believe her," he says. "You're siding with her against Dad."

"I'm not siding with anyone," I say evasively. "She's just telling us what she heard."

Wulf looks me straight in the eyes with an expression that's sharp and teary, overflowing with hate. "She's just telling us what she heard," he repeats in an attempt to mock me, but his voice wobbles pitifully. Then he stalks into the long, dim shadows of the cacti and brush and trees.

"I probably shouldn't have said anything," says Vanessa, staring after him.

"You shouldn't have come," I say, my voice quiet, the dark swallowing it.

Vanessa is silent for a moment, her arms hugged around her rib cage. "You're right," she says finally. "But here I am now. Here we are, with things the way they are now, and I'm not sure what any of us are going to do about it."

18

I'm surprised to be included in the meeting Dad convenes the next morning. The landscape is still cool and blue and quiet when Wulf comes to get me, the air scented with smoke and animal fat, the morning barely starting to stumble out of dreaming. There's a dangerous stillness in the air, broken only by the distant, inconsolable coos of mourning doves and the sound of our own feet crunching the silty ground as Wulf silently leads me to the cabin.

Dad and Herm are sitting around the coffee table, and Wulf reclaims his place on a chair between them. Dad motions me to the unoccupied armchair, and I sit down obediently, making us the four points of a misshapen square. Wulf picks at a wooden splinter on his seat. Herm is sitting with his hands folded in his lap, his eyes directed serenely at the ceiling.

"Georgia," Dad says, nodding. "Thank you for joining us. I wanted to address the information Vanessa brought to light yesterday and to make sure that all of us are on the same page. In that regard, I'd like you to know that, after considerable discussion, Herm and I have come to believe that what Vanessa informed us about Eduardo—namely, that he defected—is likely true. It aligns with the facts we have. It furnishes an explanation for those facts that we don't have. What I am less certain about is why Vanessa would provide an alternative history of our time at the settlement. I'm struggling to think of a reason why she would supply it herself if she knew it to be untrue, knowing the fabrication would discredit her. That leaves us with the explanation that Eduardo furnished the fabrications himself. But why? In some misguided attempt to lead her off his trail? Is his mental agility declining? Is confusion and decreased cognitive ability perhaps a symptom of the same malady we've been seeing kill the birds and sicken Nick? I'd like to know what you think. Whether there's anything you've picked up on in your interactions with Vanessa that might bring us closer to an answer."

It feels like a test, like it always does with Dad. Wulf and Herm watch me as I deliberate how to answer. Maybe they've already taken their turns.

"So it isn't true?" I ask. "What Vanessa said about people dying at the settlement?"

I don't know what impels me to say it. It's as though my tongue has taken on a mind of its own, flippantly asking a question I know very well is the wrong one.

Dad gives me a hard look. "True? I would have thought you of all people wouldn't have doubts about that, Georgia. You're old enough to remember that it's always been me, you, and Wulf at the settlement." Marveling at myself, at what my body is seemingly doing by itself, I shake my head. "No?" says Dad, his voice dangerous.

"I don't remember everything," I say.

"She believes her," says Wulf.

"What's that, Wulf?" Dad turns to him.

"She believes what Vanessa said."

Dad frowns at me. "Is this true?"

"She's brainwashed," Wulf says.

"I never said that," I say. "I didn't say I believed or didn't believe anyone."

"I can't say that I'm not disappointed, Georgia," Dad says.

"I don't believe her," I say, but even I can hear how false this sounds.

Dad's gaze sweeps away from me, toward Wulf and Herm. "We still don't have conclusive proof about the contamination," he says. "I admit, I may have been hasty in assuming that Eduardo was dead, and deciding his death was linked to it. But we shouldn't let that cloud the other proof, the other troubling indicators, that we have of something gone amiss. The illness Nick is suffering, the deaths of animals around the settlement. Possibly Eduardo's confused state when speaking with Vanessa. There are still investigations to be done. We shouldn't become discouraged because we haven't found the link and source yet."

Wulf and Herm nod, and my heart sinks.

He's lying, I think experimentally, thinking it for the first time so plainly. It's a cold and lonely thought, unmooring me. It's like being awash in a sea map-less, a rope tying me to a ship cut away. Dad is talking about the tasks ahead of us, the chores we left undone last night that we ought to do today. "A heavy day," he says, which makes me look up.

Vanessa and Nick are up by the time the four of us file out of the cabin. Dad tells everyone that they're on their own for breakfast, and then doles out everyone's responsibilities for the morning. It looks like Vanessa is about to ask a question, but Dad turns on his heel and retreats into the cabin, followed silently by Herm.

Wulf and I are tasked with harvesting the water from the water machine. I hold the jars while Wulf works the pump, and we watch thin streams of clean water trickle out until the jar is full. I set it aside and screw the lid off another. We repeat the process until we have two full jars and a small amount of water in a third one. Wulf works the pump harder, but the water comes out reluctantly, the pump sputtering and spitting tiny droplets of water onto his hands. He bends his head down to peer into the machine. "It's clogged," he mutters, sticking a finger in the pump.

"Can I help?" I ask.

"No," Wulf says irritably.

He opens the lid and studies the machinery, then lifts up a lever, and I hear a gurgling sound. Wulf lets go and fiddles with a different component. I let my gaze wander to Dad and Herm climbing down a wooden ladder from the low roof of the cabin after adjusting the satellite again. Vanessa and Nick are making a pile of clean empty cans. They're supposed to cut them apart and flatten them into sheets of metal with a hammer that's apparently somewhere in the shed.

Wulf makes a frustrated sound as he tugs a part that must be stuck inside the machine.

"Can I try?" I ask. "Maybe if I hold—"

"I got it," he says.

"Wulf, if you would just let me—"

"I don't need your help," he snaps.

"Why not?" I ask, exasperated.

Wulf won't meet my gaze. "Because you'll ruin it," he says.

I inhale deeply and let out my breath. "What can I do?" I ask.

"Say you don't believe it," he says. "Say you're not brainwashed by them."

"I'm not brainwashed by them."

"You're not even trying," says Wulf, staring at the machine hard.

"I am trying," I say after a pause. "I really am."

Wulf goes quiet, and for a moment—the briefest moment—I think that maybe he heard the apology in my words and maybe—maybe— that he even accepted it.

"Dad has to know," Wulf says.

"Know what?" My pulse quickens, my muscles tensing, alert.

"He has to know how they brainwashed you."

"I'm not sure what you're saying."

We hear a tinny crash and both turn to see Vanessa and Nick's pile of cans tumble down. Cans roll across the dirt, and Moonpie, who's been chewing on ashy rabbit bones, starts barking and darts to chase them. Nick stops one with his foot. Dad and Herm appear from around the back of the cabin to see what's happening. "It's fine!" Vanessa calls.

Wulf snatches the two full jars, like he's worried I'm going to take them away from him, and starts walking rapidly over to Dad. I pick up the remaining jar nonsensically and follow him. Wulf's movements are jumpy and constricted. He's staring at Dad, whose attention is occupied by the trees now, maybe thinking about cutting some down for lumber, maybe thinking of a route to take to do more investigating of the contamination. It takes him a moment to notice Wulf standing in front of him, Wulf, whose body is tight as a cord now, so tense I can feel the nervous energy emanating from him like a heat wave.

"Yes, Wulf?" asks Dad. "Is there something you need?"

Wulf swallows, his small Adam's apple moving like a stone.

"Georgia—" he says, and it's like someone hits me in the stomach, all my breath leaving me at once. Wulf's mouth moves and words come out of it, but my ears are ringing too loudly to hear all of them. Wulf says Nick's name like he's spitting out a piece of rancid meat.

I try to draw another breath, but it's so small, I feel like I'm starting to suffocate, and the world around me, the cabin and the shed, everyone else standing around, spins and blurs, the edges turning dark. I dig my toes into my shoes, clench my hands into fists, urge my blood to move quicker to my head.

"I saw them," I hear Wulf say.

I think: if I could just explain. But what's there to explain? What can I say about a heat-exhausted blur unstuck from the everyday, hours of stillness and two bodies touching, overlaid confusedly with dirt and death, a day floating like a mirage just beyond the reach of time and space. What can I say about how it had nothing to do with anything here and now—nothing to do with anything—how it would be impossible to say anything about it, to feel the words move against my tongue and teeth here, to spit them out into this air.

I open my mouth to draw in a breath.

But Dad isn't expecting me to say anything. He's looking at Nick, whose eyebrows are tipped down, who's frozen in the jaunty way he was standing, his head and shoulder tilted stiffly to the side. He shifts his weight from one foot to another. His mouth stretches across his face thinly, maybe to smooth out the fear from his face.

"Is what my son saying true," Dad says, his voice dangerously quiet.

"He's a kid," Nick says. "He doesn't understand whatever he saw."

"In what world," Dad says in the same voice, "did you think that this would end well for you?"

Nick is silent for a moment, his face strained, like he's debating his options, gambling on which route is best to go. "All right," he says. "All right. We can talk through this, man to man. Look, I realize you might be upset—I get that parents are protective of their children—but, let's be honest, what did you expect?" He motions to me like I'm a deer skull, the remains of a jackrabbit, an object to point to and discuss. "She's not a kid anymore. Did you expect her to live in your hellish Garden of Eden bubble forever? Or were you planning on propagating your own society here with the three of you? That's what would be abnormal. There's nothing wrong with what we did, when you put it in perspective."

Dad looks like someone's spit on his face, an unthinkable affront. His skin reddening so furiously that it's starting to look sunburned.

"How dare you," he manages to say. "How dare you. Get out of my sight."

"Look, I'll stay away from her," Nick says magnanimously.

"You'll stay—" Dad repeats in disbelief.

Nick laughs, a nervy, rigid sound.

"You'll leave," says Dad.

"What?" says Nick.

Dad points into the trees, his finger held like a weapon. "You'll walk away from here, and you'll keep walking until you reach the ends of the earth or until you die from exhaustion or dehydration. You'll walk to where none of us will ever see you again."

Nick shakes his head, smiling incredulously. "I'm not going to do that," he says.

"I'm not giving you a choice," Dad says, the words dangerously quiet.

"And what if I don't do it? What are you going to do?" Nick's voice is taunting, his smile is plastered on his face, and at first it seems like

Dad is going to respond, his face opening and shifting, moving through a series of strange changes. Then he reaches into his back pocket, a flash of silver in the sun, and suddenly I see everything that's going to happen.

I see it all play out before my eyes before it even starts, as though time jumps forward and then leaps back again. Nick's expression crumpling to confusion, his hands lifting and his fingers splayed out like starfish. Dad tensing his body, with both hands on the gun so he can hold it steady. I close my eyes to wipe the images from my mind, to erase them from coming true, and then the sound comes, an explosion louder than monsoon lightning. A thud, an unearthly cry, a scream, and then breathing, rapid and shallow—mine. There's a yelp and an animal whine.

I open my eyes, clinging to the hope that it all happened in my head after all, but that just makes the shock worse, the sight so physical that my stomach buckles, threatening to retch. Nick's body is lying in a pool of blood blooming from his chest, coloring his shirt redder and redder. His face is frozen with creases on his forehead, his eyes open and empty.

Vanessa's hands are plastered to her mouth. She seems unable to look away from Nick's body, unable to move at all. Wulf and Herm are immobile, too, their gazes unreadable, roving from Nick's body to Dad, who's still holding the gun with both hands, staring at it.

"Jesus Christ," Herm says.

"He was weak," Dad says, his voice breathy and confused, not sounding like him at all. His face is someone else's, a grotesque mask shape-shifting between shock and fear and rage. "He wasn't going to make it anyway."

A taut silence hangs in the air. A hot breeze, muffling sound, breathing in our ears, and sweeping hair across our faces. Vanessa wraps her arms tight around her rib cage to control her shaking, but her body continues to jerk uncontrollably. Moonpie is cowering at Wulf's feet, whimpering, and Wulf is staring at Nick's body, his eyes making tiny movements from hand to shoulder to neck to chest and feet and back over again, like he's trying to make sense of a senseless shape.

Dad breathes out a shaky breath. He wipes sweat off his forehead, off the back of his neck, and his hand comes off glistening, shaking. As we watch in silence, he walks up to Nick's body, crouches down to touch his wrist, stands back up again.

"It's for the best," he says in between heavy breaths. "We'll dig a grave."

"I'll get a fire going," Herm says.

Dad nods, exhaling slowly. "Not too close to the cabin," he says.

"The grave either," says Herm.

"No," says Dad. "We'll find a place."

He procures shovels from the shed, all different sizes. Mine is child sized, half the length of my arm. The handle is rusty, rubbing red-orange onto my skin. He leads us near the nopal field in the trees, where the earth is more giving, kneaded by the roots of hearty plants.

We follow his instructions wordlessly, without protest. It's like we're moving through a dream or underwater, where we're faceless, emotionless automatons. With Nick's body out of sight, it's easier to ignore what we're digging. Incomprehensible smoke drifts toward us from the direction of the cabin, soot settling on our skin, mixing with dirt and sweat. My throat clogs with dust, and I spit, the saliva a dark, evil-looking glob. Vanessa gags, her eyes watering. She steps to the side and gags again and again, heaving dryly. It's an awful sound, guttural and animal. Dad circles the pit, examining it. "It's wide enough," he tells us. "Now we just have to dig deeper."

We push our shovels into the dirt, and the pit deepens little by little. The dirt is packed together tightly, more stone than soil. I don't feel any hunger although we dig for hours, I don't feel any pain although I watch blisters bubbling up on my palms. We pant from the effort, a marathon of repeated motions, but nobody takes a break. When I pause to wipe my face, I look up and see a column of black smoke billowing into the sky from the cabin. Is it on fire? I wonder briefly, in confusion, then let the thought go. We dig and dig, wedging out small stones. Finally, Dad determines that the pit is deep enough. We stop our digging one by one and step back so Dad can pace around it again. He nods his head in confirmation, then leads us back to the cabin. The sky is dimming, shadows elongating. Somehow, an entire day has passed.

It's just before we reach the clearing that I make sense of the smoke and the terrible smell, an evil smell not quite like burning meat, not quite like burning rubber. It arrives all of a sudden, this understanding, and I nearly stop short, my legs ready to refuse to take another step. The trees and shrubs distort and blur, trembling frantically. A staggering wave of unreality, a dark sense that something is very, very wrong, sweeps through my body.

And somehow I keep walking, and somehow we emerge from the trees to the clearing, and then we see the pyre. The fire gone now, glowing coals and gray ash, Nick's bones sticking out at angles, dissonant with reality. Herm is picking them out one by one with tongs. He deposits them carefully in a blue plastic tub that must be from the shed. Moonpie keeps trying to stick her nose in the ash and bones, and Herm keeps having to block her with his arm. My mind leaps to the bone in my backpack, to the treks into the desert with Nick. The digging now, the digging then. The smoke in the air is so thick, that terrible smell. I can barely breathe. Vanessa is staring uncomprehendingly as Herm's hand moves methodically between the tub and the pyre.

Dad leads us to the storage shed, where we stash our shovels. He disappears into the cabin for some minutes, and Vanessa, Wulf, and I wait outside the shed, as though we're unable to do anything without clear instructions from Dad. We watch him exit the cabin and crouch beside Herm. They finish piling Nick's bones into the blue tub. When they're done, Dad hoists the tub under his arm. They trek back into the trees, and we watch mutely, knowing not to follow them. After a while, Wulf squats on the ground, poking at the dirt with a twig, and then Vanessa and I sit on the ground as well. We wait and wait, and the blue dusk becomes darkness. The air is still hard to breathe, thick with smoke, grayish. Finally, Dad and Herm return. They pass us as they put away the shovels in the shed, and we stand up when they emerge. Dad stares up at the sky, a hazy dark with a pale half-moon imprinted on it.

"We'd all benefit from some sleep," he says.

Herm says: "Feels a little early to—"

"We're going to try," Dad snaps, his calm breaking. He rubs his temples. "I think we're all more tired than we think," he says, quieter. "We'll eat a little food, and then we'll all go to bed."

Herm clears his throat. "I'll heat something up on the hot plate," he says.

Dad claps a hand on Wulf's shoulder. "It's good you told me, son," he says. "I don't want you to think it wasn't the right thing to do." Wulf shudders. He lifts his head, and I see that his eyes are bleary and red. Dad's trying to comfort him, I realize.

Anger burns at the back of my throat, numbness clearing and volition returning, the knowledge that Dad hasn't looked at me once flooding my body with a painful jolt. It's as though I've been wiped from existence, diminished beyond notice, as though a soundproof curtain has dropped and I've been ensconced behind it. There's nothing to say from behind it, no way to crawl out from under it, nothing left for me here. An aching emptiness, stretching impossibly into the future. I know, suddenly, that I can't stay here. My mind flits to the desert, to Herm's car, the keys gone, to Herm's maps and what's around us. Of walking, and where, and how to walk away without being followed. Of how to stall for time, to think.

"I'll get the water," I say.

"Good, good," Herm says distractedly.

I gather cups, a pitcher, a spoon, and a can of syrupy peaches from the shed, my arms precariously full, the bounty threatening to topple over. I fill the pitcher with the water Wulf and I harvested earlier, open the can with my pocketknife, and empty the peaches into the water. Methodically, I mash the peaches with a spoon until they turn into a murky sludge. A plan—its edges vague and soft, the parts cobbling together slowly—has started forming in my head.

I avoid looking at the cabin as I walk to Vanessa's tent. I don't check if the door is open or if anyone's looking out a window, for fear I'll stop myself. Vanessa's sleeping bag is scrunched in the back corner of the tent, her backpack underneath it. I rifle through empty jars, a hat, a shirt, a tube of sunscreen squeezed flat. And then I find what I'm looking for: a small pouch with a fat red cross printed on the side. Inside are Band-Aids, yellowing gauze, numerous small bottles. I try to remember what the bottle I'm looking for looks like, but the image is hazy in my head, too confused with memories of Nick and Vanessa, of blue pills and a deep sleep. The tiny letters on the labels blur into a crosshatch. I open bottles and shake pills into my hand, tip them back into their bottles hastily. Finally, I find the blue ones—I count five of them left—and I don't know whether this is too few or too many, but the number is as good as any guess I'd make.

I try to crush them in my hand first, but they're too hard, not chalky like I thought. I pour them onto the ground and pull out my pocketknife to try pounding them with the handle. Small pieces and shards chip off. One of the pills breaks clean in half. I bang the knife down over and over again, keeping my hand cupped around the pills so the pieces don't skitter away.

Time is slipping away from me, and my heart is beating faster. The powder I've made is like coarse sand. In a rush of thought, I consider continuing to pound the pills with the knife, looking for a mortar and pestle, even chewing them quick and spitting them out into my hand. But too many minutes have gone by already. The gravelly texture will have to be good enough. I sweep the powder into my palm and crawl back out of the tent.

By the shed, I dole out the peach water into five cups. Then I pour the blue powder into three of them and stir. Some of the larger pieces cling to the sides, leaving sticky blue streaks down the sides. I stir more rapidly, blending until I can't see anything but murky liquid. When I gather them in my arms to carry, I'm careful to remember which two are only flavored water, which three are meant for Dad and Wulf and Herm.

Everyone is sitting around the coffee table when I come in. Plates of beans are arranged on the small table in front of them, but nobody is eating, they're just staring forlornly at the food or elsewhere. My entrance seems to jolt them into motion—at least Dad and Wulf move their plates to their laps, and Wulf picks up his fork. They don't acknowledge me as I hand out the cups, trying to keep my hand steady so the water doesn't spill. Wulf gulps down half of his right away, and I look away because something indescribably painful—something like regret and grief and horror, something I know I have to stifle before it stops me—stabs me in the chest. Dad places his cup on the table. Vanessa cradles hers in her lap, staring blankly ahead. It's only Herm who looks alert, watching my movements carefully. His eyes move over the surface of the liquid, a frown developing on his face.

"Peaches?" he asks.

"There wasn't enough water," I say, my breath catching.

"Why'd you mash them up?"

I shake my head and shrug, feeling heat on my face. "I don't know," I say.

"We're all tired," Dad says vaguely.

Herm doesn't respond. He peers into the cup again, then at the others, then at me again, his look questioning. Finally, he seems to make a decision. With a strange, determined expression, like he's about to plunge into a lake of boiling water, he throws the cup back and drinks. His throat moves decisively, swallowing large gulps. I suddenly want to cry, to apologize or thank him. He sets the cup down quietly, studiously avoiding my gaze.

I spoon beans into my mouth without tasting them. Dad's cup sits untouched on the table, and I try not to look at it, but I can't help it. It's where my gaze keeps returning. Spoons clatter against bowls and plates. Someone's chair scrapes against the floor. At one point, it occurs to me confusedly that we're missing Nick, that we should have waited for him before eating, that he's sleeping and someone should have called him from his tent—and then the day's events filter back in horrific flashes of memories. Nausea creeps from my stomach to my throat, and I swallow hard, willing it away. Finally, when everyone has eaten all they could or given up, Dad lifts his cup to his lips. I stare openly, my eyes fixed on him, following his every movement. He swallows, and then his face changes slightly. He presses his lips together.

"Gritty," he says, and every muscle in my body freezes. He knows what I've done, I think numbly; he's realized everything. But then he gulps the rest of the water down. He says: "Tomorrow, we'll have to take a look at that water machine again."

19

Vanessa is awake when I show up at her tent hours later. Everyone else has gone to sleep, sure to sleep deeply, unless I've made a mistake. Everything that could have gone wrong runs through my head—the wrong pills, the wrong amount, the medicine not working in one of them for whatever quirk of chemistry. Dad bursting out of the cabin to stop us. The fallout, never having a chance to leave again. Vanessa watches me unzip the tent flap. Her body remains supine when I stick my head in, only her eyes moving—watching me, closing, flashing open again, and blinking like she's having trouble with her vision. "Vanessa?" I say. "Come on, we're leaving."

Vanessa shakes her head. "You all go ahead," she says faintly.

"No, just us two. Come on, get up. I've packed us food and water."

Vanessa casts her eyes up, staring at the ceiling of the tent.

"Vanessa," I say again, the word so sharp it startles even me.

She slips out of her sleeping bag without any further protest. I tell her what to do, and she does exactly what I say. She packs her backpack, changes her clothes and puts on her shoes, zips her tent closed behind her. We're ready to leave within minutes. There's no light or sound coming from the cabin. A few times, I think I see movement out of the corner of my eye, a shifting dark shadow in the window, and my breath catches. It takes all the willpower I can muster to avoid looking in its direction.

Moonpie is sleeping huddled against Wulf's tent. I walk up to her slowly, crouch down, and wake her up with a scratch behind her ears. Her paws twitch, and then she opens her eyes and scrambles up eagerly. I stroke her back, urging her to stay silent, and strain to listen for any sound coming from the tent. For a split second, I think I hear a swishing sound, the synthetic fabric of a sleeping bag, but it's gone as soon as I try to listen harder.

I take off my backpack and pull out the book inside, then flip to the end and tear out one of the blank pages. Balancing the book on my knee as a writing surface, I write in shaky, thin letters: *Taking Moonpie. I'll send her back to you. If you ever want to follow, she'll know where to find me.* The words spill out without me thinking about them, forming sentences that surprise me. I stare at them, unsure of whether I should crumple up the paper and start again. I meant to write an apology. Instead, I've ended up with a promise that's unreasonable, an absurd suggestion that would only make Wulf mad.

Moonpie barks twice, the sound exploding in the quiet night. I flinch, and suddenly I'm aware of Vanessa standing over my shoulder, watching me. Hastily, I fold the paper up and slip it inside one of Wulf's boots, which are lined up neatly beside the tent. I stand up and put my backpack on, my movements slow and measured so Moonpie doesn't bark again.

"It's okay," I say to Vanessa, trying to sound surer than I feel. "They won't wake up."

Vanessa glances at the cabin, and, instinctually, my gaze follows hers. The windows are dark and empty. I lead us away from the tents and then exhale unsteadily, realizing I've been holding my breath.

"Do you remember the way to the settlement?" I ask her.

Vanessa shakes her head.

"That's okay," I say, and try to believe it.

"Do you know it?" Vanessa asks, her voice vague, too distant to be troubled.

"No. Dad always takes us a different way. But I can figure it out. Moonpie will help."

At the sound of her name, Moonpie's ears perk up. She looks up at me expectantly.

"We're going home," I tell her. "To the settlement. Can you take us?" She sniffs at my shoes, bites my left toe experimentally to check if we're playing. "Come on," I say, my voice soft, pleading. "You remember how to get to the settlement." But Moonpie just stares at me with her round, dark eyes, waiting for me to give her food or throw a stick for her to fetch, eager and unsure of what she's supposed to do next. "Okay," I say, working hard to keep my voice steady. "That's okay. We'll try again when we're closer. Let's just start backtracking," I say, turning to Vanessa. "I remember the direction we came from. Moonpie's instincts will kick in later."

Vanessa stares into the trees, her expression vacant.

"Come on, Moonpie," I say.

Moonpie barks enthusiastically. Vanessa doesn't look in the direction of where we buried Nick's bones, and I don't look back at the cabin. I only glance back once toward the clearing when I know we're too far to see anything through the trees but the dark, spindly shapes of desert vegetation.

It's easy, at first, to know that we're walking in the right direction. The dirt and trees, the cacti—even in the dark, they're all familiar shapes. But it isn't long before I start to second-guess myself. The moonlight casts elongated shadows, confusing my memory of a cluster of juniper trees, transforming the mountains up ahead. And then I'll recognize a pyramid-like pile of red boulders, the certain way a group of similar trees curves, and I'll be buoyed up, certain again that we're walking the right way. Twice, Moonpie plants her paws in the dirt, glancing between us and a slightly different route through the trees, only moving when we reorient ourselves to where she thinks we ought to go. It jangles my nerves, how quickly, how easily we could take a wrong turn. I quicken my pace to expend my nervous energy.

Clouds move slowly over the moon. My eyes adjust to the dimmer light. Moonpie lurches at a bush, and a bird explodes into flight from the branches.

When it's nearing dawn, Vanessa and I stop for the first time to rest. We peel off our backpacks and sit on the ground in the thin, watery light. We drink water, splitting a jar between us. Vanessa refuses the rabbit jerky I offer, and I don't have an appetite for it either. I toss the two pieces to Moonpie, who tears into them, growling. The sun peeks over the mountains, rubbing away the last of the night's darkness. In the pinkish light, the air is already hot.

"Should we sleep?" Vanessa asks, staring at the mountains.

"I think we should keep walking," I say.

Vanessa nods. "Okay," she says, standing.

The landscape gets drier as we walk, sparser and more desertlike as we walk to a lower elevation. The trees change from pines to an occasional juniper or stunted mesquite, scattered clumps of creosote and sage. The terrain flattens out slightly, and we can see ahead of us for miles, up to the craggy range of mountains. I'm no longer sure we're walking the same way we came, but Moonpie trots confidently ahead of us, and it's all I can do to trust her. The day's light is established now, unyielding. Vanessa's pace starts to lag. She pushes her hair back, the strands clotted with sweat, and rubs her face with her hands.

"It doesn't feel real," she says, her voice muffled. "How are we doing this?"

I don't answer because the same question has been rattling around my head. How is it that we're moving? Putting one foot in front of the other? We should be immobilized, measuring time by the sun blazing east to west, specks of birds swooping in and out of the turquoise sky, ants crawling the length of our bodies. Instead, impossibly, we're walking.

"But it really happened, didn't it?" Vanessa says, as though in response to my thoughts. An animal sound escapes her throat, a sob caught and held in. "Oh god," she says, her voice a frantic wail, an unsettling tone I've never heard before. "I didn't even see where they buried his bones. I'll never see the place they buried them. I can't believe that I'll never see him again."

I look over and see that her face is wet. She doesn't blink or wipe her eyes, just takes a few audible breaths, seeming to collect herself.

We walk until the sun reaches its peak at noon. The heat is punishing, terrible. We scramble over sandstone boulders, maneuver around the scrub oak growing through the cracks, and find a patch of ground in the shade of a large rock sticking up like a tower. When we set up the tarp and I lie down under it, I'm surprised to realize that I'm exhausted. My muscles limp, my breathing labored. My eyes sticky and painful. Somehow, I hadn't felt it before. I'm asleep almost instantly, and then I'm running through a series of scalding dreams that scramble yesterday's events and replay them, trapping me in a loop that won't let me forget what's happened. I sleep through the day without waking, emerging from my dreams only when it's dark again. A nightmare? I wonder for the briefest moment, and then I feel the rocks poking into my shoulder blades, the stiffness in my legs from walking all night. Vanessa sits up beside me. Maybe she's just woken up, too, or maybe's she's already been awake, lying quietly through the day. I don't ask her. We pack up the tarp, drink a jar of water, and then start our trek again.

Moonpie stays close to our feet, a quiet shadow. She glances up at me periodically. Even in the darkness, I can see that the desert is turning unfamiliar for all of us. The mountains towering in the distance seem suddenly flatter, rounded. The cacti are few, replaced by dry grasses and shrubs poking through the rock and dirt. I can't shake the terrible feeling that we're going the wrong way, but what can I do? Moonpie, too, seems to have lost her sense of direction. Maybe we've gone so far astray that there's nothing she can do to help us.

When Vanessa and I stop for a few rationed sips of water—just one jar left now—I crouch down and hold my backpack to Moonpie's nose. "Come on," I murmur. "Take us there." Moonpie sticks her nose inside, rooting around for food. I dump the backpack's contents onto the ground and start offering her every object inside that I brought from the settlement—my second shirt, matches, the book, rabbit jerky wrapped in paper. "You know this smell," I murmur, holding the book up to her nose. "You remember."

"You think she'll smell the settlement on it?" Vanessa asks, watching.

"It was just an idea," I say, grimacing when Moonpie walks away from me to sniff at a small hole in the dirt. I start shoving the items back into the backpack.

"That's where we're going?" asks Vanessa.

I look up at her. "I told you that," I say. "I asked you if you knew the way."

"But why? Why to the settlement?"

"I thought we'd have a better chance of finding our way there than anywhere else. Then, when we get there, we'll walk to Phoenix. You know the way from there, right? I thought that's what Dad said."

There's a terrible pause, a moment in which I think Vanessa will say no, that I'm mistaken somehow, that I misheard. That this whole walk is pointless, the wrong way to go about leaving. That because of me, we'll be lost, unable to reach our destination, walking endlessly in a deadland desert. But she's just thinking it over, maybe imagining the future I've presented. "Yes," she says finally. "Yes, I know the way." Then she frowns at the ground. "What's that?"

I follow her line of sight to the bone. "A fossil," I say, picking it up too quickly.

"Is it a bone?" says Vanessa.

"It's from a whale."

"A whale?" Vanessa repeats, her voice distracted.

"All of this used to be an ocean," I say.

Vanessa shakes her head.

"It was," I say.

"It isn't a fossil," Vanessa says, and there's a strange catch in her voice.

It's the way she's looking at the bone—unmistakable even in the shadowy moonlight, a mix of horror and awe possessing her face—that makes me understand. She thinks it's one of Nick's. She thinks that, somehow, at some point, and for some reason, I managed to extract the bone from the pyre, that I'd plunged my hand into the ashes and found it. My fingers are still gripping the bone, its surface smooth and terrible. I hold it out to Vanessa, unclenching my hand. She takes it and stares at it in her palm for a long moment. Then she takes off her backpack and slips the bone inside with the utmost care, like it's a fragile piece of glass or a dangerous spider.

I turn to Moonpie, who's lost interest in us. She's burrowing her nose in the dirt, sniffing around for food. When she notices us looking at her, she looks up and barks, three ringing yelps. A faint queasiness rises to my throat, clammy dread. It's clear that she isn't going to lead us anywhere. But I take a breath, swing my backpack over my shoulder, and when I start walking, so does Moonpie, trotting happily ahead of me, guiding us in who knows what direction. We'll find out when the sun rises again.

"We're going?" Vanessa asks, swinging her backpack over her shoulder.

I nod and start walking with a more determined step.

Cacti crop up again after some hours. Tall, bulky shapes all more or less the same height, their arms twisted in different configurations. The air is turning cool and sweeter, and I don't know if it's the scent of wildflowers or my imagination. It's too dark to see the ground clearly, even with the clouds clearing from the moon's light. We walk carefully so we don't catch our feet in a crag of rock and twist our ankles. I barely notice my backpack's straps on my shoulders, the weight lighter now. For a while, we hear the faint, drawn-out hooting of an owl. Hot wind rustles through the creosote. A lizard scampers silently over a spill of rocks, dark shapes at the edges of my vision. Once, I think I hear a coyote yip, but the sound is so distant, it's only a guess.

"Do you think they followed us?" Vanessa asks.

"No," I say.

"They didn't hear us leaving?"

I clench my hands around my backpack straps. We're walking on an incline, ascending a hill that slopes up gently but is littered with large and small rocks, jutting out and blocking our path, so we have to constantly zigzag left and right. We scramble over a boulder, and then we're on a level path again, the rocks beneath our feet packed loosely together.

"You don't think they heard us leaving?" Vanessa asks again.

"I gave them your sleeping pills."

Vanessa is quiet, absorbing this. "When? How?"

"At dinner. In their water."

"But not in my water."

"No. Not in yours or mine."

"Because you needed me to get you to Phoenix from the settlement."

I look over at her, but it's too dark to see her face. "Not only that," I say.

"Why, then?"

"I wasn't thinking like that. About why. I just knew we had to leave."

"Didn't you think that I'd be angry? That I would blame you?"

"I didn't—" I stop, confused.

"That I would think, if only you and Nick—none of this—" Vanessa cuts off, and the silence is roaring. My lungs seize up, my breath trapped in my chest. "Haven't you been asking yourself that?" Vanessa asks, her voice strange, almost pleading.

I shake my head, unable to speak.

"No, I'm not being clear," Vanessa says, her eyes fixed on the ground. "What I'm saying is I can't stop replaying everything in my head and wondering how I could have stopped it. Is it just me, or are you doing that too? Or is it really my fault?"

"No," I say, my voice returning, but even I'm not sure what I mean.

"He wouldn't even have been at the settlement if I hadn't told him to get in the car with me at the last minute," Vanessa continues, as though she hasn't heard me. "It wasn't supposed to happen that way, it was just an impulsive thing. Or if I hadn't got caught up in Isaac's story. Or if we hadn't moved to Phoenix. That was my idea."

"You couldn't have seen the future," I say, as much to myself as to Vanessa.

"It can probably make you crazy, thinking that way," Vanessa says, quieter. "Maybe tragedy's always waiting around the corner, and there's no way to get around it, no matter what you do."

"Do you miss him?" I ask.

"Yes," Vanessa says, and her voice is so emphatic, the word rings so violently, that it's almost like she's said it in a different language, like a whole second or secret meaning has been imposed on that single, small word. Then she seems to change tack, her expression newly resolute. "They were strong, the sleeping pills," she says. Her voice is quiet, like she's talking to herself. "Isaac won't be trying to find us."

I glance over at her, my breath catching. What is she trying to say? That Dad's still sleeping? That he's given up on us after what I've done? That he's dead?

She stops to take off her backpack and rummages around inside until she pulls out what looks like a thick paper tube, bright blue, with faded drawings of stars and stripes decorating it.

"What is it?" I ask, stopping too.

"Fireworks," says Vanessa. "I found them that first day at Herm's, in the shed. It's too early to set it off now." She scans the desert, then looks up at the moon. "It'd be better to set it off closer to dawn, when it'll still be dark enough so it's visible, but when he's more likely to be awake."

"Who?" I say.

"Eduardo," says Vanessa.

"Eduardo? How would he—?"

"I sent him a message. On Herm's computer, back at the cabin, when I was alone for a few minutes in there. I don't know if it got to him. I didn't have a lot of time, and I had to wipe the history, so I didn't have time to check."

"What did you write to him?"

"That I was leaving from Herm's and I'd send a signal. I asked for him to come find me."

"You were planning to leave?"

"I didn't have it planned out yet. Just that the fireworks I'd found would be the signal, and I didn't even have a chance to tell him that. But maybe he got the message. Maybe he's been watching for it, and maybe we're not too far away now for him to see it."

"That's a lot of maybes," I say.

"It's worth a shot," says Vanessa.

We walk until the sky starts to turn a dusky purple, and then Vanessa sets the firework on the ground, lights it with a match, and steps quickly away. Almost immediately, it lights up in a flaming explosion of red-and-green light, sparks flying dangerously. Moonpie yelps and leaps away, then growls at it from a distance. The flame grows fatter and spits plumes of smoke, and two beams of light shoot high into the air, where they burst into starfish shapes, the arms drooping toward the ground, then disappearing.

"We'll see what happens," Vanessa says as she watches.

The sunrise that comes soon after is almost as spectacular—dim purple light, long, diffuse clouds on the horizon turning pink and orange as the sun sifts through them, shadows chiseling the mountains, then lifting. Even Moonpie, who's been walking with her snout close to the ground, raises her head to stare at it.

When the light steadily illuminates the desert and the heat is turning angry, we make camp in a shallow ravine, nesting ourselves in between clusters of jumping cholla that reach over our heads. The sand is soft and uniform, curving like the path of what was once a riverbed. I put up my tarp, and Vanessa and I lay out our sleeping bags. Moonpie comes trotting over and nestles herself against my chest. I pull her furry warmth closer, and that's how I fall asleep, with my arm around Moonpie's back and my face pressed against her oily, matted fur.

Vanessa is already up when I wake again at sunset, portioning out what's left from a can of beans for the two of us. It's barely a few mouthfuls, but it's more than either of us feels like eating. We give the leftovers to Moonpie, who scarfs them up hungrily.

We walk through the night, we sleep through another day. The sun sets, and we get up again, stretch our tired bodies, start walking. We don't have any food or water left, but we slice off pieces of cacti and chew them to dry pulp. It's barely enough to moisten my tongue. Moonpie licks the scant dew off plants and whines softly. We walk and walk, stars beaming brighter, moon arcing across the sky, the ground cooling beneath our tired feet. I'm getting more light headed and can feel my body straining, fighting against the urge to shut down. The moon arcs down, the stars fade away, and the darkness lifts like smoke, a rising sun blowing it away. It's dawn again, and we try to sleep, but it's almost like we're both too tired to. Our feet itch to keep walking, our eyes burn but don't stay shut. After a while of lying in the sun, we pack up our tarp and start walking.

It feels like we do the same thing over and over again, like we walk for days and days, the sun setting and rising, bobbing up and down as though indecisive, but maybe it's just hours. The shifting landscapes blend together into stretches of flatness and mountains, bleached rocks glinting mineral, dry expanse studded with desiccated plants. Vanessa sets off another firework, the red-and-green light fizzing, hot and painful against my eyes. This time, the flame sputters out quickly, the sparks barely rising in the air. Vanessa watches despondently, her mouth set in a thin, firm line. It isn't working, I think, the signal. Nobody's going to find us. We're just going to keep walking and walking forever. Vanessa doesn't say as much, but she seems to be thinking the same thing. She kicks up some dirt with her foot to bury the papery refuse of the firework, and once it's covered, we set off again. A dizziness creeps up on me, a darkness at the edges of my vision that I increasingly need to blink away.

Sometimes memories of what we've left behind come flooding back to me with the rush of a roaring ocean, and I nearly double over with the shock of it, my breath gone like I'm drowning, the air in my lungs unfamiliar. Like I'm a prehistoric fish that's found itself incongruously in a desert, my fossilized bones too heavy to carry me. Other times I forget where we are and why we're walking, and the only thing that propels me forward is the force of my own momentum. Can anybody recite to me the first law of motion? Dad would ask. A body walking through the desert stays walking through the desert unless acted upon by a force from outside the desert. But there are no outside forces here. Any force invading would wither dead, dissolve in sun-bleached whiteness, turn petrified. The desert would swallow it whole and silent, the way I feel the desert swallowing me. My skin the sand, my breath hot wind, the thuds of my feet the pulse of the planet churning forward mutely, drying to dust and dirt.

The longer we walk, the farther away we get from Dad, not only by miles but by a unit of measure that's deeper and more ancient. It's as though eons have passed since we've left. As though millions of tectonic plates have collided to make mountains, followed by millions of floods that eroded those mountains away. As though generations of brachiopods and fanged fish and giant plodding mammals have lived and reproduced and died, have decomposed into the dirt and left only shells and bones behind, hard minerals replacing soft tissue, lying buried until people unearthed them and put them in museums, sweeping clean a slate for another billion years of the same thing happening, events repeating into a future I can't see, even in this wide expanse, this endless horizon of desert. Sometimes it feels like that, like we've moved from one geologic period to the next and there's no trace of anyone we've left behind left on Earth. Other times, it's as though it all happened just moments ago, all of it at once, and the memories crash into and spill over each other, and how long have we been walking? and where are we walking to? and have we even left?

The sun is blinding white, the sky is high and turquoise, small black dots dancing before my eyes. I blink, and it all turns black. I direct my gaze at the ground and see a plastic water bottle half-buried in the dirt. I'm imagining it, I think. I'm still aware enough to recognize a sign of worsening dehydration. But the bottle doesn't go away no matter how long I stare at it. It's trash, I realize a moment later, old and empty, something somebody tossed away. A sign that there are people somewhere. It grounds me somewhat, a rope tying me to the earth. I try to hold on to it as we walk through the sun, the sun-scorched earth, the sun-drowned air. Sometime later, I see two metal disks lying in the dirt, catching the light in flashes. We walk toward them like they're beacons, and it's only when we're standing directly over them that we see they're crushed tin cans. Irregular shapes of red and white and yellow splayed around a perfect circle of metal. "I always tell him not to litter," Vanessa says faintly.

"Who?" I ask, although I know.

"Nick."

I bend to pick one up and examine it, moving my thumb along the creased metal. When I look over at Vanessa, she's staring at it, her gaze is unfocused. Her face is weary and strained, a sickly color where it isn't sunburned.

"We should try to sleep," I say, dropping the can. "Let's try to find some shade."

There aren't any trees around, only large shrubs of creosote, the leaves small and dusty. We walk forward, trying to see what we're walking toward, but the ground is uneven, our line of sight blocked by hills of stone. We wander to the right, trying to find an easier route to walk. Moonpie has a rare burst of energy, running ahead of us and then back again. She barks, the sound impatient, like she's telling us to hurry. When we don't, she bounds away until she's yards ahead of us. Then she halts abruptly, turns around, and watches us, waiting.

"This is probably as good as we're going to find," I say finally, nodding at a clump of shrubs wedged between large boulders. Vanessa nods and starts pulling the tarp out of her backpack. Moonpie barks from up ahead.

"Moonpie," I call. "Come here, girl."

But Moonpie's ears are pricked forward, listening to something else. She looks over her shoulder, and then back at us. She barks again, the sound authoritative, urgent. And then I hear it too. A low mechanical rumbling, faint at first but getting louder.

Vanessa pauses in unfolding the tarp and looks up, her eyebrows lowering. She glances at Moonpie, then around at the desert, searching for the source of the noise.

"Oh my god," she says.

"What?" I ask. "I don't—"

And then I see it. A movement between the rocky hills, appearing and then disappearing. A giant animal, I think wildly. My mind whirs through images of a mammoth, a saber-toothed tiger, a giant sloth dragging its arms through a dried-out prehistoric swamp. I squint into the distance, trying to see around the sun, and begin to see the shape making the noise in parts: silver metal, panes of glass, black rubber—a truck.

Vanessa drops the tarp and starts running in its direction, waving her arms.

"Hey!" she shouts. "Over here! Hey!"

The truck is maneuvering around the shrubs and rocks slowly and carefully, but it's far enough away that it looks like Vanessa isn't going to reach it in time for the driver to notice us. She continues running and waving her arms. Moonpie is at her feet, seized with sudden energy, yelping in fear or excitement. From a distance, I watch the truck stop. Vanessa stops, too, resting her hands on her knees to catch her breath. Then she stands up and waves her arms again. I watch the truck maneuver around a pile of boulders to turn around, then drive toward Vanessa. The truck comes to a halt, and a man emerges from the driver's seat. He has a stocky build and shiny black hair that reaches his shoulders. He lifts a hand to shade his eyes from the sun. Vanessa appears to say something. The man continues to look at her, and Vanessa says something else, motioning with her arm, half turning to point at me. Finally, the man opens his mouth and seems to answer her. They have a brief conversation, and the man motions toward his car and climbs back inside. Vanessa picks up Moonpie and lifts her into the passenger seat, then pulls herself up. The car starts with a loud rumble, and I watch, immobilized, as it gets closer and closer. Vanessa steps out first, then Moonpie hops out. The man takes his time turning off the car's engine and emerging. Still standing beside the car door, he looks me over. "So you're Isaac's daughter," he says.

I stare at this unfamiliar man, trying to understand.

"This is Eduardo," Vanessa tells me breathlessly.

"Eduardo?" I repeat, my exhausted mind working hard to connect this man to the name.

"He saw the fireworks," Vanessa says, gesturing frenetically to where the car came from. "He's been driving around looking for us near where we set it off. There's a road up there. Curving around the mountain. Moonpie knew, didn't she? She helped lead us to safety after all. She could sense where there were people, so that's where she led us. Maybe she even knew it was you on your way, Eduardo. I think she could sense it. Didn't you, Moonpie?"

Moonpie raises her snout at hearing her name. She trots over to Vanessa, and Vanessa crouches down to pet her.

Eduardo frowns. "How long have you been out here?"

"I don't know," Vanessa says. She lifts herself up from the ground.

Eduardo turns to me, his face searching. "So what happened, exactly?" he asks. "I could follow up to the part about you finding the settlement. Then suddenly you were at the Hermit's and needed to leave? And now you're way out here, walking?"

"We were trying to get back to the settlement," says Vanessa.

"Well, you're going in the opposite direction."

"Are we?" Vanessa says, glancing around. "Where are we, then?"

"You're up north."

"North? What do you mean? It's still so hot here."

"I mean you walked north from the Hermit's place. You should have walked southwest." Eduardo gestures behind him. "This is where I live, near the Domes on the other side of that mountain."

"That's where we've walked?" says Vanessa. "That's strange. I don't recognize it."

"This is where the Domes are?" I ask, looking around me.

"You can't see them from here," Eduardo says.

"It didn't seem like we were walking anywhere," says Vanessa, her voice flat and quiet, like she's talking to herself. "Not in any direction. Sometimes I thought we'd died already. Now, I think we probably didn't. We just took a wrong turn, didn't we?"

Eduardo studies us, moving his tongue around his mouth like he's trying to dislodge a piece of food. "I think we need to get some water in the two of you," he says. "I'm on my way to work, but what I'm going to do is turn around and bring you back to my house. Alice, my wife, she'll still be there. She'll fix you up and get you some food and water, and you can get some rest. We'll talk things over when I come back home later."

"Talk what over?" says Vanessa. "Can you take us to Phoenix?"

"Sure," says Eduardo, nodding slowly. "Sure, I can. But you'll want some rest first, like I said. We can talk it over and make plans later."

"We're not going to the settlement?" I ask.

Eduardo glances at Vanessa, brow furrowing. "You want me to drive you there instead?"

"No," says Vanessa, shaking her head. "No, there's nothing there."

"But that's where we were going," I say.

"Only to get our bearings," Vanessa explains to Eduardo.

Eduardo turns his attention back to me. "That all right with you?" he says, his voice kind.

I nod because there's nothing else I can do. My mouth is dry, and I swallow. I squat down to pet Moonpie, ducking my head to touch my forehead to her fur. I don't know what my face is showing, but I know I don't want either of them to see it. Vanessa and Eduardo keep talking, exchanging logistics, but their voices have become a faint buzz to me, irrelevant. A feeling of loss grows in my chest and starts spreading into the rest of my body. I curl up tighter, tucking my knees into my chest, leaning my head on my knees. Moonpie lets me huddle into her. There's nothing there, I tell myself, but the words are empty—stripped mesquite pods, barren soil, a hole in a saguaro long abandoned by a cactus wren. It's just a place, I tell myself, but I know it isn't. It's the knowledge, incontrovertible now, that I'll never see it again, that I'll never see Dad or Wulf or Herm. The sudden finality of leaving roaring in my ears like a sandstorm, unearthing everything I know and care about, and then obfuscating it, unreachable, in a blur of mineral and sand.

20

The desert around me is loose and fleeting. In Eduardo's car, we move through it at an unnatural pace. I try to grasp what we're doing, but I can't. It's not me listening to the questions Eduardo asks and Vanessa struggles to answer, to Moonpie's pitiful whines, sounding as confused as I am. I can't place myself, with the long walk suddenly behind me and everything leading up to it transforming into a vast before, a past that's rushing away from me, eroding at an alarming pace.

Arriving at Eduardo's house is a clash of images and sounds. I can only take it in in pieces. The house tiny from a distance, a rectangular structure raised on cinder blocks, getting closer. A woman with long, dark hair opening the door, pouring us water, making us beds. Eduardo calling her Alice, Eduardo leaving, Alice searching for clean sheets, talking to us in a soft, endless stream as she moves around the house. She pauses to show us strings of smooth pebbles with holes drilled into them, muted purples and reds. I don't catch why. She has us drink more water. The light inside is dim, curtained. Vanessa sits on the sofa and stares at her hands, and I sit down next to her. Poor things, Alice says. Her words float through my mind meaninglessly. My head aches from the sun, my muscles just now realizing how tired they are. I lean against the corner of the sofa and feel myself starting to fall asleep. Alice's voice is a deep, murky stream that I dip in and out of until I feel her hands gently on my arms, helping me stand, saying that my cot is ready.

Exhaustion engulfs me like a wave. The bright sun pushing against the curtains doesn't bother me, though my cot is below the window. I sleep lightly, then deeply, then lightly again. Alice shakes my shoulder gently, asking if I want to wash. A bowl of water and a rag, my arms moving in slow, precise motions, then I drag myself back to my cot. Moonpie sleeps at my feet, then on the floor. I reach my hand down, and she presses her nose against it. Her fur is rough and oily. Later, when I reach down again, her fur is cleaner, slightly damp. I wake to the clinking of dishes, boots thudding across the ground, low voices. My half-open eyes fall on a small figurine of a woman on a table, green robe, red dress. A tapestry on a wall, threads fraying brown and tan. Yellow paloverde blossoms in a wooden vase. The sun dims, and I fall asleep again. My dreams are colorless. I wake to a brilliant moon. Someone's opened the window, the curtain. I try to stand up, velvet darkness holding me, but my legs shake uncontrollably. I lie back down and lie unmoving for hours, thinking of nothing, aware of nothing but my labored breathing, my heart beating fast, uneven. I sleep again, I wake. My eyes roam around the room. Some of the darkness has lifted now, another dawn. Moonpie makes a sound in her sleep, her legs twitching. The front door is open a crack, swinging a fraction forward, a fraction back.

I get up to close it, then push it open instead and stumble down the steps. In the dusky light, I can make out a dirt road running past the house. I breathe in and out, my mind running through everything that's happened, my memory connecting and clicking it all into place. Eduardo's house, the walking, having left. I squint into the distance. Farther away, there are houses like this one and a few larger buildings clustered together into the semblance of a very small town, and there aren't any lights coming from any of them. The road is calm and empty, lined with a desert crowding in on either side, poised to overtake it.

"Get some sleep?" a man's voice says.

I start, and turn to see Eduardo sitting beside the house in a white plastic chair. "You can sit down if you want," he says, nodding at an identical chair next to his. "Vanessa was out here earlier, filling me in on what happened at the Hermit's. I think she went back to sleep."

"What is this place?" I ask, sitting.

Eduardo follows my gaze to the other small houses. "They built it for the workers."

"The ones building the Domes?"

"Yep," Eduardo says.

"I don't remember you," I say, turning to look at him.

"No, you'd be too young to."

"But you remember me?"

"Sure, I do." He nods.

"You were there when the deaths happened, then? At the settlement?"

Eduardo's eyebrows tip down. "I'm surprised Isaac talked to you about that."

"He didn't. Vanessa told me."

"What did she say?"

"That Dad blamed himself."

Eduardo nods slowly, his limbs relaxing back into his chair. "All those years ago—you know, you can find someone to blame for everything. You know what I think it was? Bad water. You know how many people in the history of humankind have died from bad bacteria in water? But that's just the way the world is. Sometimes you get dealt a bad hand. Isaac doesn't think like that, though. He blames the world at large for driving him into the desert in the first place."

"Driving him into the desert how?"

"If only the world had been fixing its problems better, if only half the country wasn't deadlands. If only the world was different, someone wouldn't have had to take a stand, to fight the good fight. You see? Because if someone had to do it, and nobody else was, then the responsibility fell to him. That's the way he thinks."

"And now he's fighting against the Domes," I say.

"Right, exactly. He believes that he's got the moral upper hand in sabotaging them. He's got a valid argument, I'll give him that, that hiding ourselves away is just putting off dealing with the problem. There's a sound kind of logic there."

"But you don't believe it anymore," I say, studying his face.

Eduardo sighs, twisting his mouth and scratching the side of his face. "It's not that I don't believe it. It's that when you're knee deep in problems, like we are, when hundreds of acres are becoming new deadlands daily, maybe you can't imagine a way to fix your problems without an intermediate solution to keep you going. Otherwise, it's too easy to give up and think there's no point. And my thinking these days is, there is a point. It's been like this before, you know? Not in this particular way, but in ways that also meant the end of civilization as people knew it. Plagues and volcanoes and hunting all our food to extinction. And people still went on doing all the normal, everyday things they'd always done, all while the world was falling apart around them."

"So the world really is falling apart out there?" I ask.

"Pretty much. But I don't think it's the end."

"Dad thought you were dead," I say after a pause.

"Yeah, Vanessa told me. The so-called contamination. It's better that way. He can remember me the way he wants, a true believer. I'd like that. Maybe he'll think it got you, too, the contamination. Maybe he'll think it messed with your head, and that's why you left."

"Maybe," I say, closing my eyes.

"It's better that way," Eduardo says again.

I open my eyes and nod, and Eduardo nods, and we fall into silence, watching the darkness lift from the desert. I think about the self I've left behind, preserved like a fern in shale. About my room at the settlement with its shelves of objects and fossils, exactly as I left it. That's what Dad and Wulf will be to me, too, now—fossilized relics, trapped in time. In reality, they'll grow older and change. One day, they'll die, and when their bodies decompose, they'll leave behind bones for someone else to find, skeletons shed like a hermit crab's shell. The bones will erode to calcium and phosphate eventually, to depersonalized minerals, and then they'll become a part of a different whole, of landscape itself. A landscape someone will hopefully walk through again one day. Who knows what it'll look like then. A jungle, a swamp? A deadland studded with abandoned Domes, the last remaining artifacts of our civilization? The desert was an ocean once, and I was once Georgia who lived in the settlement with Wulf and Dad. Who knows what I'll morph into next. It's strange to me that I think of this with curiosity, not dread.

The gray-purple of the sky is turning pink with sunrise, illuminating the mountains into distinct triangular shapes. For a while longer, Eduardo and I sit outside together, and then I start nodding off and go back inside to give in to more sleep, my hunger for it endless.

When I wake up next, the sun has fully risen, white light streaming through the window. Eduardo is cooking a viscous yellow liquid at the stove, and Alice and Vanessa are sitting on the ground, speaking softly and rubbing Moonpie's belly. When Alice notices me, she gets up and brings me a soft shirt and a pair of loose green pants. I change into them and return the nightdress she gave me to sleep in. We eat soft yellow lumps out of the pan, the four of us standing around the stove. Eduardo says we should get going if we still want him to give us a lift to the city today.

Eduardo and Vanessa sit up front, and I sit in the open back of the truck with my knees to my chest, right hand holding on to the raised side. Eduardo doesn't drive fast, but the moving air still roars in my ears. Moonpie huddles under my knees, overwhelmed by this strange wind, but I'm grateful for the noise, for the violent push of it against my arms and face, how it consumes so much of my attention.

We take long, flat roads that are nearly empty, then winding ones as we drive through a stretch of mountains. The asphalt is cracked and dusty black. Only twice do we pass another car: a giant truck hauling supplies that nearly scrapes Eduardo's car as it rumbles past us, and a small red car pulling a trailer. The man driving it makes brief eye contact with me. I take in his neatly cut hair, his shirt that's blue and smooth as a sky without weather. It hits me that he's coming from the city we're heading toward, and suddenly everything that we're doing comes rushing at me, a surge of deeper awareness—driving to Phoenix and knowing we won't be returning, knowing that I'm gone now, that though we're still moving, we're no longer leaving, we've left.

Eduardo speeds up when he gets to a road that's six lanes wide. We're the only car in sight, and it's hotter here, the sun reflecting off the expanse of concrete. The air shimmers at the horizon where the road touches it. I shift to sit cross-legged, and Moonpie buries her head in my lap. We maneuver around gravel that's mysteriously piled on the left side of the road, then later around a part of the road that's flat out gone, stripped of its cement, like someone thought to fix it but abandoned the project. We drive on the edge of the road for a while, the car's wheels crushing weeds and struggling over jagged stones. Eventually, we turn onto a road that narrows again, becomes only big enough for two cars to drive on side by side. Eduardo pulls into a patch of dirt on the side of the road and steps out of the truck.

"Scenic overlook," he says, nodding at the mountains. "Time to stretch our legs and take care of our business if anyone needs to." He stuffs his hands in his pockets and walks to the opposite side of the road into the scrubby desert, heading toward a copse of scraggly bushes.

Vanessa makes her way out of the car and walks to the edge of the road, where, after a small slope, it drops into a valley. She stands there with her hands holding her elbows, her back hunched a little. As though sensing me watching, she turns and smiles wanly at me. "Come see it," she says. "It's a better view over here."

I join her, and Moonpie follows me to huddle at my feet, as though wary of the wide expanse before us. The mountains alternate between rounded and jagged, mounds of dirt and sharp stone, brown flecked with olive green. They're different from the mountains near the settlement, more parched, barer. Vanessa's eyes are closed. She lifts a hand to knead the side of her head, rubbing some hair out of her ponytail so it sticks out in a bump.

"Do you smell that?" she asks. "The smog? We're getting close."

I inhale, and it's true the air feels grittier, coarse and dense. "Where are we going?" I ask.

"Phoenix," Vanessa says abstractedly.

"I know, but where in Phoenix?"

"Eduardo said he'd take me to my apartment. Sounds weird to say that—my apartment. How long has it been? I don't even know if my things are still there."

"I mean, where will he take me?"

Vanessa opens her eyes. "You can stay with me," she says. "Until you figure out what you want to do next. I don't really know what I can do to help you. I know you'll need help, but I don't know what I can do. I don't even know what I'm going to do next myself. I don't want to think about it right now. We don't have to figure out everything at once. Anyway, you're welcome."

The muscles in my arms and legs slacken, pulpy with relief. "Thanks," I say, though the word feels inadequate.

"Sure. Of course."

"I thought Nick would be my way out," I say.

"Nick?" Vanessa says, almost like she doesn't recognize the name.

"I thought he would let me come along when you somehow found a way to leave. I wasn't even sure I wanted to leave then. I don't really know what I was thinking. I just got it in my head that I would and, somehow, that he would help."

Vanessa nods, her mouth stretched thinly into something that isn't quite a smile and isn't quite a grimace. She blinks a few times fast, her face otherwise frozen. When I turn my head to look more closely at her, I realize that her eyes are damp, her nose reddish.

"I'm sorry," I say. "I don't know if I've said that yet."

Vanessa shakes her head and makes an indecipherable gesture with her hand.

I try to think of the right thing to say next—another thank-you, some kind of acknowledgment that I know it's not just a place to sleep she's giving me, it's a place to go, the only one I have—but Eduardo comes back right then and asks if we're ready to set off again. We pile back into the truck. The engine starts with a sputtering sound, then a sound like distant thunder, and then we're driving down the bumpy, pockmarked road.

After a while, the landscape starts to even out, desert covered with yellowing vegetation that blends in with the sand. Large boxy buildings appear every now and again just off the side of the road. They look abandoned, their giant doors open, their parking lots blank squares of asphalt. When we start passing houses, entire mazes of dilapidated multistory ones that look empty as well, I sit up straighter. We're getting close to the city—we're right at its edge. My throat feels like it's coated with a gray film of smog and grime, and I keep coughing to try to clear it.

Eduardo drives off the main road onto a small one, then pulls into a charging station in the middle of an otherwise empty lot of dirt. "Anyone hungry?" he asks. "I need to eat something."

He parks the car by one of the charging units and hooks the car up to it. I stand up in the truck bed and stretch. My muscles feel sore and cramped after spending the last few hours clenching them against the wind and motion. Moonpie hops off and sniffs at the ground. I wonder whether she's taking stock of her new surroundings like I am, acclimating to the new scents of the city, but she's probably just following the scent of food.

Next to the charging units is a store and a plastic picnic table chained to the ground. The store looks like a small bunker, hunkered down against the heat, the door paned with dirty, darkened plastic. The exterior is covered in graffiti, the writing all different sizes and styles and languages layered over each other, unreadable. Eduardo tries the door, and he looks almost as surprised as I am when he's able to pull it open. A bell rings when he disappears inside. Vanessa leads us to the picnic table, and we sit down to wait.

"Hotter here, isn't it?" she says. She shakes the front of her T-shirt, the fabric billowing against her body. Her face is pink, her forehead damp. "It's because of all the concrete and asphalt. And this is just the outskirts. It'll be hotter once we get further in, where there are more buildings crowded together."

I look around to take in our surroundings more fully. There are strips of desert between the opposite sides of the road and in patches in front of buildings, but they're just dirt and dirt-colored weeds cowering close to the earth, none of the desert plants I know. The few buildings I see from here are all made of cement. Huge signs poke into the sky, but whatever was once written or drawn on them is faded, bleached unintelligible by the sun.

Eduardo emerges from the store holding three hot dogs, his own already half-eaten. He hands one to each of us and sits down across from us at the picnic table.

"Tastes like home," Vanessa says, taking a bite. She licks bright yellow and red goo off her fingers, then rearranges the paper wrapping holding the hot dog together.

Moonpie whines at our feet. I pinch off a small piece of my hot dog and toss it to her. She swallows it in one bite and sits on her haunches, waiting for more. I pinch off another small piece, with bread this time, and she eats it out of my hand.

"Try it before you feed it all to the dog." Eduardo nods at me. "It's not bad. You'll get sick of them real fast, though. It's the one food we never seem to run out of in these parts. I guess they transport well."

I take a bite. The meat is salty and rubbery between my teeth. It doesn't feel like meat at all, but it tastes edible. The yellow goo stings my mouth, and the red is sweet and tangy. I'm surprised at how quickly the bread turns to paste in my mouth.

"Forgot the drinks," Eduardo says suddenly. "I was going to treat us all to some Coca-Colas. Ever had one, Georgia? Soon you'll be swimming in it. Cheaper than water out here. Still good, though." He reaches into his wallet and pulls out a plastic rectangle, which he hands to me. "Why don't you go ahead and get us a few sodas or waters. Whichever you want. Give the bottles to the cashier, then give this card to him. That's how you pay. He'll give it back to you when he's finished. Does that make sense?"

"She'll be fine," says Vanessa.

The small bell rings above the door when I enter. A boy at the register who looks around Wulf's age looks up from his phone, and moves his eyes up and down me. There's a question in his face, a vague curiosity that doesn't look friendly. I walk to the aisle farthest in the back, but out of the corner of my eye I see the boy's neck craning to keep me in his line of vision. I move to another aisle, where he has an unencumbered view of me, and then he seems to realize that I'm not a danger and goes back to slouching over his phone.

The aisle is stocked with candy bars and small bags of cookies and chips. I don't touch anything that I won't buy, but it's hard to tear my eyes away from the colors and pictures on the labels. I could spend hours staring at them, all the small words, the cartoonish drawings, the shine of the wrappers, the brilliant light blues and neon greens and deep purples unlike anything in nature. Or maybe like something in nature that's exotic and distant, some bird on another continent I've never seen. That I haven't seen yet, I correct, experimentally.

A candy bar catches my eye that kicks up a memory lodged deep and far back in my brain. Wulf and I are young, maybe seven and four, and we must have recently returned from a trip to Herm's. We have a bar of chocolate in front of us, a brown wrapper around silver foil, a little torn. Something Herm must have gotten for us on a supply run. The chocolate is chalky around the edges and crumbles easily when I break it into small pieces. Wulf watches with suspicion. Is it fairy food? he asks, his voice babyish, slightly petulant. Like in the story you read me? No, I say, Dad said it's okay. Wulf touches the wrapper with an outstretched finger, unconvinced. But what if it is fairy food? he says. What if eating it means they'll take us away and we can't get back home? I put a piece to his lips, and his face contorts until his lips part and his face lights up at the hit of sugar. Then it'll be an adventure, I say. And we'll both be there together. The memory stops there, at the change in Wulf's face, his scrunched-up nose and cheeks softening, his mouth spreading into a gummy smile. The hot dog in my stomach turns. A breathlessness rises in my chest, threatening to close up my throat. I walk to another aisle.

The refrigerator with drinks is at the back of the store. When I put my hand against it, I realize it isn't kept cold, or it's broken. It's just a lit-up rectangular box with a see-through door. Bottles are jumbled inside, the labels and liquid a mess of bright colors.

I'm about to pull it open and pick out three small bottles when the fluorescent lights flicker. Nothing happens for a moment, then the lights flicker more violently for what feels like a whole minute, and then, with a whirring sound that briefly starts up and then dies down, the lights go out completely. The store is dark and unearthly quiet, a low buzzing sound I only now realize I'd been hearing suddenly absent.

Dad, I think, the thought arriving unprompted. Despite the heat, a shiver courses through my body. It feels like all my senses are alight at once, trembling, ready to hear his message. My mind whirs frantically—is it an instruction or a reprimand? Could it be a goodbye? There's no doubt in my mind, in this moment, that it's him sending a missive, a final communication. I wait for the meaning to unfold like a Möbius strip, to become a simple strip, legible. I can almost sense it coming closer, feel it come almost close enough to call it *almost there*. The darkness is wound tight, eager to spin deliriously into the arriving message.

"Nobody move," calls a voice. "All customers—uh, just the one of you—stay where you are to minimize injury to your person. We should have the power back on in just a—"

The refrigerator lights flicker, a low drone invades my eardrums, and then the fluorescent overhead lights shudder on again, searing white. I blink, my eyes adjusting to the sudden brightness. I'm still by the refrigerator, staring at it. I pull it open and pull out the three bottles my hand reaches first. I hold them tight against my body as I walk to the register.

"Did you find everything you needed?" the boy says mechanically. He eyes me from behind his hair, and I nod stiffly. He wiggles each bottle in front of a machine that blinks red. "Fifty-six ninety-nine," he says, and I stare at him, waiting for him to add context to this number.

"That's how much it costs?" he says.

"Oh, right." Hastily, I hand him the plastic card Eduardo gave me.

The boy sticks it into a machine. It doesn't seem to respond the way he wants it to, because he frowns at it, and presses a few buttons. "Sorry," he says. "Give it a minute to get back online. It's like that after we have a blackout. Solar's been glitchy. Okay, there it is. Wait, give it a few more seconds. There, done." He hands the card back to me and pushes the bottles toward me. The small bell rings again when I exit, a clanging, jarring sound.

"There she is," Eduardo says when I set the bottles down on the picnic table. "Did you have a chance to look around? It's a heady experience, even here, in this day and age. Half the shelves empty, the bottom-of-the-barrel dregs nobody else wants, and we still have all that choice. What is this?" He squints at the small letters on the bottle. "Some kind of tea? I can't read the language."

Vanessa opens a bottle and takes a sip. "Might be tea," she says. "Or just water with some kind of flavor." She tilts her head back and downs half the bottle. "It's not bad," she says. "Have you tried it yet, Georgia? Have some. You're probably dehydrated."

I pick up the bottle and turn it over in my hand. A drink in a one-use bottle, created to be thrown away—Dad would hate it. If I were back at the settlement and had found its crushed remains, I would have propped it up on my dresser, a relic from a different world. Here, it's one of dozens in the convenience store, one of a million in Phoenix, too common to be special. And still, I hesitate to open it. Even after everything that's happened, it feels like a betrayal, drinking water that wasn't wrung from the earth by Dad or brought from the outside world by its emissary, Herm. The bottle of liquid a potion: as though drinking it will release me from the last few bonds tying me to the settlement, marking me as either free or forsaken. The green plastic catches the sun, glowing like an alien gem.

Unscrewing the bottle takes more effort than I expect. The heat must have somehow melded the plastic parts of the cap together. The liquid inside looks brackish, cloudy. For a moment, I stare down at it. Wulf's voice, childishly high, years younger, surfaces again in my memory. Herm's unbreaking eye contact as he drank the water I gave him. Dad setting down his empty glass on the table. I blink to clear the memories. I bring the bottle to my lips and tip it back. The liquid is soothing against my throat, like medicine. I take long, measured swallows until the bottle is almost empty.